MOON OVER VOLNEY

A novel by Steve Stinson

MOON OVER VOLNEY
by Steve Stinson

ISBN-979-8-9922904-8-6

Cover art by: Steve Stinson

Copyright 2025 Steve Stinson

Printed in the United States of America
Worldwide Electronic & Digital Rights
Worldwide English Language Print Rights

www.stevestinson.com

*Dedicated to
The B Girl*

CONTENTS

CHAPTER 1

THE MATCHUP

AUGUST, 1963.

Alone in his studio, Peter Basque posed in the manner of a baseball pitcher. He gripped a massive brush in his right hand. It dripped with lurid red paint. He faced off against on overlarge canvas maybe fifteen feet away. The canvas wasn't bare. It was fully obscured by a swarm of colors overlaid in splotches and strings and drips.

The brush could not contain the paint. It dripped on Peter's designer shoes. This was not a problem. They were, the paint-stained shoes, another of his many trademarks.

Peter seemed to be about 40. It was hard to tell. He was lean and tall, with a face that aged higher and stringy dark hair that should have been shorter. There was a languid grace about him, as though he had been forever pardoned from urgency. You could tell he was at one time good looking and could be again, but if he kept living the life he'd manufactured, the chance would fade away.

An isolated warthog expression was beginning to take hold, one that could someday become permanent.

For now, though, there was still a measure of

keenness about him, even as he failed to disguise it
behind acute gray/green eyes.

The room itself, and it was a big one, was a free-for-
all of escapee paint stains. Colors festooned every inch,
including the ceiling. This was a feat. The ceiling was
twenty feet high.

His clothes – loose fitting and black – made him
seem a statue alone among madness. A farrago of
unhinged expressionist works on canvas – each with
a signature smack of red paint – leaned and piled and
tumbled here and there.

The floor and tabletops were a chaos of new and
discarded tools of his trade – brushes, paint cans, paint
tubes, stir sticks, mixing knives, clean and encrusted
palettes, new rags and old rags, oils and thinners and
spirits. The scent of turpentine seemed permanent
because it was.

The jangle and brawl of heavy equipment and
industry outside his tall, open windows – the room was
well lit for a warehouse – competed with the primitive
thump of music, if you wanted to call the sound music,
belaboring his studio.

Peter leaned in for the sign. Long squint. He shook
it off with a slow and resolute no. He peered in again.
He shook again, this time to move a dangle of hair out
of the way. He looked in again. Pause. His eyes closed in
affirmation. A slow nod yes.

He went erect into the stretch, holding the brush
to his chest. He checked first base, slow-motion chin
to left shoulder. His eyes were slits. He opened one eye
and released a faint, passing smirk. Slow-motion head to

center. He eyed the target, leaned back, kicked high, and hurled the gob of red paint at the canvas.

Peter watched the blot of red maneuver its unstoppable way over the other colors. He tossed the brush aside. It melded with the muddle on the floor, where it would surely harden and die. He turned his back on the canvas.

He worked his way through the disarray toward a free-standing coat rack that pronged up in the middle of the room. He lifted his trademark black flat-brimmed gaucho hat – the kind favored by Flamenco dancers – and tapped it on. He lifted an opera cape – black silk on the outside, red silk on the inside, and wildly out of context in the late summer heat – and swung it over his shoulders. He seemed to grow taller. Stately. He swirled toward his latest canvas, which gave the cape a dramatic flow. The blot was no longer moving. It was in the upper middle of the canvas and a little to the right. He delivered a careless umpire's gesture and spoke.

"High and inside."

***

Brush Holland, 18, knew what he was doing, and he was doing it, which made him handsome in the timeless work-shirt-and-overalls look that says "farmboy." He labored close-up to a huge canvas. Long horizontal. Maybe 10 feet wide. You'd need a pickup to move it.

His eyes – azure blue in artist lingo – were difficult to interpret, especially for such a young man. They betrayed the fading presence of wonder, premature for

3

his age. More contradictions emerged upon looking. He was neat and tidy and groomed beneath an impossibly unrestrained surge of auburn hair. He was tallish and rawboned but had a languid ease about him. His hands were calloused horny but moved in an elegant way.

His temporary outdoor studio was exquisitely organized. He sat on a tall three-legged stool. The canvas was propped, balanced, and leveled before him on two homemade easels, right and left, carefully constructed using wooden sawhorses. His paint tubes were arranged by color on a three-legged milking stool to his right. His palette, brushes, medium oils and turpentine containers were arranged on an identical stool to his left. His brushes were sorted by type. Both tables were spotless.

The painting seemed complete. It depicted the prairie surrounding him. The image was magnificent. It demanded a second and third look.

The painting depicted the prairie, but it didn't. It was impossible and delicious to behold. He was creating what seemed a perfectly natural scene while using unnatural colors. Pinks and oranges and purples mixed and overlaid the usual greens, browns, and blues of a landscape. The sky was tinted with green. The wrong colors were everywhere, but the painting seemed more than right. The brushstrokes were energetic. They seemed spontaneous and dynamic, yet the picture was serene. Every square inch was thought through.

His composition removed the accidents of nature but retained the integrity of the landscape even as his brush reimagined it. The image was romantic without being precious. It breathed maturity and confidence.

But for the muffled peeps and rustles and flutters of prairie life, the field was utterly silent around him. He bent to the canvas and stroked a shadow that defined a fence post in the background of the painting.

He quickly wiped it off the canvas. He dabbed more paint on his brush, adjusted the dab with his fingers, shook his head "yes," and aimed the brush into the palette again. He took a long pause. He brought the newly loaded brush tip to his eyes. He slowly took the brush back to the palette and again fingered off some excess paint. He planted the brush tip on the canvas and glided it downward. Another shadow in the same spot as before. He quickly wiped it away and repeated the process.

He used both hands on his third attempt on the shadow stroke. Done. He cocked his head. An eyebrow lifted. Acceptance swept his face. He leaned back and eyed the canvas from there. He spoke.

"Perfect."

CHAPTER 2

THE DEAL

SPENCER GRISAILLE sat, elbows on his desk, his manicured fingers making a little tent at his chin. He had the look of a man with something better to do.

It was a tasteful and expensive desk. Just enough chocolate-box inlay to be shy of conceit. It fit into the rest of the décor, which reeked of good taste. The appointments demonstrated an astute eye for the right thing in the right place. This was a good thing. He was the acquisitions director for the Chicago Art Institute.

Spencer fit the décor, too. He was tall, with a fit carriage draped by an impeccable three-piece suit, British cut. His only nod to charm was an insurgent tie and pocket square, both just shy of reckless. His glasses were rimless. He peered over them and across his desk.

Opposite his desk, draped across a tasteful and expensive leather couch, Peter Basque eyed the ceiling as though he expected some meaning to drip from it. Peter was at that moment a living expression of his career, namely lying there and doing nothing. At least that's how Spencer saw it.

Spencer took in the transgression of Peter's trademark shoes on the couch, and let it pass. Spencer broke the silence.

"How am I supposed to justify mounting a show for you, Peter?"

Peter, eyes still upward, let a draped arm drop.

"A retrospective."

Spencer pushed back from his desk. He leaned back. The chair let out a creak. Now his eyes went to the ceiling and found nothing and returned to Peter.

"Retrospective? Peter, you've been doing a different version of the same painting for ten years."

Peter rolled up and leaned forward on the couch.

"For old time's sake."

"The board doesn't go back with you as far as I do."

Peter unfolded back into the couch. His head lolled back again.

"I need a jump start. Make that a restart."

Spencer's eyes came back to Peter.

"Peter, it's too dark to see the canvas when your head is up your ass."

Peter spoke to the ceiling.

"I may be a headcase, Spencer, but you'll always be a Sunday painter."

Neither party acknowledged that both insults were true as Peter undraped again and dismounted the couch. Once vertical, Peter slid his opera cape off the back of the couch and over his arm. He turned to go, gaucho hat in hand. Spencer's face delivered low-paced flickers of affection, frustration, disgust, and pity. His eyes dropped toward the gilded mahogany "in" tray on his desktop.

He now had the look of a man who is about to walk on burning coals. He stopped Peter at the door.

"Do you still have that traveling roadshow?"

Peter, facing doorward, raised an eyebrow. He spoke to the door.

"In the warehouse."

"But it still runs?"

Peter completed a theatrically languid about face.

"Yes."

His eyes bored in on Spencer, who slid a folder from the tray. Spencer opened the folder and leafed through it. Casual, studiously so. He spoke toward the folder.

"Let's say I get you space for a show. What would you hang?"

Peter let the transaction hang in the air a moment. They had done this dance before.

"I've got a studio full of . . ."

"Too big canvasses with your trademark red splash?"

Peter went into his version of high dudgeon. Chin and nose went aloft. Eyes away. It didn't last long. The pose gave way under its own weight. This was a dance, and Spencer was leading. Anyway, you can't hide it when you are beseeching.

"I swear, swear, I'll get you something new."

He took a half step toward Spencer's desk. He made a thoroughly unpracticed swipe at crossing his chest. "Swear."

Spencer now had the look of someone whose feet actually were upon the burning coals. He spoke to himself.

"I already regret this."

He held out the folder. Peter dropped the hat and cape. He sprang to the desk and snatched it. As Peter rifled the folder – news clippings, photos, hand-written notes – Spencer narrated.

"There's a kid, Brush Holland, in a little town in Missouri called Volney. He's a prodigy. He might be the finest painter of his generation.

Peter looked up from the folder. "Brush. He's a painter and his name is Brush?"

Spencer answered with a shrug. "Apparently his girlfriend gave him the nickname and it stuck."

He indicated the folder in Peter's hands. "You'll see a couple of shots of his work in there. Ignore the snapshots. There are two full-size glossies."

Peter halted at a photo. A color glossy. He pulled it from the folder and examined it. Brush Holland and a prosperous looking woman posed like bookends alongside a huge landscape painting. Envy trailed across Peter's eyes.

"It must be twelve feet long."

Spencer, who spotted the envy, returned to elbows on the desk.

"Ten. You don't mention that it is also fabulous. Wicked color palette. High octane handling. It's modern but it isn't. The kid is prolific. At one time, he had paintings hanging all over that town. He gave them away. And, yes, we think they are all that good."

"At one time?"

"The kid's a recluse. About a year ago he quit school and took back every painting he had hanging in that town. Now, he won't let anyone but that woman and some girl see his work."

"Some girl?"

"I guess it's the girl who gave him the name. We don't know."

"So, what's this got to do with me?"

"I want to mount a show of that kid's work. And I want that kid to be an alumnus of our school."

"So, you want to recruit a high school dropout."

"If he decides he wants to learn algebra, we'll find a way."

Peter ran his finger across the photo, tracing the flow of the painting.

"Has he got something against money?"

"I don't know what his problem is. The last guy we sent down there claims the kid's father came at him with a shotgun."

"Who did you send?"

"Perkins."

"He's a candy-ass."

Spencer sighed in a manner that suggested this was true. "Maybe, but he's the one who put that folder together."

Spencer sighed again, this time with a manner that suggested he was handing his future to chance. He took the next dance step. "Get me that kid and his paintings, and I'll get you a show."

Peter now had a glossy in both hands. The envy in his voice was fully unconcealed. "Where did the kid get training?"

"Nowhere. As near as we can tell he's an autodidact."

Peter spoke to the glossies, with a hint of larceny. "So,

he's a teenager, he's self-taught, his handling is mature, like maybe he's done a bunch of these big ones. And he already knows what he's doing."

Peter's eyes slid from the glossies to Spencer. He now spoke with a touch of slime in his voice. "Which means you need him more than he needs you."

Spencer shrugged off the slime. "The school will be good for him, and you know it."

Spencer's parry worked. Peter resumed, the slime gone. "Who else is after him?"

"We don't know. Right now, we think he's our little secret, so there is reason for haste."

"How much haste?"

"School starts September second."

"Eight days."

"And you're burning daylight. Everything you'll need is in that folder."

Peter returned to transaction mode. "My show. I'll need the contemporary wing. All of it."

"No."

Peter shoved the photo back into the folder and thrust it at Spencer, who didn't budge. Spencer's eyes met Peter's. Now Spencer's voice had a touch of slime. "You're the beggar. I'm the chooser."

Spencer watched this sink in. Ever so slowly, Peter morphed into a new persona. He donned his hat and cape. His manner became Olympian. He stood sideways to the desk and looked over his shoulder and down on Spencer. He swept a caped arm and retook the folder, clutched it to his side, turned his head away and spoke to the ceiling.

"I require a per diem."

Spencer pulled a checkbook from his top drawer and a tasteful and expensive pen from his breast pocket. He scrawled out a check. Peter, no longer Olympian, leaned in and nipped it from Spencer's outstretched fingers. He side-glanced the check and spoke with a trace of uncertainty.

"This is a personal check. From you."

Spencer spoke to the drawer as he returned the checkbook.

"This is between us, at least for now. I need to see how you handle this."

Spencer closed the drawer and eyed the man who would be an old friend if the man had any friends. "I can risk my money on you, Peter. I can't risk my career."

Peter knew this was true, too true. He paused to restore his dignity and swept from the room, cape aflowing. There was no farewell. If there had been dust in the room, it would still be settling. Spencer spoke to the void.

"Showtime."

CHAPTER 3

TRAVELING ROADSHOW

PETER'S traveling roadshow roared through the pre-dawn streets of Chicago. It was a bus, a double-decker Greyhound, modified and frisky. The lower exterior was painted black, with the addition of his signature on each side, outsized and painted in red, punctuated by an ample glob of red. The upper exterior was splattered with an interpretation of one of his color-riot canvasses.

The bus hauled a long box trailer, same paint job minus the name. Loudspeakers atop the bus bawled and howled. It was music, if you wanted to hear it that way. Otherwise, it was an insult.

Early risers on the sidewalks stopped and stared. Some covered their ears. When cars were stopped in traffic nearby, the drivers rolled up their windows.

Inside the bus, the same music played. Bad and loud. Peter, in gaucho hat and cape, piloted the bus while one-eyeing a roadmap and chewing on a Danish and drinking coffee.

The interior was bright and roomy. The original bus passenger areas, both levels, had been hollowed out and remodeled. It had the effect of a two-story room brightened by skylights. A half wall with a windowless door divided the space into two rooms – living space in front, painting studio in the rear.

The oversupply of primary colors continued inside. Two red-splotch canvasses were affixed to each side of the half wall, sandwiching the door. The living space was a party space – an extravagant bar adjacent to two swivel chairs bookending a couch that doubled as a bed. You could tell the furnishings were expensive when new, which had been many parties ago.

Peter navigated to a highway and accelerated onto it. He was going against the grain of morning rush hour, and it felt good. When Chicago began to shrink in his rear-view mirror, Peter tossed off the roadmap and stuffed what remained of the Danish in his cheeks. He settled in. It would be coffee for the rest of the day.

The map was dispensable. He was now on Route 66 to St. Louis. It would be five hours there, then a left turn onto another highway. Then another hour or so.

As the traffic thinned, Peter's roadshow lost its audience. He turned off the exterior loudspeakers. He silenced the non-music music inside the bus and switched to classical. Rachmaninoff at a listenable volume. He flicked off his gaucho hat and released the baroque clasp that fastened his cape and let it fall behind him.

Farmland opened up around him, framed by the ample windsheld. Peter's manner changed. His shoulders loosened. So did his grip on the wheel. His warthog expression softened but refused to go away. A mindful look emerged, refusing to be hidden.

He rolled south on the two-lane highway and let rural Illinois amble by. He slowed now and then to one-hand a small, professional-grade camera and shoot scenes through the windshield. He was quick and assured with the camera.

When he spotted pastured cattle with all but one cow facing the same direction – one of his favorite road trip pastimes – he slowed to frame the shot properly. If you didn't know better, you could think painting wasn't his primary profession.

In many ways, he preferred the lens to the brush. You could say he was always in the act of composing. He preferred a camera that slid easily into his pockets or could dangle from a wrist strap, always at the ready. He also preferred a small camera because it attracted little attention. Over the years he had watched as people adjusted their behavior and body language, sometimes ever so slightly, but enough, when they detected the presence of a camera.

He wanted to capture people being themselves. He rarely took photos of people posed looking directly at the camera, which to him created a falsehood.

The hours passed easily. They always passed easily for him. Peter Basque had very few small secrets. One of them was watching, observing. He knew you watched him. He didn't deny his vanity. He didn't want you to know he watched you, and everything around you. He didn't want you to know his mind was always absorbing as his eyes framed the passing day. Every moment could be a new composition, and each composition was a new secret, especially if you were in it. The hours passed easily.

He skirted St. Louis, found highway 40, headed west, and switched to coffee and sandwiches as the low hills around St. Louis gave way once again to open prairie. He pulled the map out again. Volney was about an hour ahead.

But it wasn't. Peter found himself steering the bus and trailer in and out of construction sites and detours. A new interstate highway was being laid down along the path of U.S. 40, mostly alongside it, sometimes erasing it. For Peter, this was an opportunity. He went to work with his camera as the stop-and-start, slow-and-go traffic crawled forward between flagmen. Peter had no idea what he might do with these photos, but that could be said about all his photos. This was shoot now, decide later, or as Peter preferred to label it, "Ready. Fire. Aim."

Ready. Fire. Aim. It may as well have been his personal motto. Peter Basque had spent his life, including his childhood years, in obedience to impulse. He was obedient to little else. As a child, he was considered "hyper-active" in the terminology of the day and therefore bedeviling, but almost normal.

As an adult, the assumption of normality went away, although he was never thought to be frenzied or manic. He was just unpredictable. He never said no to an impulse, mostly because the impulse had overtaken him before he got the chance to think "no," much less say it. And, like that, he would veer off to the next novelty, whatever it was.

He rarely reflected on what motivated him other than the novelty. He considered self-examination ponderous, and he feared the weight and drift of brooding. Also, he grew to relish that people found his unpredictability to be irksome.

But one thing was predictable. He left people behind. Many tried, at first anyway, to keep up. After all, his novelties were never commonplace, but, unfortunately, never fully novel enough to pursue along with him for very long.

He became friendless without even knowing it. He had only people he knew, and it never crossed his mind to make something deeper of it, or them.

Now, he pocketed his camera and gave Ready, Fire, Aim a rest. Noon had come and gone, and the detours had gone away. Peter returned to an unobstructed highway 40. Construction on the new highway plodded along, a few hundred yards to his left. Small towns came and went.

He pulled out his camera anew as he saw a sign approach, "Welcome to Volney, Missouri. Where People Come to Smile. Pop. 401." The sign was larger than it needed to be, more like a small billboard, and hand painted, especially the population number, which had apparently been painted over and updated with each birth and death.

Peter didn't continue past the sign. He was lured from the road by a newly finished, but still barricaded access road that led to an overpass a few hundred yards away. He turned left toward the overpass and swerved the bus and trailer around the barricades, knocking only one aside.

He navigated past the exit ramps and braked at the

top of the overpass. Here he aimed camera shots that followed the new 4-lane highway long into the prairie distance. He took shots of work crews adding finishing touches in both directions – sod here, a signpost there – laboring before the stirring promise of a horizon.

At the sound of angry voices, he pointed the camera downwards. Not far from his overpass, maybe 15 yards, a truck driver, arm out his window and pounding his door, was losing a heated argument with what appeared to be the worksite foreman. Peter grinned in appreciation as he watched the foreman dodge a clip board the driver hurled at him. Peter got a shot of the moment, but it was rushed. He could only hope it was in focus as he watched the truck and its angry driver lurch away.

Peter crisscrossed the overpass again after fashioning a laborious u-turn, which displaced another barricade, and headed into Volney. He one-handed the wheel. The camera never left his hand. He didn't stop to replace the barricades.

Just past the population sign he took a shot of a tallish, slender young woman toting a large scrapbook-style book. She was walking away from a produce stand with a sun-faded sign atop – "Symington Produce." The stand was shuttered. She stopped and took in Peter's passing roadshow before she slipped inside a roadworn pickup – same name painted on the door. Peter could just make out a big hand-written note on the stand front, "Back in two hours."

He spoke to his windshield. "Two hours from when, darlin'?"

On the other side of Symington Produce an empty

Sheriff's car was pulled over in front of a speed limit
sign – 25. Peter slowed as the Sheriff's car neared, noting
that It was rusted out and had almost flat tires. Past the
car,, Volney eased into view. The town was split down
the middle by the highway, which widened to allow for
generous diagonal parking on both sides. Peter left his
loudspeakers silent.

Peter's bus growled through town, nice and slow. It
wasn't a one-street burg. Residential side streets branched
away on both sides. The place had a pleasant, tree-lined
look. Two church steeples rising from the canopy beyond
lent the townscape a serene note. A church bell signaled
the arriving half hour. Up ahead and to Peter's right, just
outside the north side of town, a perfect little gumdrop of
a hill arose above the prairie. It was the only hill for miles,
and it featured a massive, stately tree on its crown.

The town was small, but substantial enough to have
one of everything – hardware store, gas station and
garage, shoes and clothes mercantile, bank, grocery,
drugstore, five and dime, barbershop, post office, bus
stop, cafe.

Volney was the hub of a farming community. As
such, the town followed the conventions of farm life.
Dinner was the noontime meal, and it was substantial
and taken at leisure. The wide, awninged sidewalks were
now silent in noontime intermission. Peter's traveling
roadshow passed unnoticed.

Peter slowed as he neared a small, white-fenced park,
or maybe it was a fairgrounds. There was a well-kept
baseball diamond to the rear. A small sign read "Jesse
James's Rock Park, Fairgrounds, and Duck Pond," so it

was both, plus a pond. Beneath the sign a smaller sign pointed toward a footpath that led toward the hill and upward. It said, "Round Hill Cemetery."

Park, fairgrounds or cemetery, there wasn't enough room to park his rig. Peter looked further down the road. On the adjacent lot he saw grain towers surrounded by an ample gravel space. He wheeled the bus there, pulled under the only shade at the edge of the lot and switched off.

He was splayed on the aging couch and napping before the angry truck driver from the highway pulled in beside him, exited and ambled into town.

CHAPTER 4

THE AYES HAVE IT

LILLIAN PERSON'S CAFE had the commonplace and timeless appurtenances of a diner. Customers entered from a door on the right side of the façade and immediately turned left. To the right as they passed through the room was a counter with stools. Behind the counter was the usual workspace cluttered with utensils and appliances.

A low, long horizontal opening behind the workspace, deep enough for a shelf with heat lamps, accessed the kitchen. The wall above the opening was bare.

The cafe was a single room that was clean, shiny, and brightly lit, with slow-motion ceiling fans and a black and white checkerboard floor. Tables for four were nicely arranged to the left of the ten-stool counter. They filled the room. There were no booths. A large picture window extended the view out to the sidewalk under the awning and Main Street beyond.

It was the post-noontime lull. The place had a visible population of four, not counting Lillian herself, who could not be seen but seemed to be there, because the angry truck driver was speaking to her, loud, like he was giving a speech. He was sitting at the counter, coffee in hand.

"So, I said, well excuse me! How could I question an important executive like yourself? Now I know he isn't going to sign any invoice. Eight thousand gallons. Screwed up."

Three old codgers discoursed at a nearby table. In the middle was Mokane, who had been a larger man in youth. He was wearing a baseball cap and faded blue work clothes over his still squarish build. Gray had overtaken his dark hair. To his left was Calwood, a small, trim fellow who sported a flat-brimmed hat, the kind they called a straw boater. He was in short sleeves, string tie, and had a trim mustache still with traces of light brown. To Mokane's right was Bloomfield, tall, hatless and bald in a checked shirt and striped pants held together by dotted suspenders. He had a long face, heavy lower lip, basset hound eyes, and a perpetually baffled expression behind ancient bifocals. All three had unlit cigars.

Bloomfield stared into the distance as Mokane shielded himself with a newspaper and pretended to not listen to Calwood.

Calwood spoke anyway. "It's an engineering principal."

Mokane, spoke to the paper. "Oh? And what would that be? Nothing is stronger than something?"

The truck driver again spoke to the empty wall behind the counter.

"So, he says it's the wrong color. It's supposed to be

yellow, you know, for the stripes, and it's his stretch of
road and he isn't going to be a laughingstock and it's my
problem."

Calwood looked away from Mokane's newspaper and
spoke to the air. "The holes create arches, see? And that's
strong. Just look at any building. The way it's built."

The truck driver drained his coffee and returned it to
the counter a little too hard, as he spoke. "And I say, well,
this is for sure my last government haul."

Lillian Persons struggled up behind the counter,
hammer in hand and a nail between her teeth. She looked
around like she owned the joint because she did. She
was in her mid-30s and attractive in a working girl way.
Blonde hair pulled back in a ponytail. Her outfit was a
one-piece, done up in uniform style, topped by an apron
with pockets over a physique kept trim by constant
motion.

Married young and widowed early, she had called all
the shots and written her own paycheck most of her adult
life. Still, there was a wistful femininity about her, even as
she looked like she could toss out a disruptive customer,
which she had on occasion done.

She poured the Truck Driver a refill with her
hammerless hand and turned to eye the wall. The truck
driver continued.

"So, now I've got two choices. I can deadhead two
hundred miles… "

Lillian let out a sympathetic "ooh" and slid the
nail from her mouth. She traced across the wall above
the kitchen window with her hammer until she stopped
in the center and drove the nail into the middle of an

X penciled there. Four precise blows. The truck driver saluted her carpentry skills and went on.

"Or I find a way to unload eight thousand gallons of pink paint that nobody on Earth wants."

Lillian silently acknowledged his predicament. She bent behind the counter and pulled up a framed print – a romantic prairie landscape, long and horizontal – and deftly placed it on the wall, finding the nail on her first try. She stepped back, tilted her head, and glanced at the truck driver for confirmation. He gestured an "up" movement with his right hand. Lillian nudged up the right side of the frame. She looked over at the codgers. Calwood gave a "down" signal with his left hand while Mokane looked around his paper and thumbed a "down" sign with his right. Bloomfield looked out the window. She left the frame as it was.

She turned to the truck driver. "So, what did you do?"

"I threw the clip board at him."

Mokane let out an extravagant sigh from behind his paper and spoke toward the paper. "Alright. How big is each hole?"

Calwood took on a look that revealed he knew the sigh was coming and was delighted it came.

"Inch and a half," he said. "Or maybe less or more."

Mokane muttered toward Bloomfield, who was now leaning in to read the newspaper over his shoulder. "Can I turn the page now?"

Bloomfield gave him his perpetually baffled look.

"Burn the place down?" he said.

Mokane shouted into Bloomfield's ear. "I said some

old fools are too stubborn to wear a hearing aid."

Bloomfield removed his glasses and polished them with a napkin as Mokane returned to Calwood.

"So, that's four and half inches. All the way through, right?" he said. Calwood nodded yes. Mokane went on.

"Which is, I estimate, about 20 percent of a brick. Which any moron can see is less brick than a hundred percent of a brick which saves them money at the brick factory where they are likely, even as we speak, doubled up laughing because they got this muttonhead up in Volney believing that holes make a brick stronger!"

Mokane slapped the paper onto Bloomfield's chest. "Here!"

"Order up!" a sharp, disembodied voice rose from the kitchen as a plate appeared on the ledge of the kitchen window. Lillian hustled over, swiped the plate from the ledge and placed it before the truck driver.

Hubbub arose out on the sidewalk as people passed before the window. The door swept open and a trio hastened in, followed by a crowd.

The trio was led by Mike Rutherford, Volney's youngish banker, business owner, and mayor. He caressed a large rolled up sheet of paper under one arm. His navy blazer was draped over the other. He was trailed by his two handymen, Duck and Pez.

Duck – big, hatless and roundfaced in T-shirt and overalls – toted a wooden podium. He made his way across the room with a rolling, side-to-side gate. He had buzz-cut sandy hair, and a healthy cheek blush that framed a sunrise smile. He seemed to be in his thirties. You couldn't really tell.

On his heels was Pez – mute, thin, dark, dour – plodding in long flat-footed strides. His upper body did not move, and his arms stayed glued to his sides as he marched in overlong strides, clutching a briefcase with one hand and a Pez dispenser in the other. He seemed to be in his late twenties. You couldn't tell. He stopped at the codger's table and stiff armed the candy dispenser in presentation.

"No thanks, Pez!" the codgers responded in unison.

As Mike swept past the counter, Lillian slipped a coffee cup into his hand. He took a swig and pointed the cup toward the far end of the room and barked an order, "Duck! Pez!"

Duck and Pez immediately set about transforming the room into a town meeting hall. Duck placed the podium at the spot where Mike had pointed while Pez slid a table beside it. Duck began shoving the rest of the tables to the other end of the room as Pez dragged the chairs forward and arranged them, audience style.

The codgers relinquished their table when Pez approached. They moved into chairs near the front as more townspeople entered and pitched in before taking seats.

Helen Bellamann, all business and dressed for it, entered chin high, gliding like a ship sailing through the assembly. She maintained the noble posture of a dancer while she managed to avoid making physical contact with anyone as she made her humorless way through the room and took a seat at the head table.

Lorelai Bellamann, Helen's dolled up younger sister, danced in and brushed up and flirted with anyone, but mostly Mike. This obviously discomfited him. She was extravagant, her hair permed immobile – platinum with an aluminum sheen – above a lace layered dress that arrested ice cream scoop cleavage escaping an hour-glass form. She somehow stayed balanced on tri-colored heels. She brandished a matching parasol, which townspeople dodged as she maneuvered to a chair, with stops along the way to pose in coquette mode.

Susannah Symington, the young woman from the produce stand, entered quietly with her book and took two seats near the rear. More townspeople flowed in.

Person's cafe was now full. Overflow townsfolk sat and leaned on the tables that were pushed to the rear, making a sort of balcony. The hubbub rose as all but Lillian and the truck driver gravitated toward seats. Mike rapped a gavel on the podium. Pez plodded to the head table, turned to the assembly, and unfurled a small American flag.

The crowd spoke in unison.

"I pledge allegiance to the flag of the United States of America. And to the Republic for which it stands, one nation under God. Indivisible. With liberty and justice for all."

After the pledge, Pez presented his candy dispenser to the assembled crowd. They answered in unison.

"No thanks, Pez!"

During the pledge, Peter had swept in, cape aflowing, pausing to remove his gaucho hat and hold it over his heart. Now, all eyes turned to Peter.

The truck driver saluted him with his coffee cup, "Afternoon, pardner."

Peter took a half bow, "Half your nouns are correct. It is indeed afternoon."

He turned to Lillian. "Swiftly lass! Though it be past noon, I require the elixer of cocklight!"

Lillian glanced toward Mike, uncertain. Mike mouthed the word coffee as a question. She poured a cup. Peter took a hearty swig and spoke to the ceiling.

"Midday! Mild blushing goddess! Fortified, I ravish thee!"

Peter turned back to the room, leaning, elbows on the counter. He settled in and toasted all with his cup. The townspeople glanced at one another, performed a group shrug, and turned again to the podium. Peter's eyes went there, too.

Mike was at the podium. Helen was seated alongside at the table. It was impossible for Peter to miss that they were a team, but an incoherent one. They arranged themselves a little too close but held themselves a little too far.

Helen was prim in a starched, blazing white, high collar blouse and light gray summer suit. Peter took her in the way he saw all women. He observed women first as would-be models. He catalogued the features and proportions as he searched his mental encyclopedia of types – a source of never-ending fascination for Peter. Some people would look and move and sound like other people he'd met in far apart places, and, for Peter, this was a delightful mystery lodged somewhere in the long records of ancestry and pedigree.

It wasn't until after he had made this initial appraisal – an act that required maybe a second or two – that Peter considered attraction, if he did at all. Beauty, for him, was issued from the sketch pencil, and it wasn't determined by classical or cultural standards. It came from nature and disposition.

As he had told himself many times, you can tell a great deal about a person by observing their clothing. You can tell a lot more about the person if there is no clothing at all.

He found Helen's firm, clear features severe, but falsely so, which somehow made her fetching. She had naturally wavy dark hair that was too long to be short and too short to be long. She had wide-set eyes that would be expressive if she let them, and a perfectly angular nose over full lips and a turned-up chin. She would have pleasant dimples if she ever smiled. She was trim and fit in a well-ordered life sort of way. Peter guessed her age as mid-thirties. Other than being fully English/American, she fit no type.

Mike was in shirt sleeves rolled up past his wrists, loosened necktie, and darkish hair that he had combed with his fingers. He had a way of moving that hinted at restlessness. He was a man in his prime, but he didn't appear to fully know it. He had a competent bearing, yet he seemed too earnest in the moment, and Helen looked to be the reason why.

It was also evident that Mike and the townspeople were a team. There was an air of integrity to him. Mike didn't want to be mayor. They wanted him to be mayor.

Mike spoke in a semi drone. "This is the 831st recorded Volney Town meeting. August, 1963. Helen Bellamann recording. Michael Rutherford presiding. Do

I hear a motion to dispense with the reading of the July minutes?"

Helen attempted to protest but was cut short by her sister.

"So moved!" squeaked Lorelai.

This was followed by Peter, "I second!"

The townspeople paused and turned his way. He toasted them again while Mike closed the deal. "Moved and seconded. All in favor?"

All but Helen delivered a throaty "aye!"

Mike lost his drone voice and became fully engaged in the meeting. "Do we have any old business?"

Lillian, behind the counter, raised her hand. Mike responded.

"The Chair recognizes Lillian Persons."

Lillian slipped away from the counter and came to the podium. She addressed the room. "As outgoing chairman of the July Fourth Events Committee, I know I speak for everyone when I thank Pez. . . please stand . . ."

Pez came to his feet.

". . . Pez for the best fireworks display Volney has ever seen, and Susannah Symington..."

Pez returned to his seat.

". . . Please remain standing until all names are called. . ."

Pez returned to his feet.

". . . and Susannah Symington for organizing the Covered Dish supper. Susannah?"

Susannah stood. Lillian checked her notes.

"And. . ."

Lorelai vaulted to her feet, her dress flouncing along,

her parasol vertical.

". . . and Lorelai Bellamann, recently returned from her tragic life in Kansas City, for the modern dance demonstration at the Holiday Lunch and Learn. We are grateful to you all."

The townspeople delivered a healthy dose of applause and attaboys as Pez and Susannah bowed and took their seats. Lorelai continued to bask, even as the applause faded to quiet.

Helen turned to Mike, her voice steely, "I believe, Mr. Chairman, there is no further old business."

Lorelai let out a pout and sat down. Helen continued, the steel gone, "While we're thanking people."

Mike didn't look at her as he spoke, "Chair recognizes Helen Bellamann."

Helen didn't rise to speak.

"I'd like to extend our gratitude to the Rutherford Grain Works for their civic-minded repainting of the grain towers in the wake of the recent unfortunate fire."

Peter watched Mike shrug off the compliment. Out of the corner of his eye he observed Duck going into a hangdog posture while Pez shielded him.

Mike returned to the moment, "Is there any other old business?"

The eyes of every single man in the room bore in on Mike, forcing him to avert his. He shifted in place. Helen gave him a glance that said, "what's this?" Mike didn't answer. He looked back into the room. The eyes of every man in the room had not moved. Mike let out a sigh. He spoke to the floor, like maybe there were fire ants down there.

"I guess I have some old business that might be new business."

Now the women's eyes were on him, too. He went on.

"We, the men of the volunteer fire brigade would like to express our appreciation for the fine uniforms provided to us by the Ladies Auxiliary."

The women in the audience beamed.

"But that was more than a year ago," said Helen.

"Yes," said Mike, eyes on the room. "In fact, it was two July 4th parades ago. Of course, that's when we wear them. The fourth of July. You know, when it's so hot. Nobody wears them to a fire . . . well, nobody but Pez, and, well, some of the men wanted me to mention . . ."

He shifted again. The men were not going to let him slide out of the moment.

". . . well, all of the men have pointed out to me that there's no shade on the parade route, and how the festivities last all afternoon when it's really, really hot, and the uniforms are . . ."

You could almost feel the pause hanging in the air.

". . . well, the uniforms are made of. . ."

All the men leaned forward in their chairs.

". . .heavyweight . . ."

The men seemed about to spring forward.

" . . . wool."

Helen went erect in her chair as all the other women tensed and a very dark cloud gathered and churned in the room. Helen spoke in an unbending monotone. "Move we table this discussion."

"Second!" called Lillian.

All the other women declared "aye" before Mike

could call for a vote.

"The ayes have it," said Helen as she watched Mike absorb his own overthrow.

Mike, who seemed grateful to see the moment pass, gave his gavel a feeble thump.

"Is there any other old business?" he said.

"I'd like another cup of coffee," said Peter.

All eyes turned to him as Lillian, who had returned to the counter, refilled his cup. Peter offered the room another abbreviated toast. With a little cough, Helen brought the eyes of the crowd back to the podium and table. She paused and began to speak while glancing at pages of notes laid out on the table.

"I will report for the Progress Committee. As you know, the Volney leg of the new Interstate highway is due to open in 17 days. The Progress Committee is concerned that Volney will be left behind when the new four-lane highway bypasses us, so we've been collecting ideas. Mike?"

As he prepared to speak, Mike had one eye on Helen and one on the room. He addressed the room.

"Well, the thing we've got going for us is you can see the town from the new Interstate. But you've got to give them a reason to pull off."

Lorelai dove in, punctuating with her parasol. "What better reason to stop than Bellamann House, our town's historic home. Once featured in Time Magazine."

Duck rose to his feet. "I'm Duck."

The crowd responded in unison, "We know, Duck!"

The crowd waited for more. So did Duck. He startled, then continued, "Jesse James Rock. Me and Pez, Pez and me, I. We say put up a sign for the rock. It's history."

At his side, Pez nodded in agreement. Lillian waved from the counter.

"Speaking of signs," she said. "See, we've got my place here. And we've got Frank's full-service 66 station across the street."

She reached under the counter and tugged up a largish sample sign: "Eat and Get Gas." The sign received a general crowd approval.

Susannah rose. "Well, I . . ."

Mike nodded toward Susannah. "Chair recognizes Susannah Symington."

This was met by a communal low groan. Susannah ignored it. Peter's antennae went up. He watched her intently. She squared her jaw and addressed the crowd. "I don't think the four-lane should be there at all."

Another groan, perhaps louder. Susannah, undaunted, continued, "It should be moved. The way it is now, it's a, a thing. Okay, we're part of something. We're.
. . "

She produced her large book. Another communal groan.

" . . this is my guest register from our produce stand. It's signed from every state in America and 14 other countries."

All the townspeople except Helen and Mike mouthed the words "fourteen other countries" along with her. Susannah pushed on.

"If you come out to my stand and look, you can see it. The two-lane. Perhaps you didn't know, but U.S. Route Forty goes from San Francisco, California to Atlantic

City, New Jersey. One coast to the other."

All except Helen and Mike mouthed "one coast to the other."

Susannah, who didn't see the mockery, continued. "It is often referred to as America's Main Street, and, well, it actually is our Main Street here in Volney. You step off of it and you're in Volney and you're part of the life here. You step back onto it and you're part of something else. There's something happening way down the road that you can't see, but you're part of it just the same. So, I don't think they should open it. The four-lane."

Susannah closed her book and sat. Peter, amused and warmed by her artlessness, found himself drawn to the scene before him. Mike, again with one eye on Helen and the other on the room, executed a little neck roll, took a breath, produced the rolled-up paper, and barked an order.

"Duck, Pez!"

Duck and Pez stepped forward to the podium, where Mike handed them the paper roll. They spread the paper and held it for the crowd. It was an architectural drawing with a map alongside. There was an extended pause as the audience took it in.

Helen let out a gasp. "It's a giant gas station!"

Mike sighed and spoke to the ceiling, "It's a traveler's plaza, complete unto itself. Fuel. Traveler's rest. Shopping."

Helen looked like she had just seen a Martian, "Why on earth would anyone stop at this hot treeless place when they could come to Volney?"

Mike spoke to the room, but his voice was directed

to Helen, "Any town on the four-lane can build one of these. But if we get the biggest one started first. . ."

Helen broke him off, "What my family founded will never come to this. . ." She waved off the drawing. "This . . . thing!"

Mike turned to Helen, "Helen, this will save the town, but only if we do it before any other town. Even Robley . . ."

The crowd erupted at once, "Robley!"

Mike eyed them and delivered a solemn truth, "Yes, Robley. They will have an exit, too."

"But what about the 66 station?" said Lillian. "Have you told Frank about this?'

Frank, the only man in the audience except Calwood and Mokane who wore a hat indoors, touched the bill of his cap and nodded at Mike.

"Yes, Frank and I have talked it over," said Mike. "He'll offer gas at the exit and repairs at his current station."

Lillian seemed hesitant. She couldn't hide her alarm.

"Are you planning a . . . a restaurant there?" she said.

Mike reassured her directly. "Only if you want one." He returned to the room. "I've also talked to Mattingly at the Five and Dime. He will operate the curio and snack shop at the new plaza. It's something they call a convenience store."

Mattingly, the only man in the room with a bow tie, acknowledged this. Helen let out a voluble harrumph and spoke to the ceiling.

"Well, everybody seems to know about this but me. But even if you move the whole town out there, this . . .

this isn't Volney."

Mike turned back to Helen, "Okay, it isn't Volney, at least it isn't your Volney. . . "

They were now leaning into each other, the room forgotten.

"But it is our property," she said in an armour-plated voice. "Your big gas station . . . plaza thing . . . wants to be on the southwest corner of Bellamann property. I can see it on your little map. When were you going to tell me about . . . "

Peter planted his coffee cup on the counter with enough thump to draw all eyes. He pushed away from the counter and addressed the podium, "My good mayor!"

Mike and Helen, brought back into the moment, turned their heads to Peter. Mike, still leaning into Helen, spoke to the room. "Chair recognizes . . ."

"Peter Basque, artist extraordinaire," declared Peter, carnival barker style. He worked his way to the podium, stage managing his entrance. At the podium, he spun with enough flourish to sweep his cape, black and red.

"My arrival is fortuitous," he declared. "Brush Holland, Volney's favorite son, will soon agree to come to Chicago and mount a show of his fine paintings."

The response was quick and mixed. Oohs and aahs and murmurs of approval mixed with mutters of confusion and doubt. Helen, instantly suspicious, grew dark. She didn't try to hide the wariness in her voice.

"This has been arranged?"

Peter ignored the conjecture.

"This will put your fair village on the map!" he said. "Press coverage! Television!"

The crowd responded in unison. "Television!"

Mike wanted to hear more. "How?" he said. Peter swept around to him, cape aflowing.

"So glad you asked," he said. "Brush Holland's fine images of Volney will be reprinted and will adorn the walls across this nation!"

More murmurs and mutters and mumbles and whispers arose as Brush Holland quietly came into the cafe, hauling a milk can. Susannah perked up, her eyes never leaving him as Brush deposited the can at the front of the counter. He looked up and found Susannah in the crowd. She patted the saved chair and shined as he came her way.

"Brush!" said Mike.

The crowd followed Mike's eyes and spoke in unison, "Brush!" Some rushed to him.

For a moment the bewildered boy was mobbed by hugs and back pats, congratulations and attaboys until he escaped to the chair next to Susannah. As he slid into his seat, a sketchbook – the boy always carried one – slipped from his pocket and landed beneath the chair, unseen. Brush and Susannah whispered. She filled him in as Brush repeatedly glanced up at Peter, who offered twinkly half salutes in return.

Peter's eyes never left Brush and Susannah while they conversed. They were like a matched pair. She was almost as tall as he, and her hair, although darker, was as abundant as his, and it framed features arranged in an angular diamond-shape – medium-set brown eyes over slightly high cheekbones and barely parted lips that unveiled a more penetrating perception than she revealed. He had noticed on seeing her at the produce stand that she had a touch of agile elegance and a graceful carriage that was accented by a long neck.

They both wore fatigued jeans and sun-faded work shirts over the lustre of outdoor complexions. She wore sunlight and air the way other girls wear makeup. The two whispered using a personal shorthand, in a very deep interplay of lifelong affinity.

The hubbub died down and the room seemed to take a deep breath. The truck driver slid off his stool and met Lillian at the cash register. Mike went into mayor mode and addressed him, "Thank you for dropping by Volney. If there's anything we can ever do . . . "

The truck driver didn't look up from his exchange with Lillian. He spoke over his shoulder, "You can tell me what I'm supposed to do with eight thousand gallons of pink paint."

This brought out murmurs and chuckles from the room. Calwood's voice rose above them, "Eight thousand gallons? Shoot! You could cover every building in Volney with that much paint."

More chuckles and murmurs and general babble carpeted the room. Meanwhile, the idea hit Peter, still at the podium, like a sack of hammers. As the crowd's attention shifted back to the podium, Peter's face grabbed all focus. He was in his Olympian pose now, with the addition of a beatific glow. He seemed frozen in time and floating on a vision. One by one, the townspeople grasped, as if by magic, his thought. Low murmurs, first of doubt and distrust, then low debate, then a quiet boldness, and finally an approval of sorts swelled until

Peter, eyes upward, punctuated it.

"Every building! Every lamppost! It will be my greatest work!"

Bedlam ensued. Voices arose all at once, some speakers standing, some sitting, some alternately sitting and standing. Mike pointed toward the truck driver and barked, "Duck!"

Duck hustled through the chattering crowd, nimbly for a man of his size, and collared the bug-eyed truck driver.

Mokane could be heard shouting into Bloomfield's ear, "He wants to paint the town pink! He wants to paint the town pink!"

Mike gaveled the room quiet. The truck driver, jittery, eyed Duck and the room.

Helen pointed to the driver, "Duck, let that man go!"

Duck eyed Mike. Seeing no directive from him, Duck shifted his weight and renewed his grasp. The truck driver balanced on his toes.

Lorelai bounced up, "I move we buy that man's paint!"

The truck driver seemed stunned by the notion, then he could be seen quickly warming to it.

Peter sent an arm skyward, "I move and I second that we put me in charge of the project!"

Mike whispered to Helen, "Can he do that?"

Helen returned an icy glare. Bedlam returned. Mike tried to gavel it down, but it was no use.

"Put him in charge?" declared Mokane. "Who is he?"

Lillian rose and addressed the podium, "We can't put anybody in charge of anything until we vote."

"They sure as hell won't miss us from the new highway, now," said Mattingly.

Lorelai beamed and did her best Marilyn Monroe, "We'll be irresistible. I know all about irresistible."

Brush spoke to the room. "I don't want to go to Chicago."

"Chicago's in a whole 'nother state," said Duck.

"He doesn't want to go to Chicago!" exclaimed Susannah. "Is the paint in buckets?"

Above the group chatter Helen could be heard pleading, "Wait! Stop! This is crazy!"

"Lunacy?" answered Peter. "Ah, who is to say? Only the sane man knows doubt."

"It's no crazier than golf," said Lillian.

"It's not crazy if he doesn't want to go to Chicago," said Susannah.

"No not that," said Helen, trying to speak to Lillian and Susannah at the same time. "I mean yes. I mean, no."

"I used to play golf," said Calwood.

Duck rose and spoke towards Mike, "What about the fire hydrants? Are they still red?"

"I think that's a hydrant law," said Mike.

"You take a club and hit this little bitty ball and you drive to it in this little clown car," said Lillian.

Peter became even more Olympian. He raised a finger skyward and spoke toward it. "Oneness!"

"And what are they doing when they squat down like that?" said Lillian.

"This is going to take at least a month," said Mokane.

Susannah pointed to the truck driver. She spoke with urgency. "You can't hold that man for a month!"

Duck and the truck driver both considered this. Duck re-adjusted his hold. The truck driver was now less resigned to his condition and more curious about the outcome.

"Lillian, that's how you line up a putt," said Calwood. "That's what the squatting is for."

Peter's voice rose over the others, "We will do it in sixteen days!"

All in the room responded at once, "Sixteen days!?"

"When the mighty road opens, so shall we," said Peter. "Reborn! A Phoenix!"

"That name's taken!" said Bloomfield.

Helen, weary, continued to plead, "This is crazy, I tell you."

"We can't change our name," said Bloomfield, speaking to no one in particular.

"We're talking about tourists, Helen," said Lillian. "It's not supposed to make any sense."

"Me and Pez, Pez and me, we tried tennis once," said Duck. "Not golf, though."

Pez affirmed.

Susannah, almost writhing in uncertainty, spoke mostly to herself, "It's. . . it's. . . well. This is. . . see? Chicago? You could, I mean we all could. . . well. Just, just, just, just. . . errrgh!"

"We actually could do it in a week," said Mike. "Everybody would have to pitch in."

"We're gonna need a lotta tools," said Frank.

At this, all eyes turned toward a heavyset man in the back of the room, the owner of Callaway Hardware on Main Street. He had not spoken since the meeting began.

He came to his feet slowly. His eyes met no others as he counted something on his fingers. His eyes came up.

"If I don't have enough in stock, I can get it by Wednesday," he said. "I'll sell at cost." Cheers and whoops filled the room.

"What about the grain towers?" said Lillian.

"Especially the grain towers!" said Peter.

Lorelai's voice carried above all the others, "I move we buy that man's paint!"

The truck driver nodded in agreement, even as he looked around in something like absolute fear.

"We could use money from the deer and dog fund," said Mike.

"How much does he want?" said Mattingly.

The truck driver, alert, could be seen calculating.

"Mostly, he just wants out of here," said Calwood.

"Ladders, buckets. We could store them at the firehouse," said Frank.

"Did he say it was in buckets?" said Mokane.

Helen continued to plead, "Volney will become a joke."

"I already asked about the buckets," said Susannah.

"We could sell those souvenirs made of cedar," said Mattingly.

Peter declared to the ceiling, "Yet, still, beneath the pink veneer, a town seethes and pushes and yearns!"

"Little pink replicas of Bellamann House!" said Lillian.

"Oh my God," said Helen.

Duck, addressed the driver in his grip, "Latex or enamel?"

"Paint the animals?" shouted Bloomfield.

"You can't paint the animals!" said Susannah.

"Sure you could," said Calwood.

"And how's it supposed to stick to fur, muttonhead?" said Mokane.

"It's a free paint job for every building in town!" said Lillian.

Mike eyed the calculating truck driver. "I don't think it's going to be free," he said.

"We'd better vote," said Frank. "Duck can't hold that man forever."

Lorelai rose above the crowd and let out a glass-shattering scream, "I move we buy that man's paint!!!"

This silenced the crowd. The truck driver nodded eagerly.

In the silence, Peter's voice rose like an evangelist, "We will rise from the prairie."

"Buy it with what?" said Helen.

"From many, adjoined yet inchoate, we become one!" intoned Peter.

"With money, Helen," said Lillian.

"Pink is Communist!" said Bloomfield.

This brought the room to a quick pause followed by a low, many-voiced grumble.

Helen spoke up in a desperate voice, "Wait. Not everyone here has spoken. Brush Holland, you're an artist."

The low grumble turned to silence. All eyes turned to Brush.

"Brush, what is your opinion?" said Helen.

"I don't want to go to Chicago."

"See!" said Susannah. "He doesn't!"

Peter continued to intone to the ceiling, "The seer sees what is seen, even when the sayer says it isn't so."

"Give me strength," said Calwood.

"Brush, we are seeking your opinion as a recognized artist," said Helen.

Brush was cornered by the attention of the room. His eyes searched the room. No escape. He was quiet until the room became restless. Then he raised up, but he couldn't look Helen in the eye. He spoke toward the floor, "I guess maybe if, well, if everything was painted . . . "

"You endorse this hideous notion?" cried Helen.

Brush shifted. He looked this way and that. No support.

"I . . . I don't know," he said.

Helen grasped at the moment. "There! See? He's not sure."

"I think there's enough in the emergency fund," said Mike.

"That's what this is!" cried Lillian.

Bedlam again. Mike gaveled as Helen's voice rose above it. "I will not disfigure Bellamann House. Mike! Point of order!"

Mike pushed on, "There is a motion on the floor. There is a motion on the floor. There is a motion on the floor!"

Helen pleaded, "Mike! Wait. It's a . . .a strange motion. Procedural grievance!"

Peter responded to Mike, "I second."

Helen became curt and snappy, "The architectural review board must approve it before you . . ."

Lillian stopped her, "Oh, Helen, that board has no authority. We just put it in to make you feel good."

Helen, now in full desperation, reached for Mike's gavel and shouted, "Move we table this . . ."

Mike pulled the gavel out of her reach, held it aloft, and addressed the room, "The motion has been seconded. All those in favor signify . . ."

Helen cried out, "Not Bellamann House!"

Mike continued, "By a show of hands.

Peter, Lorelai, and Lillian shot their hands up. Calwood followed along with Mokane. Bloomfield, clueless, went up with them. As Mike, avoiding Helen's eyes, slowly voted yes, so did Duck and Pez. The rest of the townspeople raised their hands. Brush raised and lowered his hand a few times until he finally left it aloft. Susannah followed. The truck driver, still in the grasp of Duck, raised his hand.

"The ayes have it!" declared Mike.

He gaveled the vote closed, but Helen's obstinate eyes told him this was only the beginning. The crowd, most of whom were already on their feet, shifted into post-meeting hubbub. Peter made his way through it, sidled up to Brush, and spoke in a forced offhand manner.

"Are you by any chance armed?"

Brush regarded him, eyes wide and flummoxed, and turned to go with Susannah.

The unseen sketchbook remained on the floor.

Peter felt a piece of paper slipping into his hand as he watched Helen Bellamann glide beside and past him. He looked over the paper. It was her card. He spoke to himself.

"Ready. Fire. Aim."

CHAPTER 5

"WE'RE BOTH PAINTERS, KID"

THERE ARE no good or bad neighborhoods in a very small town. The town itself is a neighborhood, and it's always a mix, house to house. Volney was no different, but upon closeup, a first impression of prosperity proved true enough. The town was delightfully walkable.

There was a grid of streets off both sides of Main Street. Six streets paralleled Main Street on the north side. Five on the south side. These were broken into short blocks with cross streets.

As he ambled along, Peter required no directions. The grounds of Bellamann House spread out and emerged on their own within his view. The house had a tower. You could see it above the trees. And it was on Bellamann Street.

Even so, Peter held up a card with the house number and confirmed it. It was the card that had been passed to him silently by Helen as she exited the cafe. The words "four o'clock" were hand-written on the flip side.

Bellamann House was a soaring wedding cake of a home, with too many fairy tale turrets and gingerbread porches (each hinting at a small secret) to count in a single look. They ascended five stories to a circular tower with a conical slate roof of many colors. Downward, it arrayed all the Victorian trimmings you could think of and then some, until a deep, wicker-furnished porch opened up to the main door.

A dandelion-free lawn tucked itself under topiary near the house, then spread away beneath ancient oaks. Flowers bloomed along a picket fence that was freshly painted brilliant white. Centered in the fence, a little swing gate opened to a serpentine brick walkway.

Even Peter, who relentlessly braced himself against sentiment, had a sharp little intake of breath when he approached the house. It didn't last long. He exhaled and ignored the serpentine walk and trod straight to the front door, over the grass and through the scent of boxwood. A single knock, and he was ushered inside.

He now found himself, hatless and capeless, leaning, one elbow over the fireplace mantel in the living room, with a delicate teacup in one hand and saucer in the other.

A folder from the Art Institute of Chicago was balanced on the mantel, which centered a wallpapered room, floral, with stained glass transoms and a wide, civilized, undraped bay window that pleaded in vain for the presence of children. Behind Peter, the magnificent landscape painting he had seen in the photo at Spencer's office spread across the wall and made the rest of the room insignificant. When the painting came into his view, Peter had done his best to obscure his second sharp little intake of breath since he'd seen Bellamann House. Again, he failed.

Helen sat opposite him in the wing chair that she occupied when he entered the room. He had accepted the unavoidable tea after tossing aside his gaucho hat and cape and assuming his fireplace position, there to await the faceoff. Other than the tea, which was presented silently, there had been no formalities. There was a charged stillness to the room. Peter broke it.

"I spoke no untruth."

"If you had an agreement with Brush, I would know about it."

"Brush Holland 'will soon' agree to come to Chicago and mount a show. That's what I said. And so, he shall."

"Who are you?"

Peter placed the cup and saucer on the mantel, swiped away the folder and came to Helen's chair. He dropped the folder in her lap, which unsettled her.

"Who am I? The lad's future."

Helen inspected the folder unhurriedly. There was a glossy promotional brochure and a manila envelope with a scholarship offer that was also a contract. She scanned the brochure and read every word of the scholarship offer. The room was still charged, and Peter could still sense her wariness, but it was now leveraged by curiosity. He spoke when she leaned away from the contract.

"I shall need your assistance. I'm told he has a shotgun."

Helen slid the brochure back in the folder but left the contract out and placed both on the table. She paused to size up Peter, who welcomed the scrutiny. She looked away before speaking.

"His mother left three years ago. His father has been a wreck since. Brush runs the family dairy by himself."

"All good reasons for a departure."

"He has one friend."

"The lass."

Helen sized up Peter anew. He continued.

"He clings to her."

"Yes, he does."

Peter could sense unease in her voice, or maybe it was apprehension. Either way, she didn't want to approve of their matchup, that much was clear. She softened and became almost wistful.

"I've been his guardian, so to speak, through these troubled years. He welcomes a maternal presence . . ."

The softness vanished. The wariness returned. She eyed Peter. ". . . and I am also his champion. He will not come to you unless through me."

Peter dismissed the challenge. "I need to know two things. During these last three years of turmoil, did the lad continue to paint as before?"

"Yes, he did."

"Did his paintings get better?"

The question startled Helen, but it also triggered a shock of recognition. She replied as though she were speaking to herself.

"Why, yes. They did."

As if on cue, the front door semi-slammed, and Brush let himself into the room. As soon as he saw Peter, Brush turned on his heel. Helen rose from her chair.

"Brush. Stay. Please."

The boy rocked in hesitation. Helen gestured to the open wing chair opposite her little table.

"Come."

The boy shuffled to the chair and threw himself into it, slumped and staring through his knees. Helen nudged him with the folder until he took it. He took his time before opening it. He perused the brochure, spending more time than Helen, a lot more time, taking it in. Peter searched Brush's face as the boy eye's lingered on photos of student life at the school, returning to some photos again and again. A trace of satisfaction came and went from Peter's expression.

Helen handed Brush the scholarship offer. He scanned it and dismay flooded his face. He looked up to see Peter, now in gaucho hat and cape, looming over him.

The room was once again charged and silent. There was the atmosphere of a duel. Again, Peter broke the silence.

"You are Bulkington."

"Who?"

"Bulkington, who sailed with Ishmael to confront the Leviathon."

"Leviathon?"

Peter swirled around, his back to Brush.

"The earth scorches your feet. You must sail against the very winds that would blow you homeward. There is no sanctuary. Out there lies the intolerable truth, and thy apotheosis. You must go."

"Apotheosis? Go? You mean Chicago? I don't want to go to Chicago."

Peter swirled, cape aflowing, and leaned in on Brush.

"Who is staying home?"

"Me. Brush Holland. Me."

"Do you mean the Brush Holland who slogs the mud and pulls teats in the pre-dawn? Is the ping of the milk upon the pail music to him?"

"We're mechanized."

"Or the Brush Holland who would linger late over coffee with the other students. Callow demigods. Is the clink of the spoon the rhythm of his new anthem?"

Brush squirmed a bit, his eyes traveling to the brochure. Peter pounced.

"Ahhh . . . you have a vague notion of it."

Brush tossed the brochure aside. He spoke with false bravado.

"I don't need that."

Peter leaned in further.

"Oh, yes you do."

Brush, cornered, made a feeble attempt at defiance.

"My dad and I are putting in a drainage pond."

"Kid, do you really think you will make your mark on this world with a shovel?"

Still cornered, Brush turned away, eyes to the bay window.

"My paintings aren't ready to show."

Peter's persona changed. He turned away and regarded Brush's painting. He spoke in a voice laden with melodrama and overdone sadness.

"Sad. There's an entire town counting on you . . ."

He turned slowly back to Brush.

" . . . we're not going to let them down, are we?"

This struck home. Brush rose from his chair, eyes pleading Helen for help. Her eyes had never left him as the little duel had unfolded. More than once she had begun to intervene before thinking better of it. Softly, she took a side.

"Brush, maybe it's time."

Peter, seeing the momentum shift his way, swung a caped arm around the startled boy and started to march him slowly back and forth in front of the painting.

"Kid, I don't have time for some random walk to self-discovery, so I'm just going to hustle you through the five stages of grief right now, if that's okay."

Brush, confounded, looked to Helen for guidance. She shrugged a "yes." Peter took it from there.

"Good."

He gently pushed the boy up against the wall next to the mantel.

"You've got your head up your ass because your mom blew Dodge and your old man jackknifed into a bottle. You can't believe it happened. You're pissed and hurt. Part of you, probably a big part of you, thinks it's your fault. How am I doing?"

Brush nodded a wide-eyed agreement.

"You think maybe if you keep running that dairy by yourself, everything will return to normal someday, but it's too big a job and it's killing you."

Peter eyed the boy. Brush agreed again.

"So, you give up. Why bother? And you take your ball and go home. You take down all your paintings and hide them from the world."

Brush flinched on this one. Peter leaned in and went

into hypnotist mode.

"That's the bullshit part. How do we know this? Because you left one hanging. Right there. It's your best one, too, at least you think so, isn't it?"

Brush nodded an agreement.

"So, we've got this ten-foot-wide cry for help hanging in the home of the nearest thing you have for a mother. Bingo."

Peter leaned in further and spoke quietly into Brush's ear.

"We're both painters, kid. We both know that nobody, and by that I mean nobody, sweats out a ten foot canvas just to hide it from sight. You don't give a damn about me, kid. Just let me have a look at them. All of them."

Ever so gently, Helen, now standing next to Peter, reached in front of Peter, grasped the boy's shoulders, pulled him from the wall, and turned Brush her way. Their eyes met before Brush's went to the floor. He nodded "yes."

CHAPTER 6

"THAT, BY GOD, IS PERFECT"

THE LONG driveway to Holland Dairy was fronted by a hand-painted sign that swung from an L-shaped post. It displayed in black and white outline the form of a Dutch windmill with the words "HOLLAND" curving down over it and "DAIRY" curving up below it. "Since 1927" was lettered at the bottom. The sign needed fresh paint.

In the distance, three skinny silos climbed above a long barn roof. Brush, piloting the Holland Dairy delivery truck, lurched down the dirt drive toward them. Helen and Peter, in Helen's unadorned sedan, trailed in the August dust until they passed over a cattle gate and more barns came into view. They, too, needed a coat of paint.

Brush pulled up to the smallest of three barns. It was fenced off on its own. Helen and Peter parked beside him.

Brush was already out of his truck. His uncertain look had returned. It was clear to Peter that the boy wanted to open the door and didn't want to open the door with equal intensity. For the first time since they spoke in Helen's living room, Peter grew gentle. In a wordless gesture, he turned the boy toward the door. Brush went to it.

Peter watched light crawl across the interior as Brush pushed the large sliding door open. Then Peter took a step inside and stood in absolute wonder. The barn had been converted into an art studio, including the addition of skylights.

The place was magical. Ten-foot canvasses seemed to float about, hanging on two rows of support poles that passed down the length of the room, which was immaculate, the dirt floors covered and layered with rugs and scraps of carpet. Over to the right side, easels, shelving, and a sink signaled the working end of the studio.

Brush came up alongside Peter. He semi-whispered an apology.

"They aren't perfect. I think they are when I finish them, and then later…"

Peter stayed him with his hand. He returned the semi-whisper.

"You just described every painter on the planet, kid. And there is no such thing as perfect."

Peter left Helen and the boy at the door as he began to wander from canvas to canvas. Quiet overtook the room as Peter walked, hands clasped behind his back, spending reverential minutes at each painting. Standing back, and then peering inches away, and then standing back again.

Peter silently knew he would never forget this
moment. It ignited something inside him. Something
very old made very new. He also knew he could not put
that something into words, at least not right then.

The quiet was broken by the roar of an approaching
tractor. Even from inside the building you could tell it
was coming in too fast. The roar was halted by the sound
of metal crunching against wood, followed by a splash,
hysterical laughter, and witless, off-key singing.

Brush and Helen rushed out the door, with Peter
trailing. He followed the pair around the corner of
the barn and past an open gate, where he stopped and
marveled in a state hovering between chagrin and delight.
There, floating in a large circular aluminum water tank,
was a very inebriated man. The tractor, still idling, rested
in a heap of lumber that had moments before been a
cattle chute.

The man stopped singing when he noticed he had
an audience. Other than the weathered look of a farmer
– his face was long bronzed permanently, his forehead
white – there was little for Peter to make of him there in
the water. The man waved a greeting – as merry as it was
ossified – while attempting to adjust himself and make
his situation seem perfectly normal.

Brush, standing at the edge of the tank, pointed to
the man. He spoke in the flattened voice of someone who
has witnessed too many moments like this one.

"My dad."

Peter walked up beside Brush.

"I stand corrected, kid. That, by God, is perfect."

Peter leaned in and examined Carl Holland's sozzled

face.

"You have a week or two to sober up, champ. That's about how long it will take me to pack up these canvases and get this town painted. Then, I'm taking your kid to Chicago."

As if by magic, Peter, still facing Carl, produced a pen and contract from his cape with one hand and held them back toward Brush.

"Sign here, kid."

Helen took the pen and paper. She handed the pen to Brush and presented the contract by making a little table with her hands.

Brush glanced at his father and began signing.

CHAPTER 7

"WHAT ARE YOU UP TO?"

SPENCER GRISAILLE worked too many long days in his office. He liked to think it was because he was busy and important, which he was in a way. Mostly though, he was alone at his desk late in the day because he had so little else to do. Other people, including all his friends, had children and hobbies. So, he was pleased when his tasteful and expensive telephone rang. Peter, in Volney's only phone booth, dispensed with any preamble, as he always did on the phone.

"How long can I have on this thing?"

"Peter! I assume you are there. In Volney."

"Yes. How long?"

"And you have contacted the boy."

"Yes, that's why I'm asking how long. Again."

"School starts the first of the . . . what are you up to?"

"I can't get him out of here until everything is covered."

"He has to be here when the semester . . . what do mean 'everything is covered?'"

"What, so he misses some orientation nonsense. We might need a week. Okay, two."

"We can't hold the scholarship. If he's not here, it goes to somebody else."

"I know what I'm doing for the show."

"Is it new?"

"Oh, yeah."

"No red splashes?"

"Not to worry, amigo. I need more money."

Spencer delivered a long silence. Peter banged the phone against the wall.

"Do you want this kid or not?"

"Guaranteed delivery? On time?"

"Yes. And no."

Another delivery of silence from Spencer. Peter, going into hypnotist mode, interrupted it.

"There aren't words to describe these paintings."

Spencer let out a tasteful and expensive sigh.

"What's the money for?"

"I can't tell you. Let's just say it's for art supplies. You know, like paint."

"You can't tell me. Why can't you tell me?"

"Because then you might not send it."

"You can't deliver the kid on time, and you need money and you can't, make that won't, tell me what the money is for and you expect me to buy into all of it."

"Perfect! You've nailed it!"

Spencer considered his surroundings, like maybe he wasn't actually there at all. He reached for his tasteful and expensive drawer.

"Tell me what it is you need."

"I already said. A week, maybe two."

"No, I mean money."

For a moment Spencer could be seen listening. Then his eyes bulged and he fell backward in his chair and upon the tasteful and expensive rug.

CHAPTER 8

"PART OF ME REALLY WANTS TO STOP DISLIKING YOU"

INSIDE HELEN'S living room, the heat of the day had broken. Outside her bay window, the golden hour retreated. Peter was again hatless and capeless with elbow on the mantel. The delicate teacup was gone, replaced by a martini glass.

Helen, again at her wing chair, warily observed her own martini glass on the nearby end table. This was supposed to be a celebration. She wasn't good at celebrations, and she knew it, but one was needed.

So much had changed in one afternoon. So, it was a celebration. She had invited him. Still, the air in the room remained charged. Peter had a way of making that happen. She felt herself unbalanced by his presence and constantly so. He raised his glass and toasted, mostly to himself.

"Ahh, 'the ineffable pleasure of eating and drinking at someone else's expense.' I believe that was Oscar Wilde."

He brought the glass to his lips and took a generous sip. Helen's glass remained on the table. The two considered each other. Her appraisal had an academic feel, but she couldn't hide her mystification or her gratitude.

"It was wonderful what you did today. Here and at the dairy. With Brush," she said, reaching for her glass. "Weird, but wonderful."

Peter's eyes traveled over his glass and rested on Helen.

"You should consider changing your hair."

Helen ignored the feint but paused before grasping her glass. She didn't touch it. Her eyes came back to Peter.

"You accomplished in an afternoon what I've been struggling to achieve for three years."

Peter cocked his head, like he was examining a canvas.

"And showing some cleavage."

Helen let out a so-this-is-how-it's-going-to-be sigh.

"Part of me really wants to stop disliking you," she said.

Peter drained his martini.

"Is it the part that is standing between me and the most provocative artistic statement in a decade?"

"So, we're back to that, are we? Bellamann House is on the National Historic Register. I won't disfigure it."

"Or is it the part that wants to succumb?"

"You mean give in to this freak pink paint notion."

"Actually, I meant that in two ways."

Peter glided toward Helen's chair. He reached across her to the end table, bringing their faces too near. Helen stiffened and retreated as far as her wing chair would let her, eyes wide in indignation. Peter's eyes met hers. He winked and grasped her martini, came erect and toasted her with her own glass. He slurped her martini.

"Or is it the part that can't hide her hots for the mayor?"

Peter swept away, placing her martini next to his on the mantel, and nabbed his cape and gaucho hat on his way to the hallway. Lorelai, coming into the hall and looking the other way, bumped into him, which Peter made no secret of enjoying. As they recovered, a martini glass sailed over his head and smashed against the wall. Lorelai's eyes went round.

Peter, his face now too near hers, took in Lorelai, the smashed glass and the remains of Helen's martini dripping down the wall. He spoke, mostly to himself.

"Outside and high."

And he was gone.

***

That night, the final night of a waning moon blinked into darkness over Volney.

CHAPTER 9

TUESDAY, AUGUST 27

HELEN HASTENED through the elaborate, but sober doors of The Bank of Volney and into a tall – it was two stories – open room with narrow stairs on the left leading to a mezzanine at the rear.

She made her way toward one of the two teller windows, making a bit of an echo as her heels clicked the marble.

The room was windowless on three sides, with a large picture window fronting the street. Through it, and through the reversed bronzed lettering that identified the bank, a hurly-burly scene swelled across the morning sidewalk and into the street.

Helen had just passed through it, her silence as loud as her contempt, slaloming 50-gallon barrels of paint arranged the length of Main Street. Next door, under the wide awning outside Callaway Hardware, Peter commanded, movie director style in gaucho hat and cape, as townspeople emerged from the store brandishing brushes, paint rollers, sandpaper, buckets, tarps and mops.

Several of the diagonal parking spaces in front of the store were blocked off. A long table had been pushed up against the store window beneath the awning and under a hand-lettered sign – "Paint Project Headquarters." There, Lillian operated a coffee and donut stand with a smaller sign, "Free to Volunteers!"

Back inside, Helen arrived at the teller window and served up a chilled greeting, her eyes rolling as the teller put down her donut. She handed the teller a check.

"Cash, please. And two stamps."

She flourished another eyeroll when the only door on the mezzanine above, the one she knew led to Mike's office, swung open and the truck driver from the cafe ambled out, a donut in his mouth and a wad of cash in one hand that he finger-counted with the other. Mike followed. He brightened when he saw Helen below. He darkened when he saw her expression. He and the truck driver passed down the stairs and into the main room. Mike gestured to shake the driver's hand, but they were both full. The driver exited as Mike came beside Helen, who acknowledged him by speaking to the ceiling.

"So, how may I help you Mr. Rutherford? Perhaps a calliope in my garden. Or should I just grow a beard?"

"Dammit, Helen. I didn't hear any better ideas from you yesterday."

"Profanity is the tool of the ignorant."

Helen snatched the cash out of the teller's hand while she was still counting it. She delivered a curt "Thank you" and stuffed the cash away. She headed for the door, Mike dogging. When she pulled up at the door, Mike almost ran over her. He clutched her from behind to keep them both balanced. She shook him away and spun around.

"Just like you. Childish and impulsive."

She slapped through the door, letting it close on Mike, who just stood there. He sprang back when the door opened again and Helen tramped back in and arrowed in on the teller window, her heels letting out sharp angry reports against the marble. She snatched two stamps from the teller's outstretched fingers, wheeled and clicked her way out the door. This time Mike followed.

On the sidewalk, Helen huffed through the press and surge of volunteers, disregarding Lillian and scorning Peter. Mike scrambled after her until the din of the painting crew faded. When they got to a sidewalk bench, Mike raced around the front side as she paced behind it. The bench now between and insulating them both, he confronted her.

"Helen, please."

He knew she was angry with him, but he also knew that, deep down, she didn't like being that way. They had been at odds for years, but they had also been close for years. Theirs was a deep understanding based on a long refusal to understand. It formed a barricade of ice that couldn't be cracked, much less melted, but it was transparent enough they could see through it.

It went back years to an incident with Helen's sister Lorelai, an incident that managed to surface in any conversation between them that lasted more than a few minutes. It was also an incident they refused to discuss with anyone else.

In this way, Mike and Helen had long been a wellspring of amusement for the people of Volney. Ask any citizen of the town to make a list of favorite pastimes, and sooner or later you'd get "watching Mike and Helen wrangle."

Mostly, this was because the wrangle was always the same. Mike would fall out of favor with Helen and then he would attempt to preserve his dignity and grovel at the same time until she relented. Even as they were amused, though, the people of Volney took no delight in Mike's suffering. Given a choice between the two antagonists, he was by far the favorite.

As the tongue-waggers at the barber shop put it, "Mike was either on the way into Helen's dog house, in the dog house, or on the way out."

Alas for Mike and Helen, their center of attraction was the chill between them. It never occurred to either that they were also an attraction for an outside audience.

Now, Mike could feel his nose coming out the door of the doghouse. He saw progress when her eyes finally met his. He came around to her side of the bench. He groveled.

"Helen, don't you see? We're a team. Always have been. This can be our next . . ."

High heels tapping on the sidewalk alerted the pair that Lorelai, in yet another provocative dress, even lower cut than the day before, was headed their way. She walked between them, artfully brushing against Mike, which caused her scarf to slip. He caught it as a reflex. She retrieved it from his hand and slowly dragged it across

Mike's chest as she moved on, hips like pistons. A long moment of icy silence from Helen followed. Mike broke it.

"God Almighty, Helen, I didn't ask her to come back. You did. And you've been driving me nuts . . ."

"I haven't the slightest idea of what you speak."

Calwood, Mokane and Bloomfield, each with a paint brush and donut, muttered to the bench and took seats, their backs to Helen and Mike. Mokane, on the left, gestured at Calwood, in the center, with his brush.

"First off, who's going to catch them? Second off, how are you going to hold them until the paint dries?"

Helen, hands now on hips, her face a living tempest, leaned into Mike.

"How many members are on this team?"

Mike, hands also on hips, his face a swarm of exasperation, leaned into Helen.

"Two. I've been trying to make that. . . her . . . up to you for ten years. Ten! No. Two! The answer is two. On this team. Two."

Mokane poked Calwood's chest with his brush as he spoke.

"And how long, Mr. Muttonhead, do you think those squirrels are going to stay pink?"

Helen leaned away from Mike. Her hands remained defiant on her hips.

"We were engaged. Engaged."

Mike dropped his hands. His shoulders sagged.

"I was a stupid kid, for crying out loud."

"That's not how Lorelai describes it. We have to make choices in life.

Bloomfield eyes came alert. He peeked over his bifocals and into the air. "Horses in stripes?"

Helen stabbed a finger in Mike's chest. "That night, not so long ago, it didn't look to me like you had narrowed your choice to one."

Bloomfield turned to Calwood and Mokane. "You can't paint the horses, too!"

Mike accepted the stabs and stood his ground. "Not so long ago? Helen, that night was ten years ago. What about now? Now! Look, this traveler's plaza is a big deal. I have a group of investors lined up. Doctors from St. Louis. Solid people. But they need a commitment by Monday."

The sound of flat feet slapping the pavement turned every head. Pez slouched up to the bench, he, too, with a donut in his maw.

Mike, restless, speaking with his arms, turned back to Helen. "We could lose this deal. Eighteen acres. Eighteen! It's not even decent pasture."

Pez presented his candy dispenser to the three codgers.

"No thanks, Pez!"

Helen's eyes widened in mock surprise. "We?"

Pez circled around the bench to approach Helen and Mike. Before he could offer his candy dispenser, Helen pulled the donut from Pez's mouth, rammed it into Mike's mouth and whisked away. Calwood, Mokane, and Bloomfield turned Mike's way, took in the moment, and allowed a moment of silence. Pez handed Mike a note. Mike scanned the paper and looked back toward the bank. Mike finished off Pez's donut as he hustled away,

Pez in tow.

The three codgers turned back to face the street. Calwood removed his straw boater and fanned himself with it. "Well, she bulled up on him again."

Mokane shook his head. "Twitchin' like a mule's ear."

Bloomfield cupped an inoperative ear and spoke to the air. "I couldn't hear, either."

Calwood replaced his hat. "It's a high price for a roll in the hay with Lorelai."

Bloomfield's face performed a calculation. "Six cents a bale!"

Mokane regarded Calwood with tender scorn. "Pay the price? You would in a heartbeat. If Lorelai Bellamann were on the other side of the fence during rutting season, you'd bust through just like Mike did."

Calwood ignored the charge. "Helen's a different story. She's the only one who can bullyrag Mike."

Mokane waved off the comment. "She's just rattling his cage."

Bloomfield's perpetually baffled expression became even more baffled. "His battleship's late?"

Calwood looked up, suddenly in thought. "Was Mike in the Navy?"

Bloomfield chewed on his donut. "You can't bring a battleship to Volney."

Calwood leaned backwards, elbows on the bench back. "Sure you could. Bring it up the Missouri River."

Mokane rolled his eyes. "That's about what I'd expect a muttonhead to . . ."

Lorelai rolled back in and took over the moment. She swayed to a stop before the bench and breathed a greeting, "Calwood, Mokane, Bloomfield."

She bent forward, letting her bosom suspend just so, hypnotizing the codgers. She tipped a little deeper, planted a kiss on Calwood's bare forehead, composing an almost perfect bright red, cupid-bow lip print. She withdrew and performed a silent, slow-motion exit. A long moment passed. Mokane elbowed Calwood hard and walked the other way, grumbling.

***

Brush tilted backward on the sloping hood of Susannah's aged pickup, his eyes to the sky. Susannah leaned toward him, close at his side, elbows on the hood. They were alone in the ample shade of a tree on the fence line of a prairie field, the grass knee-high and tickling the bottom of the truck's open doors.

It was their tree, at least that's how they considered it, and it shaded a small sanctuary. It offered just enough seclusion on an otherwise open prairie. Their names had been carved into the tree so many years ago that the letters had been re-carved several times.

An undisturbed picnic basket rested on the truck seat.

In the distance, the silos of Holland Dairy poked up, half visible. On the other side of the fence, Holsteins silently grazed the low grass, their black and white markings somehow different and the same, each one.

It was an idyll, and the two were wholly comfortable in it. Even so, there was no hiding the uncertainty in the air.

Susannah plucked a blade of grass from the soil, twisted it in half, and slipped it toward Brush's lips. He gripped it with his teeth. She returned to elbows on the hood.

"I was thinking we could go swimming tonight, up at the pond."

"I have a game."

"Maybe after? Or let's go Saturday."

Brush shrugged in assent. Susannah plucked another blade and curled it in her hands.

"Do they play softball in Chicago? I mean, is there room in the city?"

"Parks, I guess."

"Are there girls in Chicago? I mean, at the Art Institute."

"I guess so. There were some in the brochure pictures."

"Do they were clothes? I mean, the models."

"I don't know. Suz, what am I supposed to do in Chicago?"

"Nothing, I hope."

"What am I going to draw in Chicago? Who is going to run Holland Dairy? Who will cut and rake and bale this field? Who? What about my friends? What about Dad? I don't have a car."

"Okay, now tell me what's really bothering you."

Brush lifted from the hood. He turned away, slumped under an immeasurable weight. He pulled the grass stalk from his teeth and coiled it in his hands. All at once he looked like a little boy.

"Suz, what if they laugh at me?"

"Oh, Brush . . ."

She came up behind him and caressed his shoulders. He spoke to her and away from her at the same time.

"They're so . . . there. And I'm . . . I'm . . . so . . . so here."

Her caress turned into a clutch. She rested her head on his shoulder and spoke in a whisper.

"Why is it that I have to be the only person on Earth who knows how smart you are?"

Brush twisted around, tangling the grass around his knees. Now his hands moved to her shoulders.

"Because you are . . . you."

Their faces inclined until their foreheads rested against each other. Susannah, eyes down, spoke to the grass below.

"Brush, I want you to do something. For me. This is a Gottado."

Below their faces, she offered her hand, pinky extended. Brush rolled his eyes at the ground and wrapped his pinky around hers.

"Okay."

"Stop worrying about me. Now."

They gripped pinkies, eyes closed, and held the moment. She abruptly pulled away and feigned a sudden trance, regarding her surroundings as if they were utterly new. Brush hinted a knowing smile and took up a sketchbook, one of the dozens, if not hundreds, that littered his life. He always kept a few on hand. Now, the two engaged in a long familiar game. She pointed as Brush opened up the sketchbook and took up his pencil.

"Butterfly."

Brush laid down lightning quick strokes as the butterfly – rough but unerring – surfaced on the page.

"Tree."

The tree emerged in seconds.

"Two cows looking."

Now there was a rhythm and cadence to her directions.

"Mockingbird . . . gate . . . truck . . . road to nowhere."

She paused and reclined on the hood of the truck.

"Me."

Brush rested his pencil and drank her in. He turned to a fresh page and began to sketch, now with an easy, unhurried measure. Susannah luxuriated in his attention. Again and again, her image emerged plain and sublime on the pages in pose after pose, filling the sketchbook.

***

The Holland Dairy farmhouse was a center-hall Colonial, mid-1800s clapboard, painted white – the paint was peeling – with a pitched red tin roof and chimneys on both ends. There were four rooms upstairs and four downstairs, each a corner room. A kitchen and mudroom and bathroom had been added to the rear in the 1920s. Otherwise, it was unchanged. It was fronted by a small two-story covered porch with a walkout on the second floor. The house was on a rise in the prairie, which made it seem taller than it was.

The home was surrounded by flower gardens long abandoned, and shrubbery grown bristly and uneven.

It was night. The house was darkened but for one room. Light glowed from the southwest corner of the second story. It was Brush's room, and he was up late, especially for someone who kept dairy farmer hours.

Brush knew his father was elsewhere in the house, but he didn't know which room and he didn't try to find out. It wasn't because he didn't care. It just wouldn't do him any good to know.

Clutter, thoroughly absent a woman's touch, bedecked Brush's bedroom. The room was large, but in no sense grand, and high-ceilinged enough for a transom that pulled the night air up from the window. There were droopy, lame attempts at drapes that floated and shifted with the breeze. Lamplight bounced off the black windows peeking between them. The room needed paint.

His bed was an antique four-poster that had a leftover look. It was, the bed, free of clutter. A well-loved quilt spread over it.

The clutter around the bed revealed a dual nature. On one side of the room, there was no method to it. Baseball equipment, hunting gear, car parts, caps, boots, gloves, fishing tackle, and an abandoned chemistry set loosely layered the room. On the other side, a host of art supplies was arranged systematically and with evident care – brushes here, palettes there, and paint tubes arrayed just so.

The duality extended to the walls. They were overlayed with inexpensive prints – sports heroes and movie posters mingled with painted landscapes, mountain scenes, and seascapes of all kinds.

Only one picture was framed – a wide landscape over

the head of the bed. It was a watercolor of Susannah and her truck at their sanctuary tree.

A floor-to-ceiling bookshelf recalled the same division. The upper and lower shelves were jammed with a mix of paperbacks – Western novels, adventure and sports stories, and classics of American literature. The eye level shelves were laden with hard-bound books, coffee-table sized, with dust jackets in brilliant colors. They were art books, the expensive kind, lined up in alphabetical order – Benton, Botticelli, Constable, Goya, Hopper, Leonardo, Manet, Michelangelo, Monet, Rembrandt, Renoir, Titian, Turner, Van Gogh.

Every book was well-thumbed. The art books were especially worn and crammed with dozens of bookmarks.

The house was quiet. Brush stood before a chest-high oak dresser. A mirror with photos, prize ribbons, and souvenirs tucked into the frame on all sides, hung above it. He had pushed aside enough clutter on the top of the dresser to spread out the brochure from the art institute. He lingered over each page, reading again every word. He was arrested, again, by a wide photo of the student union. Young artists at ease in cafe chairs at tables. The scene breathed sophistication. "The clink of the spoon" echoed in Peter's voice at the back of his mind.

He put the brochure down and began to unbutton his shirt. He quit halfway, picked up the brochure and opened it to a two-page spread. A photo covering the left-hand page showed students laboring at easels in a wide, brightly lit room. In the center was a model, but it wasn't a person. It was a copy of a statue – a Greek god, he wasn't sure which one. He bored in on the photo. It was large enough to see that the student's work was exquisite. The scene breathed competence.

On the right-hand page an equally large photo showed a single artist with his painting. He seemed to be about Brush's age. The canvas itself was a superb, if not magnificent, large-scale cityscape. But that wasn't what seized Brush. It was the young artist himself. He was urbane, poised, and self-possessed beyond his years. Brush's eyes traveled from the photo on the page to the mirror before him. He regarded himself for an unlovely moment, closed his eyes and closed the brochure.

***

That night, Peter stood outside his bus and looked skyward under a new moon. Like all new moons, it could not be seen, but you knew it was there if you thought about it. Peter did. His eyes lowered and traveled across the old highway and down through the little town that opened up to his left. Time was on his mind.

Peter Basque gave very little of himself away, and this included time, especially so. He structured his associations with people to be like a passing spectacle. A parade that never paused or lingered. He did not want to be the object of too-long scrutiny because he knew a once-over was all he was equipped to deliver. In his own words, "shallow and beguiling is all they get."

Now, he had committed himself to a place, and he had committed himself to time enough for scrutiny. Committed. There beneath the unseen moon, Peter came to understand that he could not walk away from what he had started. He didn't know why he had done it and he didn't know how it would be done.

Ready. Fire. Aim.

The parade had stopped, and he had no clue what he would look like when standing still, naked under the opera cape.

CHAPTER 10

WEDNESDAY, AUGUST 28

MIKE, at his office desk, leaned into the phone, face downward, his features twisted into equal parts irritation and grievance. His voice sounded weary.

"I already told you, Fred. I can get this done by Monday. . . She'll come around. I'll get the land. . . Yes, Fred, I know how to read a calendar."

Before hanging up, he looked at the phone in his hand like maybe it was the problem. He spoke to the silent phone.

"Dammit, Helen."

Mike pushed away from the desk, rolling his chair, and spinning it around. He rose, his back to the room, and turned his attention to a file on the counter behind his desk. The office was undecorated. Mike told himself that this was because he never had the time for it, but he had, in fact, been waiting for Helen to do it.

The walls were bare except for an overlarge corkboard that was pinned with a forest of notes and clippings and pictures. Beside it was rack of hooks laden with keys.

86

Duck sidled in, wearing sunglasses. He seemed to be attempting subtlety, but his heavy, rolling footsteps weren't letting him get away with it. Mike spoke to him without turning around.

"Duck, get the flatbed. The tandem axle. With the ramp. Go over and pick up Mrs. Horton's Ford. Got it?"

He swung around, got a good look at Duck, and dropped the file on his desk.

"Dammit, Duck! How many beers did you have? Duck. Duck? How many tallboys? Look at me."

Duck removed his sunglasses and looked to the floor. Mike persisted.

"I said look at me."

Duck raised his head and exposed bloodshot eyes. Mike fumed.

"Dammit, Duck!"

Duck shifted his feet and looked back down. He spoke to the floor.

"I only do it once a month. Only once."

Mike leaned forward, hands extended to his desktop. He spoke in a lecturing tone.

"Once before was one too many,"

"I'm of age. Old enough."

"Where do you hide your beer, Duck?"

Duck, cornered, put his hands on his hips and attempted to darken his rosy-cheeked aspect with a scowl. Ferocity wasn't an attribute that Duck possessed, but he attempted it from time to time, and the result was, unfortunately for both Duck and his audience, comic.

"You're not the boss of me!"

Mike didn't have to hide a smile. There was enough

ache in Duck's voice that Mike softened. He spoke a little more tenderly.

"That's always been our deal, Duck."

Duck swiped his hand across the room as though to cast aside all before him.

"Nobody is the boss of anybody."

Mike raised an eye and caught Duck with it.

"Didn't I make you the boss of Pez?"

Duck extended his arms, the ferocity put away, and pleaded with both hands.

"Well sure, but Pez, he don't . . . he doesn't talk or drive or swing his arms when he walks."

Mike came around his desk. The two were planted face to face.

"Duck, there isn't a person in Volney who doesn't trust you. But that could change if there is another incident like the grain tower. Duck, you burned it down."

"I saved it, too! I'm on the Fire Department! I'm not a pilot-maniac!"

Duck let his shoulders fall and his gaze slide back to the floor, which he half-kicked. "You just don't smoke at a grain tower."

Mike returned to his chair, took a seat, and eyed Duck.

"You shouldn't smoke, period. Duck, if something like this happens again, I can't keep it a secret. It wouldn't be right. You know that, too."

Duck, still eyes to the floor, spoke as much to himself as to Mike.

"Beer kills your brain. And me, I'm stupid from the get-go."

Mike softened more.

"You're not stupid, Duck. Sometimes what you do doesn't keep up with what you think, and sometimes it's the other way around. But mostly you know it, so it's okay. Usually."

Mike leaned forward in his chair, forearms on his desk. "Duck, if you want a beer, you can have one with me."

Duck raised his head.

"How are you gonna know to be around when I want one?"

The two considered each other for a moment until Mike pointed toward the rack of keys.

"The flatbed. With the ramp."

Duck sauntered over to the rack, fingered a few sets of keys, picked one and whistled out the door. Mike reopened his folder, pulled out the design for his traveler's plaza, unfolded it and spread it out and bent to work.

"Dammit, Helen."

***

Brush's studio barn was still cool as midday passed. The sliding doors were closed against the rising heat. Peter's bus was parked outside, the trailer unhitched and pulled aside, cargo doors open.

Inside the barn, the room had the look and feel of a construction site. Sheets of plywood, lengths of lumber, sawhorses, boxes of screws and nails, hammers, saws, and screwdrivers scattered over the rug and carpet floor.

Brush and Peter lifted a newly-made shipping crate –

plywood sheets over a frame constructed of 2x4 lumber –
from the floor and set it on its edge, the top and one side
still open. It was large enough to contain one of Brush's
ten-foot canvasses. Brush held the box upright while
Peter, with exquisite care, slid a painting into the side
opening. It was a gallery-style canvas, two inches deep.
They both watched it progress steadily through the box
until it was fully inside. No scrapes. The fit was dead-on,
nothing touched the painted side, which brought a small
sigh of relief from both.

"That's one," said Peter. He fetched two screwdrivers
and a box of screws from the floor. He dropped a handful
of screws into his shirt pocket and passed the box and
a screwdriver to Brush, who began attaching a plywood
cover to the top while Peter did the same to the open side.
The two worked silently.

When the final screw was lodged, Peter dropped his
tool. He and Brush lifted the box and rested it against a
wall. Peter slapped his hands together. "There. Nineteen
more of these and we're out of this burg."

Brush became hesitant. Peter questioned him with
his eyes.

"What?"

"So, you want to take them all?"

"They're all good, kid."

"But that one," Brush spoke as he indicated a canvas
on a back post. "See how the cloud formations . . ."

"What's the problem kid?"

"They have flaws. All of them."

Peter's manner suggested he was about to say
something he'd said many times before.

"Paintings are like people, kid. Even God started with two perfect ones, and they blew it."

Peter knew, although he couldn't bring himself to admit it, that they boy's misgivings should not have been so nonchalantly tossed aside. He also tried not to admit to himself that the boy's paintings were singularly transformational. At this, Peter failed.

It had been a long time – too long Peter inwardly knew – since he had lingered in the presence of paintings that deserved more than a passing glance. There had been a time for Peter when spending time in an art museum was like idling in a warm bath. He would amble and muse long after his feet began to ache.

Over time, this went away. He would enter an art museum or gallery only if he had a work hanging there and then only to bore in on his own work, ignoring all others. He would release his tunnel vision only to consider if his own piece was hanging properly relative to the rest.

Now, in the presence of what he knew to be magnificent works, and works that only he was able to view, the warm bath refilled, so to speak.

He had abandoned the Volney painting crew as early as possible that morning. He knew he should have stayed on the work site longer, but he was drawn to Brush's barn studio. Peter also knew that it wasn't a whim that drove him to the studio early. He wanted to be there. He would not allow himself to ask why.

Peter's warm bath drained when the sliding door to the barn rumbled but didn't move. Another rumble was followed by irked cursing. Peter and Brush regarded the door as it shuddered open about a foot, letting sunlight in. Another foot, and the lower part of the door was blocked by Carl Holland, who squeezed through and straggled in, his snarled bed-head hair framed before the sunlight.

He took a moment to let his eyes – telltale bloodshot even from fifteen feet away – adjust.

Peter spoke to no one in particular. "Fresh from the arms of Morpheus!"

Carl spotted Brush, steadied himself and ran his hand through his hair. He addressed the boy, part question, part accusation, "Did you make the morning run?"

Brush started to answer, but he was halted by Peter's hand on his shoulder. Peter. who had donned his gaucho hat and cape, now glided past Brush and swirled toward Carl. He threw his caped arm around the dazed man's shoulders.

"My good man," he said. "Let us perambulate."

Peter ushered a thoroughly mystified Carl back out into the sunlight. He began to march Carl back and forth in front of the barn door.

"Champ, we don't have time to do the whole Serenity Prayer bit. 'Hi, I'm Carl and I'm a stumbling tosspot.' So, I will have to go with fear and intimidation, if that's okay."

Peter paused and gave Carl a look that asked him if he understood. Carl peered back at Peter – one eye wide, the other a slit – like he'd seen a carnival freak. Peter accepted the look and spoke in a strangely fatherly way as he nodded toward the shattered cattle chute.

"I'm not the lunatic here. I met you yesterday."

Carl turned hangdog and directed a beseeching eye to Brush, who was now outside the door. Peter waved off the boy and slowly pulled the man's chin, directing Carl's face back toward his.

"You ever stared down a Docent?"

Carl shook his head "no."

"Ever locked horns with a pack of vainglorious pansies at a museum board meeting?"

Carl shook his head "no."

Peter's demeanor abruptly changed. He shoved Carl up against the barn door and spoke in a baleful tone.

"I have felt the white-hot fear that comes when you bullshit your way into a massive federal grant and have nothing to show for it when the deadline arrives. I spit nails. Pitbulls whimper at my name."

Peter eased up on Carl enough to let the man's feet fully plant on the ground.

"Your wife didn't leave you because of that kid over there. It was you. Or it was her. I don't know why. I don't care why. Brace yourself, Champ. I'm going to go Freud on you now."

Carl flinched, but did, indeed, brace himself.

"The lad's got it in his head that he's the problem and now he can't see his own worth. So, we're going to fix that."

Peter shoved Carl back up against the wall.

"You are going to be sober as a judge while I am here. You are going to show that kid you can still run this dairy. You are going to let him know that your wife left you because of reasons that are between you and her alone. And you are going to get some high-test breath mints."

Peter went into hypnotic mode.

"If you don't do these things, I'm going to . . ."

Peter paused. His eyes swiveled until he found what he wanted.

"See that pitchfork over there?"

Carl lolled his head and looked toward the pitchfork. Peter released Carl's shoulders, took Carl's head in his hands and nodded it "yes." Peter backed away, leaving Carl propped against the barn.

"If you don't, someday when you're not looking, I'm gonna take that pitchfork and put three holes where you now have one."

Peter walked away, paused and turned back to Carl.

"Maybe I didn't come through clear enough to you the first time we met, champ. In about a week or so, I'm going to take your son to Chicago whether you like it or not."

Peter climbed into his bus and drove off, leaving Carl wide-eyed.

***

The glass door to the Big Three barber shop proudly proclaimed "This is a union shop" in professional-style hand-painted letters, all red, white, and blue. Peter pushed his way into the room to see a single barber chair in the center beneath a ceiling fan. Peter wasn't there for a haircut.

To his left a mirror covered the full length of the wall above a counter packed with the tools of the trade, and a sink. To his right, five chairs were aligned against the wall. Four were filled. The barber, identifiable by his apron, arose from a chair to meet him. Peter waved him back down.

"Keep your seat, my good man, I just came in to find out where everybody is."

Peter recognized only two of the customers, Mattingly of the Five and Dime in his bowtie, and Frank from the 66 station, in his baseball cap. The other customer wore a white straw cowboy hat.

"Everybody?" said the barber.

"Well," said Peter. "Nobody is painting. The street is dead."

"It's August," said Mattingly.

"What happens in August?" said Peter.

"Nothing," said Cowboy Hat.

"Nobody is going to work in the afternoon heat," said Frank.

Peter let this sink in as a recalculated the number of days it would take to paint the town. He headed for the door. The barber interrupted his thoughts.

"So, you think this stunt is going to work?"

The question arrested Peter. To the extent that he had given the scheme much thought, he had never doubted its success, and it never crossed his mind that anybody else would. That, along with finding himself with nothing to do for the afternoon, delivered him into a reflective state. He had spent the morning in the company of Brush's paintings. They stirred a long-buried feeling in Peter, one he couldn't as yet put a finger on, and one that he couldn't shake. Now, there was a question in the air.

He turned back to the room, removed his gaucho hat

and cape, and took the empty seat along the wall.

He now spoke as men lined up in barbershops do. He addressed all in the room via the mirror on the opposite wall, his voice now absent its theatrical tone. All this felt oddly natural to him. He had no idea why.

"Actually, I do. I do think it will work. It's something new. It's a real work of public art. A work of public art performed by the public. It's big. It's unexpected."

"Nobody cares about that," said Cowboy Hat.

"Will this pink stunt bring people to Volney?" said the barber.

Peter eyeballed his audience in the mirror with a new understanding. He knew that Mattingly and Frank had both bought in to Mike's truck stop venture. If Mike got what he wanted, they were good either way, or perhaps both ways. The barber and Cowboy Hat, though, had something to lose. They cared.

Peter Basque did not spend very much time around genuine, authentic people. His was a world of canapes, air kisses, and champagne flutes. The people he knew were the people he was supposed to know, mostly because they could someday be of use to him. The things he said to those people were the things he was supposed to say, namely things that made them feel refined. They preferred to believe their own air was rarified, even if it was counterfeit, and he was there to complete the illusion.

In other words, he had never sat in a barber shop, a circumstance that now compelled him to go with the truth.

"I don't know."

The response he received was unexpected, at least to

him.

"Then, tell us what you do know," said the barber.

In the unhurried environs of the Big Three barber shop, Peter felt no need for a hasty reply, although the answer came to him quickly. It was though he'd already thought of it but had never told himself.

"I can only look at this the way I would look at it, if that makes sense," he said. He looked in the mirror at the faces of his audience. Apparently it did make sense. "For me, the place, the town, will be irresistible. It will be a visual mystery from the highway, especially the grain towers. A real diversion. It asks a question: 'How did this happen?' So, if most people are like me . . ."

Peter again examined the mirror. this time to see if this last statement was met with incredulity. Nothing.

" . . . then, yes, I believe the stunt will work. It's a visual treat."

"Well, you've got everybody believing it," said Cowboy Hat.

"And I think the treat will be fulfilled when they pull off into town," said Peter.

"How do you fulfill a treat?" said Frank.

Peter thought on that one for a moment or two.

"By being a place where people want to linger," he said. "Like the motto on your town sign, 'where people come to smile.'"

The barber rose and crossed the room to the counter behind the chair. He produced a box and selected four cigars from it. Peter observed they weren't the expensive kind. No need for a cutter. He returned and handed Peter, Mattingly, Frank, and Cowboy Hat a cigar each. Cowboy

Hat unpocketed a lighter, flamed it to his cigar and passed it down the row. Peter was last. After he lit his cigar, he presented the lighter to the standing barber.

"No thanks," he said. "This is a union shop. There's no smoking."

Again, Peter looked in the mirror for traces of incredulity from his companions. None. He passed the lighter back down the row, blew a smoke ring, and regarded the single barber chair.

"How many people work here?" he said.

"One," said the barber. "Me."

"Who owns the Big Three?" said Peter.

"I do," said the barber.

"And it's a union shop," said Peter. He eyed the mirror again. Again, he saw no trace of incongruity from the other three.

"What about Brush?" said Mattingly. "Will making him famous work for Volney, too?"

Peter went with honesty again.

"Will prints of his work be seen all over the country? Yes. Will they put Volney on the map? No, at least not for a long time, if ever."

Frank tilted forward and looked down the line toward Peter while thumbing at Mattingly.

"That's not what he meant."

"Is this school thing for Brush real?" said Mattingly.

"We don't want to lose him," said the barber.
The concern in his voice launched Peter inward. He arrived at a place that was new to him, or perhaps long shrouded, and he could feel he was content to be there. Contentment. At first it unsettled him. It was too new

and peculiar, but he also knew that it would be fleeting. Still, he had the vague sense that he had returned for a moment to a place he walked away from long ago. He wasn't sure what he was going to say before he spoke.

"A talent like Brush belongs to the world."

Peter slowly came to his feet. His warthog look faded behind a veil of musing.

"What is it about paint on canvas? Why is it magic? How is it that a painting can stop you in your tracks? Make you want to linger? What makes people travel a great distance to see one painting when they can look at another one right there on the wall? How is it that one still life of sunflowers is worth millions while millions of other paintings of flowers are worth nothing? Why is that one painting magic? How is that a painter can reach out and touch you across centuries?"

Peter became aware in the mirror that he had been pacing slowly, forward and back, in front of the row of chairs. He also became aware that he was time-traveling through thoughts he had long shelved. He scanned his tiny audience in the mirror. They seemed to be listening. They were listening. The barber had slipped into his barber's chair. Peter went on.

"I think it's because the great paintings ask a question."

Peter stopped pacing. He spoke to himself as much as his audience.

"The question. Why the idea? That's the question. The painting of the sunflowers doesn't show sunflowers. It shows the idea of sunflowers."

"That's from Plato," said Cowboy Hat.

Peter did his best to conceal his astonishment as he stopped and searched his audience in the mirror for any sign of astonishment elsewhere in the room. None. He continued.,

"Yes. The form of sunflowers. The idea. An idea that poses another question. If I'm looking at an idea, who, or what am I? So, the question in the painting becomes, 'what is it to be human?'"

Peter returned to the moment. Were his barber shop boys still with him? A glance told Peter "yes." He started pacing again.

"Not just any painter can ask the question. Wait! That's not so. Anybody can ask the question, but history tells us that only a very few painters are treasured for centuries while thousands of others are discarded. Their questions matter."

Peter stopped pacing again.

"You aren't losing Brush," he said. "History is gaining him."

His mini-audience seemed to ponder that one. Peter posed a question.

"Have you ever said, 'I don't know much about art, but I know what I like?"

All four nodded a "yes."

"Do you think maybe it's because you like it when you look at a painting and see the question and you don't like it when you don't?"

Mattingly stirred in his chair and pointed with his cigar. He had adopted Peter's veil of musing. "You might be on to something there, Mr. Basque . . ."

"Peter."

"You might be on to something, Peter. That could be why so many people like impressionism."

Peter did his best to not look gobsmacked again.

"You might be on to something there yourself, Mattingly," said Frank. "With impressionists, it's like they ask half the question and let you fill in the rest."

"Yup," said Mattingly. "People who try to understand things favor the belief that the known is only an extension of the unknown."

"A good painter can connect the two,' said Frank. "At least I think so."

"I think it's the same with Edward Hopper," said Cowboy Hat. "It's like there's always something about to happen in his paintings and you get to study on what that might be."

Mattingly, still veiled, looked at Peter, who was still attempting to conceal his astonishment.

"What about when the paint is just thrown around, like on the side of your bus? What's the question, there?" he asked. Peter didn't answer because he didn't have one.

"What is paint?" answered Cowboy Hat. "I think that's the question there."

The statement went deep into Peter. He had just engaged in the most cogent discussion of art he'd attempted in years, and the conversation was with what at first he took to be four hayseeds in a small room in the middle of everywhere.

It was unexpected, to put it mildly, but Peter knew without being told that it was because his expectations were false. He saw himself in the mirror with his companions and he saw that his long habit of placing people into types had decayed into cartoon dimensions.

He looked at himself and saw a man who had become lazy or perhaps satisfied with what he considered his version of certainty. He looked again at his companions and understood they were people who had gifts, private gifts, gifts they owned. They were people who were certain about realities, and that these realities he knew were beyond his own grasp.

It dawned on Peter that he genuinely liked this room, this place, these people. He took a long look at himself in the mirror. Even without his hat and cape, he appeared out of place. He appeared to be at arm's length from the others. A notion came after him. He turned to the barber before he had time to consider it.

"You know, I think I will have a haircut," he said.

The barber regarded Peter's shoulder-length hair.

"What do you expect me to do with that?" he said.

Peter reached over and lifted Frank's cap to reveal a short to medium cropped cut with a long, straight part. He eyed the barber and pointed to Frank.

"I'll have what he had."

It was done leisurely, but swiftly. The barber swiveled the chair around to face the mirror and showed his handiwork to Peter, who once again attempted to hide his astonishment.

He looked younger and older at the same time. The droopy hair no longer dragged his features downward. The trim revealed the onset of a distinguished hint of gray at the temples. He looked better, and he liked it that way.

He paid the barber and took up his cape and gaucho hat. As Peter slid one arm into his cape, Cowboy Hat asked, "Does that look good somewhere?"

"And it's hot outside, if you've noticed," said Frank.

Peter once again saw himself in the mirror. He removed the hat and let the cape drop and hang over his arm. After a pleasant farewell salute, he exited.

When he passed through the door and went onto the sidewalk, he caught a glimpse of his reflection in the window. He looked himself over and chose not to reflect on what he'd just done. He spoke without a hint of irony.

"Ready. Fire. Aim."

***

That night, the waxing moon came to life over Volney. The night was almost as dark as the night before, but the moon was struggling to be seen.

CHAPTER 11

ELIZABETH HOLLAND

THE HANDS of the clock rested at 4:30. It would be an hour before light. Brush was already semi-vertical, sitting up in his bed, legs to the floor. There had been no alarm. There wasn't an alarm clock in the Holland farmhouse. The timetable at Holland Dairy, like any dairy, was permanent and unalterable. Brush had spent his life working in and around that timetable. He knew the Holsteins would be grouped, waiting outside the barn door in 30 minutes.

After a stretch and a yawn, he dressed in the dark - overalls and shirt. His gum boots were downstairs in the mudroom by the back door. He silently descended the center hall staircase, yesterday's socks in hand, and was brought up by the scent of bacon in the pan and the sight of light from the kitchen.

He stepped into the kitchen to see his father at the four-square table, nursing coffee. Upon seeing Brush, Carl silently went to the stove and cracked a few eggs into a ready pan, swirled them around with a spatula and let them bubble while he prepped a pair of plates with bacon and toast.

Brush took a seat at the table and pulled on his socks while his father poured him a coffee. Brush noted that his father's hands shook a little. Carl replaced the coffee pot, piled eggs on the plates, hands still shaky, and returned to the table.

It was a scene that had been played out uncounted times, enough that words weren't needed because both the boy and the man knew there was nothing they needed to say. They downed breakfast the way that men do when there is work to be done, and they pushed their chairs away.

The staff of Holland Dairy, now returned to full strength, headed out into the morning.

***

Carl's was a sudden transformation, but Brush had grown becoming accustomed to these. So much had changed since the day Peter Basque swept into his life. The town, his father, and Brush himself were recast. Peter's presence was spellbinding and his power to sway people seemed to Brush like a sort of sorcery.

But Brush knew it wasn't sorcery. It was just common sense. He knew his own assessment had been right all along. His father wasn't a drunk. He knew Carl would return, and Carl did after Peter pulled off the one thing that the socially hobbled people of Volney, including Brush, could not. He spoke the brutal truth.

But even that couldn't sober up a man on a dime. It was something deeper. Carl Holland sobered up overnight when he heard a man he'd never met tell him he was taking his son away.

Carl actually did sober up overnight. He laid in bed, staring upward and feeling the alcohol work itself out of him until he felt the familiar tug that told him it was time to rise. Even in his sleepless state, he felt lethargy vanish in the face of work to be done. It felt good.

For Brush, Peter's magic was fruitful. Brush had almost forgotten how much he liked working the dairy. It's a life that most people would find confining. Every day needs to be the same and there is no day off. The herd had to be milked, and it had to be milked on schedule, every day. It was that simple, and the simplicity, if you liked it, was fulfilling.

For Elizabeth Holland, Brush's mother, it had been a prison. The repetition – dairy cattle don't even take Sundays off – wore on her. She bore it until the day came – the day it dawned on her that Carl would never make the operation grow. The dairy had been in the family for three generations, and Carl was fully content with his insignificant patch of dirt and grass. He would never increase their holdings. He would never grow the herd. He would never take on the responsibilities of managing a crew of workers and a fleet of vehicles and expanded territory. He would never be somebody.

It was the day she knew that every day, now and forever, would be the same.

It never occurred to Elizabeth that she had not shared her aspirations with Carl. She had sent hints, and comments, and what she thought were signals, and then she just waited. She waited for her dreams to bloom inside his head on their own, just as they had in hers. And every day that passed without a bud of new ambition rising from Carl was one more day in a row of disappointments. She came to think of him as a failure who was too dense to know what failure is.

She stopped seeing Carl as a husband first. He was just a man who was content, ridiculously so, with a life of endless sameness.

She never understood how much Carl needed her. And in her growing hollowness, she never understood the depth of love he had for her and that he expressed it by treating his content as her content. He simply thought they were both happy. How could they not be? He was the man who brought milk and cream to the town of Volney, and she was his partner. It seemed to him to be more than enough. But she could imagine a larger future. Why couldn't he?

And then her disdain began to extend to the people of Volney. For more years than anyone could count, the Holland Dairy Ice Cream Sunday was a summer event that all looked forward to. You brought your own chairs and planted them in the shade for a day of easy company and ice cream at the ready. Any time. All day. You took your little shift turning the ice-cream churns and then you took your turn at the games, mostly horseshoes, until the shade inched long, and the children began to chase fireflies.

She could no longer cherish the goodness of the moment. She no longer valued the elegance of small talk. She had no interest in sharing her too small life with the small lives of others. She began to fade early from the festivities until her presence was no longer noticed, or missed.

Her mirror became her enemy. Would her youth fade to gray in isolation? The sweeping prairie sunsets lost their magnificence. They just meant tomorrow is another day.

Her bed became cold. Brush would be an only child.

What she wanted became too distant from what she had. What she did have became too distant from her heart. Then, after reading a magazine article, she came to believe there was more to her condition than her domestic situation, that her longing for something new was somehow spiritual. The emptiness wasn't around her. It was in her.

What she needed, she decided, was to be fulfilled. With what she had no idea. It would have to be discovered. And with this, she closed the loop of heart-searching from herself to herself.

In her self-absorption, she never took a mother's delight or pride in her son's rising artistic ability. It was just something Brush did, an amusement with Susannah Symington, the girl who lived on a neighboring farm, and who was always around and usually hungry. She dismissed it as that, even as she resented Helen Bellamann for her gifts of art supplies and expensive art books for Carl to pick up at Lillian's cafe on his morning rounds.

She barely noticed when Carl and Brush cleared out a barn and her son disappeared into it, there to construct his own world, usually with Susannah.

By the time brush was 12 years old he was prolific.

Remarkable paintings piled up in his studio barn until he began to give them away. Everybody in Volney wanted a Brush Holland painting, but his mother wouldn't recognize one if you held it before her. And then the paintings grew larger and larger, mostly because Helen left larger and larger canvasses for Carl to pick up at Lillian's.

A year later, Elizabeth Holland stopped seeing Brush as a boy at all. On the outside, even nearing the age of 14, Brush was tall for his age and as good a farmhand as any grown man. This was about the same time she also decided that her husband was wed to his dairy, and therefore not to her.

She decided she wasn't needed. She didn't want to be needed, and these excuses were as good as any.

She left on a spring day while Carl was on a delivery run and Brush was out with Susannah, where she didn't know or care. She took her clothes. She left a note.

With her new freedom, she instantly described the boundaries of her imagination. She went 60 miles to St. Louis because she had been there before. There, the circle of self-examination continued, but it remained in vain.

The promise of the city was never fulfilled. She was never fulfilled, and she had to hunt for new people to blame. The circle became a vortex, ever darker.

Her salvation was an arm's length away. One telephone call would have told her that welcoming arms awaited at Holland Dairy, but she couldn't see past an arm's length in the darkness of her mind, a condition that grew ever more bitter as she struggled to see the rightness of her future while being gnawed upon by the wrongness of the present.

She took on the fixed eye that comes with perpetual discontent.

She was wrong about her husband and her son. Very wrong. After Elizabeth left, Carl could not bring himself to believe what had happened. A numbness came over him. The unchangeable days still came and went, but now they seemed relentless. Carl went through the motions. The dairy routine had been rooted in him so long he could perform without thinking.

After his final chore of the day, Carl would take a seat in an old rocker on the little front porch and stare down the long driveway. The gate and sign just peeking up in the distance. Surely, she would pass through the gate and come up the drive where he would meet her and they would embrace and all would return to normal. Carl would wait into the evening and into the night. It wasn't long before Brush stopped asking him if he was going to bed.

As the summer wore on, Carl could be seen at his vigil earlier and earlier. As the summer faded, he stayed on the porch later and later. He began pouring a small glass of bourbon as a nightcap to put himself to sleep. With the passing nights, the glass got bigger and bigger and then it became the first glass, not a nightcap. Brush began finding his father asleep in the chair in the mornings. By fall, Carl was permanently on the porch. So was the glass and the bottle. It was remarkable, really, how quickly it all happened.

Brush now managed the dairy alone. He was now almost 15 years old. No man is equipped to work endless

12-hour days. Brush may have appeared as a man on the outside, but on the inside, he was very much a boy who was forced to become a man overnight.

He sustained himself and the dairy by making a single assumption that saved Holland Dairy – that his father would return to his old self.

Brush stopped attending school. There were calls and letters from the county school system, but all went unanswered until they finally stopped coming. When Susannah wanted to stop school, too, Brush insisted she stay.

Brush took over the deliveries. He was a year shy of driving legally, but he looked old enough and he drove well enough that nobody questioned him. He just did it.

Brush shortened the days and eased his burden by sticking to the minimum. He ceased the afternoon milking. The twice-a-day routine was hard enough when he and his father were both on hand. Now, it was impossible.

It didn't take Brush long to figure out which cows could make the adjustment, and which couldn't. The one's who couldn't adjust, he called the "empty cows." Brush sold them without his father's permission or knowledge. The money helped.

After that, the herd had to be milked and the milk delivered in the mornings. Then the milking barn, milking machines, and bottling apparatus had to be cleaned and prepped. Except for the afternoon feeding, which didn't take long, that was it. Everything else could be put on hold for the day when Carl returned.

There had been a time when Carl prided himself on

his cluster of gleaming white barns under red roofing. He never let the paint job weather. A dairy "needed to look healthy and clean" he would say. The barns were due for a paint job before Elizabeth left. As the seasons passed, Holland Dairy took on the weary paint-peeled look of a place where everything was scheduled for another day.

With the help of Susannah, who came over and put in two morning hours at the milking barn each day before heading to her shift at Lillian's, which she followed by opening the Symington Produce stand during the summer months and fall weekends, Holland Dairy stayed afloat.

Brush was also the face of Holland Dairy, especially after he started driving the delivery routes. Nobody saw Carl, so his problems remained unknown, and nobody missed Elizabeth.

Susannah never mentioned the situation, not even to her parents. So, it wasn't until the usual notices for The Holland Dairy Ice Cream Sunday failed to appear – in the past they were little hand-made posters taped to the shop windows in Volney and notices in the church bulletins – that people began to talk.

Volney was a small town. The Hollands were a small puzzle. It didn't take long for the pieces to fall into place. Both Helen Bellamann and Lillian, especially Lillian, had their suspicions about the situation all along, or thought they did, but both remained silent. Like everyone else in Volney, Lillian and Helen were their own obstacles when it came to dealing with difficult personal matters. The residents of Volney and the surrounding farms were people for whom the word stoic had a narrow application.

It wasn't that they couldn't become excited or express joy. This, they did. It was inner disquiet and emotional pain that was untouchable. These were deemed to be private and nobody's business. There was no available vocabulary of therapeutic notions. If one were spoken, it would be considered unseemly. This was true even in the churches, both Presbyterian and Baptist, where you could expect a Biblical prescription of "snap out of it."

This had been part of Elizabeth's problem, and also part of Carl's inability to grasp it. Now, after the fact, nobody knew what to say, especially to Brush. So, nobody said anything, although they told each other that they all saw it coming.

When Brush went house to house to ask, ever so politely, for the return of the paintings he'd given away, people attributed his behavior to the trauma they couldn't talk about with him. They were wrong. He had come to think his early paintings weren't good enough and he didn't want them to be seen.

This was because the one part of Brush's life that changed in a good way was painting. Even after a long day, Brush returned to his studio barn, where Susannah inevitably awaited. Forced to paint indoors under lamplight, Brush began to abandon his natural palette.

The results were odd at first. There were times when Susannah, watching him work from her seat at his shoulder, would reach over and wordlessly mix an odd color on his palette. Brush would try it here and there and keep it if it worked. Over time a distinct and novel palette emerged. The results were spectacular, and they were the

reason he withdrew his old paintings.

CHAPTER 12

DUCK & PEZ

NOW, THE state of gloom that had cast a pall over Holland Dairy for three years was lifted. To Brush, it was like mud-colored skies were turned blue. It was all he had wanted, really, to see his father restored.

In a way, everything was on its way to restoration. Brush, who had long before made his peace with his absent mother, although it cost him the presence of wonder in his eyes, was ever so ready to witness the same peace in his father.

Now back on the job, Carl still had work to do on himself, and he knew it. He'd been at it for more than a year, the drinking, and for a time going forward he had to confront a familiar tingle at sundown, a feeling of being drawn away, but he resisted. Carl was not much given to musing over the science of the mind, but he came to think of his lost year as a sort of cleansing. He had to face the loss of Elizabeth, and he did it with time and bourbon and an empty driveway.

And a steadfast son.

The Holland Dairy produced enough milk to supply

Volney and neighboring towns, with enough remaining to sell to larger distributors. A new post-milking routine emerged – Brush delivered to the towns while Carl delivered to the distributors. Brush continued to be the face of Holland Dairy in Volney. For now, Carl wanted it that way. He wasn't sure of the reception he'd get in Volney. Even though he had never gone into town during his time with the bottle – he had traveled to Robley to buy his bourbon – he feared, implausibly, that he had made social errors there.

The Volney run wasn't complicated – Lillian's cafe and McIntire Grocery – and then on to the next village.

***

The morning highway traffic was light as Brush cruised into town. It always was in the morning. The blocked off parking spaces and sidewalks extending from Paint Project Headquarters, though, were filled. Busy volunteers painted away in a holiday atmosphere. They waved as Brush passed by. Their plan was to paint from the east end of main street to the west end, building by building, before branching into the residential streets. On the edge of town Brush noticed Peter. He had to look twice to see that Peter was working his camera.

Brush passed by the painters and pulled his truck – it was a refrigerated panel truck with the Holland Dairy logo on both sides – in front of Lillian's. He leapt from the cab, swung open one rear door of the truck, and yanked a knee-high stainless-steel milk can from the shadows. He disappeared into Lillian's for a moment, and returned to the sidewalk with a milk can swinging empty. He placed the empty in the truck and pulled out two dozen bottles of milk nested in two metal totes, each with a long handle. He lugged them, both arms straining, as he worked his way down to the grocery.

He disappeared into the grocery. He returned carrying both totes packed with empties, loped to the truck, and placed the totes in the rear. There were sounds of glass clattering as he leaned into the truck. In moments, he leaned back out, again with two full totes. He lugged them into the grocery, returning again with empties. He slammed the rear door closed.

He backed out onto the highway, proceeded through the rest of town, and pulled into the small gravel parking lot outside the Jesse James Rock Park & Fairgrounds and Duck Pond.

He parked alongside the fence. There was just enough room. On the other side, a large boulder was centered in the grass. It was nondescript, but for the words "Jesse James 1880" carved onto the side facing the road. Duck and Pez awaited there, dressed as usual, with the incongruous addition of neckties.

Brush had known Duck and Pez for as long as he could recall. The pair was in many ways the face of Volney. They had been a very public presence for years.

They arrived in Volney as orphans. A Greyhound pulled away from the post office bus stop one afternoon – nobody except Helen had a record of exactly what year – and two small children stayed behind, standing there on the sidewalk. Nothing was known about their lives before that moment.

Duck was a little boy, although he was already big for his age, and Pez was an infant still in a basket. Along with the basket, Duck carried a small satchel containing some clothing items and a hand full of silver dollars. There was no note.

The postmaster called Cyrus Bellamann, Helen's father, who sent some people over to pick up the boys and take them to Bellamann House. A week later, Cyrus called a town meeting where he said the boys were now wards of Volney. He had given them names. The older boy would be Noah Volney, because he carried his brother to safety. The infant would be Moses Volney, because he arrived in a basket.

Cyrus announced at the meeting that, as wards of the town, the boys would be placed in foster homes in Volney for periods of six months to a year. Then, they would move on to a new foster home. The Bellamann family would pay all expenses. Cyrus told the people at the meeting that he put the boys in a rotation of homes because he didn't want to burden any single family for too long. What he knew, though, was that sooner or later, one family would keep them.

It turned out to be an older couple whose children had moved away. They were a caring couple, but hardly young enough to monitor two boys, so Noah and Moses became familiar characters on the sidewalks of Volney. Actually, they were more than characters. They were mascots. This is when Noah became known as Duck, due to his penchant for following the ducks into the Jesse James Duck Pond fully clothed, and Moses became Pez, named for his favorite candy, which McIntire Grocery supplied at no cost.

At first, people thought they were brothers, but as the years passed, there just wasn't enough resemblance to support the assumption.

When Noah arrived at school age, he lasted about a month before his stepfather pulled him out. "Leave that boy at a desk and he'll wander away," he said. "But he has a knack with his hands and he's dependable."

When Pez arrived at school age, the classroom was never considered. And so, Duck became Volney's itinerant handyman and Pez became his assistant, a condition made permanent when Mike Rutherford made them employees of the Rutherford Grain Works.

Pez never spoke. Duck did the talking for him. Over the years this became the natural state for the people of Volney, although nobody knew how Pez talked to Duck, mostly because nobody ever asked. The two could be seen, though, in what people came to call "nonversations."

Pez would gesture and stomp and roll his eyes and glare or sneer or smile as he pointed out features of the world around them while Duck interpreted. Pez also carried a small notepad that fit into his shirt pocket. If his facial expressions and body gestures didn't work, he would pull out the pad and write thoughts – nobody knew how he learned to write, but he had his own very peculiar vocabulary – and draw images while Duck translated, a process that occasionally caused Pez to heave his notepad to the ground and stomp away, only to return and resume the nonversation until Duck got it right.

The silver dollars were never spent. They could still be viewed at the Volney History Museum. You had to ask to see them. They were in a locked drawer.

Little of their history was known to Brush Holland. He'd never bothered to ask. Duck and Pez were just two guys who had always been there.

Now, as Brush approached the Jesse James Rock, the two stiffened into something like military attention as Duck straightened Pez's tie. When Brush arrived at the rock, Pez, wordless as always, offered his candy dispenser.

"Hey, Duck. No thanks, Pez," said Brush.

"Hey, Brush," said Duck.

Duck and Pez still at semi-attention, beamed. A long moment passed. Brush broke it.

"So, why did you guys want to meet me?"

Duck jostled himself and came into "at ease" position.

"Well, me and Pez, Pez and I, we're in agreement. The two of us."

Brush awaited more. It was another long pause. He broke it.

"Good. What about?"

"Oh! I was waiting for Pez to talk, but he won't. Not at all."

Pez nodded in agreement.

"Duck, I know," said Brush. Duck continued.

"Oh! Me and Pez, and I, we decided it's okay, now that you've decided to go away, it's okay for you to use our bill."

A look of wonder and appreciation passed over Brush.

"Oh, fellas, I . . ."

Pez stopped Brush with a hand. Duck continued.

"You're gonna need the rules. You gotta know 'em."

"Guys, everybody in town knows about your bill."

Duck was not to be denied. He had a thing to say, and he was going to say it.

"Mr. Mike, he gets our bill at the end of every month. He pays it. You can't use it for beer or Playboys. Neither one. Or guns. Them, too."

"Okay."

"But you can put anything else on it. Anything. Pez, he put our trailer on it."

"You're kidding."

"Nope. It excited Mr. Mike at the time. But you could tell he liked it. The trailer. Anyway, we think it'll work in Chicago. Our bill, not our trailer. Pretty sure."

Pez nudged Duck and a look of concern passed over him. "Our bill won't work in Robley, though. Pez and me, and I, we got two Roy Rogers drinks at the counter there. When they wouldn't put it on our bill, Pez, he got mad."

Pez nudged Duck again. "Mr. Mike, he came to Robley and paid all the damages. So, be careful. Pez says, well okay, he don't, doesn't say it because he won't say it, but you know what I mean. Pez says to ask first about the bill from now on."

Brush considered accepting their offer just to make them happy, but he was unsure what Duck and Pez might actually do if he did take it.

"Well, thanks guys, but I don't think I'll need. . ."

Pez stopped Brush with a hand and gestured for Duck to continue.

"Pez wants to talk about life. To you. It's advice. See, Pez, he's got this way of looking at people. Pez, he says you can always tell about a fella after he makes a mistake. Some fellas'll pretend it didn't happen. Some fellas try to throw it off on somebody else. Some fellas own up right away and try to make it right again. Pez says you want to be a Number Three. That's his thinking."

Pez nodded, solemn, in affirmation, Brush treated the moment with equal solemnity.

"Well, I think that's a good philoso . . . a good idea."

"It came to him natural. Me, too. See, me and Pez, we're mistakes."

Pez nodded his affirmation, while Brush suffered an inadequate melting feeling inside. Duck noticed Brush's discomfort and clarified.

"Well, Pez, he's more of a mistake than I am because he don't talk or drive or swing his arms when he walks."

Pez nodded his affirmation. Duck saluted.

"Okay, Brush, that's it. Bye."

Duck sauntered away, whistling. Pez remained motionless before Brush. After a few steps, Duck looked over his shoulder and his whistling stopped. "Aw, cmon, Pez."

Pez stood firm, his back to Duck. Duck turned to him and went into negotiation mode. "Brush has more deliveries. We can't hold him up. He doesn't have time."

Pez looked at Brush, who shrugged. Pez held firm. Now, the moment had a feel of confrontation. Duck pointed at Pez, although Pez couldn't see it. "You aren't the boss of me. I'm the boss of you."

Pez dug in, raised his shoulders, and hunched toward Brush and away from Duck, who tried to appear nonchalant.

"I don't care if it is my job," he said.

Pez pointed to the ground in front of Brush. Duck let out a sigh and trudged back toward Brush, who had watched the small drama play out with equal parts concern and mystification.

Duck announced his intentions to the air. "Okay, but I'm going to say it my way. It's my voice and you aren't the boss of my voice."

With the trio reassembled at the rock, Duck attempted in vain to ignore Pez as he addressed Brush.

"Pez is not the boss of me, but Mr. Mike says it's my job do his talking for him 'cause he won't talk. So, I'm going to say something to you now because Pez, Pez he won't leave until I say it. But for this, I'm not me. I'm Pez. I mean, I'm not really Pez. That's Pez right there. But my voice is acting like the voice of Pez 'cause he doesn't use his but you knew that already. So, it's not me talking even though it's me talking. It's, it's Pez. Okay? Okay. Well, okay. From now on, after this, it's Pez. Him. Pez."

Duck took a deep breath and let it out. His eyes begged Pez for liberation from the task. Pez stood firm, pointing toward Brush. Duck took another deep breath.

"Duck, Duck, he's in love with Susannah but that doesn't make him glad you are leaving. I'm just telling you this because if he pays special attention to Susannah, it's because he's protecting her until you come home. So, don't worry. Duck, he had his heart broken once, but that's a secret and it wasn't about Susannah. Now, that's it. Bye."

Pez nodded in affirmation.

Duck wheeled on his heel and hurried off, his

saunter gone, while Pez marched straight-armed and flat-footed in overlong strides behind him. At the gate, Duck, his natural rosy blush heightened by a forehead now turned scarlet, turned on Pez.

"Just tell me how that can be a secret now that you've told him!"

The pair marched away, Duck hustling to leave Pez behind, Pez laboring to keep up. Brush held his position at the rock as he watched them head back into town. He stared into the air, mouth slightly agape, before coming too. He made for his truck.

If a day went as planned, Brush completed his rounds in time to meet Peter at the barn studio for the afternoon, and that way he could still spend his evenings with Susannah. On that night with Susannah, Brush found himself watching her in an altogether new way. Part of him was happy that she'd be under someone's protection.

***

If you looked hard enough that night, you could see the waxing moon had grown just enough to be easily visible.

123

CHAPTER 13

FRIDAY, AUGUST 30

BRUSH'S DAYS now had a new and welcome routine. With Carl back in the barn, the daily milking went faster and smoother. Carl never questioned Brush's decision to eliminate the afternoon milking, and Carl made the workday even easier by taking over the afternoon feeding. Brush, now also freed from the daily run to the distributor, could be back home and in his studio barn by noon, where Peter, who had spent his morning directing the paint crews in Volney, would be already at work on the shipping boxes.

At the end of each day there was spare time before Susannah closed Symington Produce and came over. Brush used the time to clean out stalls and rooms and corners of the barns that had been neglected for three years. Brush began ending his day with a pitchfork, rake, and broom, cleaning out one spot at a time.

For the first time in a long time, things felt normal for Brush, but it was bittersweet. It made him happy to be normal again, but it also heightened his growing sense of loss. With each canvas that was slipped into a shipping box, the day when Brush would leave for Chicago neared. With each passing hour, an inner disorder fermented inside him.

Everybody, including Susannah, and now his father, was telling him he needed to go, had to go, to the school in Chicago. Since the day Peter walked into Lillian's café, this change in Brush's life seemed inevitable.

He had come to understand it was for the best, and he had pored over the brochure from the Art Institute countless times. He could almost picture himself there now. Still, he couldn't balance the lightness of anticipation with the dread of the unknown. He couldn't escape the heaviness that came over him when he acknowledged to himself how much he would have to abandon.

He had never dwelled on Susannah over their years together. He never had to conjure her presence. She always seemed to be there, an unfailing part of his life. Now, even though he had promised her he wouldn't worry about her, thoughts of Susannah returned to him again and again across the hours, each time triggering a suffocating loneliness. There was an unshakeable wrongness about her absence. It kept him awake.

While driving on his morning route, he had never waved to people he knew – and in Volney, you knew everyone – as if it were goodbye. He had never looked at his own house as something impermanent. He had never felt empty in the company of other people, as if there was no future with them.

But for at least an hour or so at the end of the day, he

could push all that aside. There was long-delayed cleanup
work to be done, and Brush was driven by an instinctive
conviction that he needed to leave things just so when
he went off to school. And so, he applied himself to the
conviction with a pitchfork, a rake, and a broom. It was a
diversion most boys his age would dislike.

In addition to Brush's studio barn, the Holland Dairy
had four others. The long, low barn beneath the silos was
for milking, prep, bottling, and refrigeration. It was the
only barn with a concrete floor.

A taller, squarish, barn was for the tractor, wagons,
implements and agricultural machinery. It was adjacent
to a smaller barn that functioned as a shed and workshop.
These were clustered near Brush's barn and connected by
a network of wooden fencing and metal gates.

Outside the network was a fourth barn. It was
an open pole barn for hay storage. It was about three
quarters filled. There would be one more cutting.

The milking barn was hosed and cleaned every day.
The hay barn never needed cleaning. The other two had
not seen a good cleaning for three years.

Brush was in a side room off the workshop,
alternately stacking and sweeping, and raising leftover
lumber from the floor before stacking it in a vertical pile
against the wall. As he lifted a sheet of old plywood, a
large, square piece of wood underneath caught his eye.
It was painted white. He leaned the old plywood in his
hands against the other sheets on the wall and lifted the
white piece.

It was the Holland Dairy sign, same style, but
rearranged. The Holland Dairy windmill logo was

painted on the left. The words "Holland & Son Dairy" were stacked next to the logo on the right.

As his eyes absorbed the sign, Brush took on the look of someone who had been punched in the stomach. At that moment, the fragile balance of the light future in Chicago tilted under and the weight of what he would leave behind.

He recovered from the punch, and, in a thoroughly needless gesture, looked about to see if anyone had witnessed what he had just seen. He carried the sign to the vertical pile by the wall. He spread the vertical pile from the middle out, slid the sign in, and let the stack fall into place, concealing the sign.

Brush found himself drained. He put his broom away, closed up the room and went out of the barn.

***

The shadows were long and fading, and the afternoon heat had broken when Brush stepped up to the back door stoop of the Holland home. He pulled off his gum boots in the mud room and came into the kitchen in socks. He was ready to wash up and get supper started, but he paused before the sink when he heard a scraping sound in the adjacent dining room.

He walked to the doorway, silent in his socks, and stopped short. Carl was in the dining room, his back to the door, grasping an old suitcase on the table. He was gently scraping it, attempting to remove the hand-painted lettering: "Just Married."

Brush, punched again, backed away from the door

and silently walked out of the kitchen and into the night.

***

The front door to Bellamann House was wide and heavy, oak, and splendid. It was hand carved in arrangements of fruits and vegetables falling away along ribbon lines extending from a cherub's face in the center. Tall, narrow windows of stained glass bordered each side, framing long-stemmed, elegant Tiffany-styled flowers embedded in the glass, pirouetting upward.

Helen swung the door open to see Brush standing in the night in work clothes and stocking feet. His face was in shadow. The porch lights were not on. She stepped back to let him in.

"Brush, you never have to knock, even at this hour."

Brush stepped forward into the light, paused at the doorway and held out a sheet of paper.

"I'm not going to Chicago."

When she wanted to, Helen Bellamann could be completely in the moment. She could assess the particulars and align them with the mood and the feelings around her. She could read people. With the exception of encounters with Mike Rutherford, she never let her feelings get in the way. In other situations, she could summon a remarkable measure of empathy, a trait she normally tried to conceal.

She wanted to be in this moment. She could sense there was something at stake, a big something. She silently took the paper from Brush's outstretched hand. It was the contract from the Art Institute. Her empathy was on full display.

"Brush, let's talk. Something has happened."

Brush stayed put. "Something came up. Let's just say I saw a sign."

With that, he turned and faded into the dark beyond the unlit porch. Helen followed him to the edge of the porch but knew not to pursue him. Her eyes followed him into the night.

***

Before she turned to re-enter Bellamann House, she looked up to see a crescent moon and wondered for a moment why she noticed it at all.

CHAPTER 14

SUSANNAH SYMINGTON

PERSON'S CAFE was empty in the post-breakfast lull. Susannah, who worked the morning rush because "nobody buys vegetables before breakfast," bussed the last table. Lillian could be heard through the clatter and tinkle of the kitchen, gearing up the dish-washing sinks.

Through the large picture window, and out on the sidewalk, townspeople could be seen hauling painting gear toward the eastern end of town. Helen, walking the other way, passed by the window and spotted Susannah in the cafe. Seconds later, the door came open and Helen entered. She was absolutely not in the moment. There was a forced cheeriness about her.

"Susannah, I'm so glad I caught you."

The words caught Susannah by surprise. She had always felt invisible in Helen's presence, which she had been until Helen noticed Brush's artistic talent. From that point on, Helen saw herself as Brush's mentor and guide, and she saw anyone else who occupied Brush's time as a rival and an obstacle to his best interests.

Helen never took the time to consider what the

boy and the girl might mean to each other. And if she had taken the time, she wouldn't have comprehended. Effortless devotion of the kind that Brush and Susannah shared was something Helen had known only once, and now couldn't let herself imagine.

Lillian came out from the kitchen. "Tea, Helen?"

"Please," replied Helen, "And Susannah, would you join me?"

Another surprise for Susannah, who looked around like maybe there was someone else in the room. "Me?"

"Yes, of course," said Helen.

"Well, I just cleaned this table," said Susannah, gesturing with a sweep of her arms. She removed her apron and waited for Helen to take a chair.

Lillian appeared and placed a tea service on the table. Pot, two cups, tea bags, two creams in plastic single servings, and sugar in cubes. Helen acted over-delighted and angled her hand toward the chair opposite her.

"Oh, good! Have a seat?"

Susannah accepted Helen's offer and scooted to the table, where she began to prep the tea. Helen, trying too hard to be nonchalant, placed her handbag on an adjacent chair and watched Susannah a little too steadily.

"Susannah, your busy time must be approaching."

"At the stand?"

"Yes."

"Well, we've already got corn in and it's going well. You know, we plant early and late so it's there all fall. The pumpkins are coming and the apples are there."

"That's when your produce stand looks the best."

"The store. That's what we call it. It's a joke. The store

just, just, just glows in fall."

Helen's artificial cheeriness faded, replaced by an artificial wistfulness.

"Fall, it will be here so soon. September's only three days away."

Susannah slid Helen her tea. Helen let it steep.

"Thank you, Susannah. You're here every morning, aren't you?"

Susannah, fully engaged in her own tea setup did not see that Helen's eyes never left her. Susannah's response was genuinely cheerful.

"Mostly. I don't mind helping out with Lillian, you know, like this."

"And do you still help Brush at the dairy before coming here?"

Susannah sensed a change in Helen's tone, but she couldn't place it. If she had, she would have known that Helen was fishing for information, and doing it badly.

"Yes. And no. I mean . . . yes, I help out, but no, I didn't today."

Helen's fishing pole extended.

"So, you haven't spoken with Brush today?"

"No."

"Or last night?"

Susannah didn't like the question. The night before had been different, almost uncomfortable, a situation that had never happened to them. She'd gotten a call from Brush around supper time. He told her they couldn't get together. He had to run an errand in Volney. This was unusual but not especially concerning.

Brush and Susannah also had a nightly ritual. It was

a brief, good night phone call, and it was the last thing either of them did before going to bed. Last night, Brush didn't seem like himself. He was preoccupied. Susannah could hear it in his voice, but she decided not to press him, so the phone call was shorter than usual. It was during last night's call that Brush told her to sleep in today, that he didn't need help.

Susannah's eyes stayed on her tea.

There was something about Helen that told Susannah she didn't need to be her usual self at that moment. She didn't need to be truthful.

"No, we didn't talk last night."

Helen lifted her teacup. Now she was artificially casual, and transparently so.

"Brush stops here in the morning, doesn't he?"

Susannah grew more guarded. Where were these questions going? Everybody in Volney knew that Brush delivered milk to Lillian every morning. Susannah spoke into her teacup.

"He didn't make it on time today. That's very unusual for him."

Susannah put down her cup and slid a small saucer toward Helen.

"Here's a little dish for the teabag."

"How thoughtful, Susannah. You and Brush have been seeing each other for a long time, haven't you?"

A wariness crept over Susannah. There was an imbalance to the moment, and it didn't seem to be tipping her way. Her eyes rose and met Helen's.

"Seeing each other? We don't call it that."

Helen returned Susannah's gaze. She had never paid

much attention to the girl other than as an appendage of Brush. Now, and for the first time, she sensed something else. The girl had grit. Helen decided to ignore it and went on.

"I can't remember a time when I didn't see you two together, even as children."

Susannah's wariness vanished. She took on a faraway look.

"Neither can I. I mean, not see us, ourselves, but you know."

"How do you intend to deal with missing him?"

The question was delivered in a tone of interrogation. It wasn't a question Susannah wanted to dwell on in the first place. Coming from Helen, it put her further on guard.

"Well. . . "

"It would be a terrible mistake. For Brush to stay here."

"I know . . . "

"We need to think of him, now."

"I am . . . I do. I always do."

"And not about ourselves."

"I don't understand."

"It's easy for a young man to make the wrong decision if he's guided into thinking about the short term."

"What do you mean?"

"About what's next with a young woman."

"What's next?"

Helen slid a sketchbook – the one that fell from Brush's pocket at the town meeting – across the table. It was instantly familiar to Susannah. She had watched him fill so many of them. She picked it up and leafed through routine sketches. She stopped when she saw sketches of herself nude from the waist up. For a moment, she was stunned into a fog. Helen seemed to be speaking. She could hear Helen's voice, but it was as though the sound came from another room. Even so, Susannah detected that the forced cheeriness was gone. The fog lifted, and Helen's words came to her.

"The last thing Brush needs right now is to be seduced into remaining here."

Susannah closed the sketchbook and placed it on the table. Her eyes leveled at Helen. The earlier imbalance of the moment was gone. Helen immediately understood she was about to see grit played out. Susannah spoke in an even voice.

"Seduced? Seduced."

Helen indicated the sketchbook.

"Well, yes."

Susannah pushed her chair back, a little too hard, a little too sudden, reached for the sketchbook and brandished it.

"This is because I'm a Symington, isn't it?"

There was more than hurt and resentment in Susannah's voice. There was an indignation that unsettled Helen. Instantly, Helen knew she had stepped out of bounds. Still, she began to protest.

"I'm only . . . "

"You wouldn't be saying this if I were a Bellamann."

"Of course I would . . . "

Susannah's voice swelled.

"You think you can just decide for everybody. You think because you're a Bellamann you can just go and, and, and just change things the way you want. Well, I like things the way they are around here. Seduced. You think you're better. You don't have to say it. I can feel it. Everybody can. Because I'm a Symington, there's nothing, nothing I can ever do to make me good enough for a Bellamann. Seduced! It's always there. Ooh, I hate the way things are around here."

Lillian, drying her hands with a dish towel, entered from the kitchen. She watched the scene in wonder and disbelief. Helen, seeing that the mess she was making now had an audience, tried to smooth things.

"Susannah, you're overwrought. Perhaps we should . . . "

"You don't even know me, but you go ahead and decide that I'm so selfish that I would try to, try to . . . trick Brush into staying with me. Sure, I guess that's the kind of thing that people like me just naturally do. Well, maybe you've never stood for ten hours in a fruit and vegetable stand, and you think it's a bad life for low people. But I'll tell you this, everyone who walks up to that stand is glad to see me. That's more than I can say for you."

The words landed hard on Helen. She was not accustomed to being addressed in this way, but one glance Lillian's way told her there was no denying the truth in what she'd just heard. Lillian couldn't conceal it. Lillian hastened past the counter and neared the table.

"Susannah!"

Susannah turned away, her back to Helen and Lillian.

"You, all of you, you've just noticed Brush. But I've been. . . I've always . . . we've always . . . you think he's just this, this thing you can send off."

Lillian came behind Susannah and touched her shoulders. "Oh, Suz . . ."

Susannah waved her off.

"Just stay away. All of you."

She turned back to confront Helen. "Everybody's thinking about Brush, but what about me? Me! What about me? Brush can't . . . Chicago . . . alone, I mean, it's just, errgh . . ."

Susannah slapped the sketchbook onto the table. "So there!"

She stepped toward the door, paused, wheeled about and returned quickly. She snatched up the sketchbook, paused again and leaned into the table and toward Helen.

"If Brush stays, I don't care what you say about me. When he goes there's only one thing that scares me. He might come back like you."

Susannah beelined to the door just as Brush entered, dark circles under his eyes, milk can in hand. She grabbed him and kissed him long and hard, and stormed out, leaving the boy dazed and mystified.

He directed an inquisitive glance at Helen, who made herself artificially busy. She spoke toward her purse.

"My, look at the time. Well, that was an informative chat."

CHAPTER 15

LILLIAN PERSONS

HELEN GRABBED up her handbag and shouldered past Brush and out the door with as much dignity as she could muster. Brush let the moment play out and continued to the counter. He placed the milk can next to it.

"Sorry I'm late. Did I miss something? Or something?"

Lillian slid an empty milk can his way. She took a minute to consider whether she should inform Brush about what she had just witnessed. It turned out to be a long minute. She was returned to the moment by Brush's voice.

"Miss Lillian, is everything okay?"

Lillian knew she had to say yes, things were okay. The fact that the incident happened in her café didn't make it her business. She perked up and dismissed his concern.

"Helen just made a big mistake and doesn't know what to do about it."

"She should talk to Pez."

Peter reeled through the door, bleary eyed. Lillian reached for a coffee pot.

"The elixer of cocklight?"

"Swiftly, lass."

Peter sized up Brush as Lillian filled a cup.

"You look worse than me."

Brush ignored the comment, although it was true. Brush had more urgent things to say.

"Mr. Basque . . . Peter . . . we need to talk. I've . . . "

Lillian broke the moment by placing a shopping bag on the counter in front of Peter. He looked into the bag, and then back to Lillian.

"It's from the Ladies Auxiliary," she said.

"Is it wool?" said Peter. He reached into the bag to find out and pulled a blue garment out. "What is it?"

"It's a shirt that isn't black," said Lillian. "Now that we're all seeing less of your cape, we thought you could use it. And it's cotton."

Peter spread the shirt out before him. It was light blue with small white checks, and short-sleeved.

"Black is also hot in summer," said Lillian. "If you haven't noticed."

Peter was rarely at a loss for words. He was speechless now at the sight of the gift. A gift. He could not recall the last time he had received one. He was confused, but pleased, and his expression revealed both. He took in Lillian and immediately saw more than was there before.

She had a story.

Lillian Persons had lived three lives, and the last one took her by surprise. She grew up in Volney to become the just-pretty-enough girl next door at the county high school, where she was a well-liked cheerleader. After high school she watched as some of her friends in Volney moved off to college or to work in bigger towns. It never crossed her mind to leave.

Her next life began when she met and married Dave Persons, a World War II veteran and travelling salesman who dealt in commercial pipe. Dave was an easy-going man, and many attributed his success as a salesman to his manner. He was the same at home, which was a small, porched, bungalow-style house in Volney after he moved there to marry Lillian.

They had dreams. Dave would work in sales and travel only long enough to build a nest egg. Then he'd go into business for himself. Lillian would continue to work – she'd taken a job beneath her skills at McIntire Grocery – until they started a family.

The dreams ended the day Dave set off in his car and never returned. He collapsed during a sales meeting in St. Louis and died almost instantly. It was later learned he had an aneurism.

The president of the pipe company had the sense to call Bellamann House with the terrible news first. A young Helen Bellamann was sent to McIntire Grocery to inform Lillian.

And so, the third, and unexpected, phase of Lillian's life began. She wasn't alone in the world. It was worse than that. She needed to care for her mother.

Her father was the only man from Volney who did not return from World War II. Upon his death her mother had begun descending into a premature senility.

There was no known diagnosis for it at that time. People just said she let old age take her early. By the time Lillian married Dave, her mother already required the measure of attention a young mother would give a child. The difference was, and Lillian understood this deeply, her mother would never grow out of it.

Dave left her a meagre insurance policy. It was all they could afford at the time and neither imagined that it would be needed soon. That, plus her job at McIntire Grocery wouldn't be enough to make ends meet, and Lillian wasn't about to go husband shopping to make them meet.

A few weeks after Dave's death, Cyrus Bellamann asked Lillian to come to Bellamann House. There, in the study, he conducted what Lillian considered to be a curious, wide-ranging conversation but was, in fact, an interview.

The interview came at the request of Helen Bellamann. Lillian, she explained to her father, was on her own and over-burdened. There wasn't a job in Volney for a woman that could meet that burden. She needed to support herself.

Cyrus had doubts. He couldn't count how many times he'd been asked to stake a business or a farm or a venture of some kind, and not one of the requests had come from a woman. Lillian didn't even make a request of her own.

Lillian, though, passed the interview she didn't know was an interview. She had the one trait Cyrus always looked for in people. She wanted to be reliable. Maybe it was the cheerleader in her, but Cyrus could also see that she was game for the chance. And it carried unmeasured weight that Cyrus had known her father.

Lillian was called again. Cyrus invited her to meet him on Main Street. There, the two stood in front of a recently emptied storefront two doors from McIntire Grocery. The question to Lillian: What can you do with this?

And so, with crossed fingers and a stake from Cyrus Bellamann, Person's Café was born.

Lillian chose the restaurant business because she already knew how to cook, and she had an invaluable collection of family recipes. She learned quickly these were just two pieces of an elaborate puzzle.

As Cyrus Bellamann explained to her, "Forget what business you or anybody else thinks you are in. You are in the manufacturing business. You will make and deliver products all day, every day. Every single product you deliver will be judged on its own. You need a system. You need a way of working that makes your products consistent, and consistently good. You are in the people business, too, but good products make for good people."

Lillian found that way of working. Mostly it was through trial and error and coming to understand that she needed to be able to perform every task in the restaurant. She also had to be willing to accept every task. This included emptying the grease pit and keeping the bathroom clean.

Person's Cafe worked. Still, when she surfaced from the early scramble to get the restaurant up and running, and this included finding a dependable grill man who would stick around, she found herself young and single and in a very small place. Her friends who had gone off to college or to larger towns had met people. There were few prospects remaining in Volney. As the women in town would say, "All the good ones are taken."

Lillian, though, wasn't looking for one, good or bad. After Dave, she just couldn't bring herself to even consider the prospect of another. There was one man, though, who came into her life every day, a man whose appeal she couldn't ignore, although she had to. It was Carl Holland.

Carl delivered milk to the café every morning. As one visit followed another, Lillian and Carl went from the daily hello-nice day-goodbye exchange to something like a conversation. He started having coffee. He lingered. The conversations lengthened and deepened.

She came to think of their talks as the best part of her day. Her only awkward moments with Carl happened on those rare days he arrived and the café was empty. She couldn't be alone with him. He was married. She knew she lit up when he entered the room, and she knew she couldn't hide it. She also knew that this could not remain a secret in Volney. She didn't want to put Carl in a position that could sully his name. If the restaurant was empty when Carl arrived, she found a way to cut their conversation short. It agonized her to do so, but she did it.

Over time, she felt she had come to know him deeply. She knew there was something wrong with his marriage long before Carl knew. After Elizabeth Holland left, Lillian found herself in the worst of both worlds. Carl Holland was available, but he had made himself unavailable. Her daily visits now came from Brush, a connection she nourished, but was careful about it. She didn't want to appear to be pursuing the father through the son.

Even in Carl's absence, she still had that cheerleader in her, and she pressed on at the café, day after day. She had never counted the passing days before. Now, with Carl isolated and tormented, and she all the while knowing she could ease his pain, she did count the days. Every one felt like a missed opportunity.

But now, here she was in Person's Café with two great artists at her counter.

Lillian changed the subject. She gestured grandly toward her new print on the wall.

"Neither of you has commented on my new picture."

Peter looked up from his shirt and shrugged a little too casually. Brush examined the print while Peter shoved his new shirt back into the bag and lifted his coffee.

Brush went all in on his criticism. "The artist is lazy."

Peter instantly lifted his eyes and peered over his coffee cup. He watched Brush go around the counter to address the painting closeup. Brush pointed to the foreground.

"See here? A gob of brown, a little yellow, then highlights poked on it with a fan brush. Instant Autumn Branch. It's a cheap trick."

Intrigue passed over Peter's face. He put his coffee down and leaned, elbows on the counter. Brush pointed to another spot on the painting.

"But look here, this is worthy of Vermeer. And he's hidden his tracks. I don't know how he did it, but it took some effort. So, he's got the ability, but he takes the easy way out."

Brush peered at the signature. "Robert Garrett. Never heard of him." He glanced over to Peter for affirmation or argument. He was answered with a shrug. He snatched up the empty milk can. Peter stopped him.

"What did you want to talk about?"

"I changed my mind about Chicago. I'm not going."

Brush headed toward the door, leaving Peter in a stew. Peter stopped Lillian with his hand when she tried to refill his cup. Her eyes followed Brush to the door.

"All I wanted to know is if he thought it was pretty," said Lillian. "And by the way, I like your new hair."

Peter grabbed the shirt bag and bolted for the door, leaving Lillian wide-eyed for the second time that morning.

CHAPTER 16

CALWOOD, MOKANE & BLOOMFIELD

WHEN BRUSH hit the sidewalk outside the cafe, he found Calwood, Mokane and Bloomfield muttering his way. Calwood and Mokane collared him and marched him arm in arm to their customary bench, sat him down and sandwiched him there – Mokane took a seat on the left, Bloomfield on the right. Out of the corner of his eye, Brush watched Peter steam out the cafe door and sprint the other way, shopping bag in hand. Calwood produced cigars, handed them out, and directed one toward Brush.

"Smoke?"

Brush shook his head "no" and tried to wave it off.

"No. I don't . . . "

Calwood shoved a cigar into Brush's mouth. Mokane lit it as Calwood paced before the bench, hands clasped behind his back, his straw boater tilted on the back of his head. He spoke to the air.

"Chicago's a big town."

Brush tried to speak through his cigar, a feat he'd never attempted.

"Guys, I'm not . . ."

Mokane stayed him with his hand.

"You need to hear this," said Calwood.

"Don't play poker 'til after you've bought the groceries," said Mokane.

Bloomfield opened a newspaper and spoke into it.

"The little fork is for the salad."

"Buy beer in brown bottles. It won't have that skunk taste," said Calwood.

"Always check your fly," said Mokane.

Bloomfield looked up from his paper.

"If you're on the American Plan, order the salmon."

Calwood lit his cigar and then used it like a pointer, jabbing it toward Brush.

"You're going to need a big ego."

"And a good sex drive," added Mokane.

Calwood returned his cigar to his teeth and grew reflective. "When you think about it, the rest doesn't matter much."

"If your socks don't match, wear boots." said Bloomfield.

"After awhile, you're gonna narrow it down to one girl," said Mokane.

Again, Brush attempted to speak through his cigar. "I already have . . ."

This time Calwood stayed him with a hand.

"You wonder how two people could be such a perfect fit," he said.

Bloomfield spoke into his newspaper. "Take your

own water. Town water gives you the trots."

"But then she starts making plans," said Mokane.

Bloomfield lowered his paper and spoke over it. "Brown liquor melts the ice faster."

"She starts trying to change you," said Calwood. "Well, you aren't gonna do that. You got a bug on your shirt, Mokane."

"In church, never sit where the preacher can point at you," said Bloomfield, now returned to his paper.

"It's not a bug," said Mokane. "It's a coffee stain."

"Smooth your sheets first thing after you get up and you won't want to go back to bed," said Bloomfield.

"Your coffee stain just moved," said Calwood. He swiped Bloomfield's newspaper and whacked the bug on Mokane's chest. "Now it's a stain."

Calwood handed the paper back to Bloomfield while Mokane watched him, disgruntled and annoyed, and then attempted in disgust to wipe off what remained of the bug. Calwood leaned back and looked to the sky, hands on hips.

"Now where was I?" he said.

Brush, now fully resigned to his captivity, spoke through his cigar. "She wants to change me."

"Oh, yeah," replied Calwood. "The thing is, you don't want her to change, but she starts to. It's like little pieces of her mother are hiding inside and they start to sneak out."

Bloomfield spoke into his returned paper. "In town, wear a clean hat."

Mokane leaned forward and spoke with gravity. "Long about forty, you're gonna turn into a lunatic. Go ahead and enjoy it. It goes away."

"If you get gas, take it outside," said Bloomfield.

"That's about the time they give up on you," said Calwood. "The women. The wives."

Bloomfield dropped his paper again. "Trim your fingernails round, but your toenails square."

Mokane leaned back. "Then again, she might start liking you again, just the way you are."

"Never eat cucumbers before you go dancing," said Bloomfield, his paper again raised.

Calwood waved his cigar in the air, like he was clearing out his view. "Or she might just decide that no man can be housebroken."

"Those are the ones that turn into old biddies," said Mokane. "Get twitchy. Complain about the church."

"They stop looking both ways when they cross the street," said Calwood.

"Butt in line in front of you," said Mokane.

"While she thanks Almighty God for giving her forbearance," said Calwood.

Bloomfield dropped his paper again. He pointed into the air.

"Spam!"

This brought a moment of silence. Calwood, no longer pacing, drew on his cigar, as did Mokane and Bloomfield. Brush removed his. Smoke clouded the bench and drifted away.

"Always check your pockets for rare coins," said Bloomfield.

Calwood turned to Brush and stabbed his cigar. "That's a fact. You could have a fortune right there in your pocket right now." He replaced his cigar, drew on it and blew smoke. "I've had three."

Mokane rolled his eyes and removed his cigar. "Three? Three fortunes. Oh, I'm just dying to hear how you know this."

"Sure," said Calwood. "It's obvious. For every million coins, how many do you think are rare?"

Mokane shrugged. "I don't know."

"Let's say three," said Calwood. "And let's say that over a lifetime you have a million coins in your pocket."

Bloomfield spoke to the cloud of smoke. "When you're moving furniture, let the other guy walk backwards."

Mokane blew an exasperated cloud. "Muttonhead. You couldn't fit a million coins in a pickup, much less a pocket."

"Sure you could," said Calwood.

Mokane rose from the bench and dug around in his pocket. He produced a coin. "See this quarter? How big is it?"

Calwood took the quarter in hand and held it before his eyes, turning it back and forth.

"I was thinking dimes," he said.

He strolled away from the bench, still with the quarter and with Mokane barking at his heels.

Bloomfield rose from the bench and braced to follow. "Well, that's about it. Good luck in the big city."

He tapped the cigar in Brush's hand. "Too bad ya got the habit."

CHAPTER 17

"WE'RE RUNNING OUT OF TIME"

PETER'S BUS lurched down the Holland Dairy driveway in way too big a hurry, a storm of road dust trailing. The bus was almost too broad for the driveway in the first place. Now, it ricocheted from edge to edge, ditch to ditch, Peter joggling at the wheel and bouncing in his seat. He wheeled it past the house and lurched it to a slide halt at the door of Brush's studio barn. The air brakes were still exhaling as he leapt to the ground and slammed aside the barn door.

Inside, only two large canvasses remained still hanging. Peter's trailer had been pulled inside and it was almost filled with shipping boxes, loaded sideways in a tight row. Carl was leaning into an eight-foot length of 2x4 lumber, sawing it in half. He halted mid-thrust, looked up and tracked Peter, who barreled toward him.

Peter grabbed Carl by his overall straps and pushed him backwards into a support pole, forcing Carl to drop his saw. Carl rebounded, knocking Peter's hands away. He grabbed Peter's shoulders and shoved him back on his heels. There the antagonists stood. Peter righted himself into a menacing stance and laid a baleful eye on Carl.

"I told you. You get hammered. I hammer you."

Carl stepped away from the pole and toward Peter, equally menacing, equally baleful.

"This is my farm. This is my barn."

Peter was unimpressed. He straight-armed a finger at Carl. "Are you back on the sauce?"

Carl slapped the hand away. A staredown followed, giving both men time to size the other up. Carl was sober, which Peter realized he should have known the moment he saw him working with a saw. For Carl, there was an urgency to Peter that pierced Carl's established impressions. Peter wasn't performing. He was for real. They were both taken aback. The air remained charged, but Carl won the staredown.

Peter unplugged. He exhaled, relaxed his hands and arms, and held them up in the universal sign for truce. Carl, too, relaxed.

"What's got you this way?" he said.

"Brush says he's not going to Chicago," said Peter.

Peter could see that the news of Brush's decision was new to Carl, who acknowledged it with a cool, deliberative look.

Peter let loose a helpless shrug. "I'm out of arrows, champ. This one's on you."

Carl remained deliberative. Peter couldn't tell if Carl was looking at him or inside himself. Either way, Peter's guard was down, utterly so, and at that moment, Carl didn't have a guard. This was a man-to-man encounter, and both men were defenseless. Peter continued.

"Champ, I gotta tell you, I need this as much as he does . . . "

A quick glance at Carl informed Peter that, somehow, Carl understood this. He could also tell they agreed about Brush. Peter continued.

". . . and we're running out of time."

Carl remained cool, but the deliberation was gone. Whatever decision he needed to make, he'd made it. He moved easily back to his saw and lumber. He picked up both and gestured them toward Peter.

"Then let's not squander time," he said.

Peter came to him and accepted the tools. The two men set about completing the shipping box.

CHAPTER 18

THE DISCOMFORTS OF HOME

THE SUN was setting on Volney as Peter, returning from Holland Dairy, guided his bus quietly onto Main Street. He had passed Brush on the way back into town.

Peter had been living in prairie country long enough now that he had adopted the habit of the "country wave," in which drivers, even perfect strangers, of vehicles that meet one another on the road offer a gentle wave of the hand to each other. Peter had waved to Brush and gotten no response.

It was the only unrewarding moment in an otherwise captivating drive. Peter was no stranger to prairie landscape, but more and more he felt what he could only describe as a magnetic pull from the countryside around Volney, especially on sunset drives like the one he had just taken. His high, wide windshield seemed to frame the land just so. He could feel himself breathe out and unknot as the horizon spread before him. He watched the distant colors – the cool blues on the edges of the horizon encroaching on the hot yellows and reds and oranges in the middle – as the nearby colors shifted and changed and danced with the retreating light. To him, it was as though the land had captured and held onto what the day had given and was now hurling the heat and light back into the sky where it belonged.

To Peter Basque, observing a prairie landscape was like watching a ceaseless, hypnotic patternless form of running water, except that nothing moved, except the light.

And he knew, somewhere inside himself, that sunsets themselves have meaning. The recipe for a magnificent sunset has to include clouds.

Now, as Main Street ambled by, he felt himself breathe out more and regard the little town anew in the golden bath of day's end. He recalled the first time he drove down the street. It seemed so long ago, but it was, what? How many days? He didn't bother to count. So much had changed, including the way he felt about the little town. He couldn't describe the new feeling until he heard himself say it out loud.

"Home."

As soon as the word passed his lips, Peter quelled it, along with the feeling. Both scared him.

Ahead on Main Street, Peter discerned Duck in Double Secret Agent Mode making an elaborate effort to sneak across the street, concealing an unconcealable object, which turned out to be a case of beer. Duck opened the driver side door of a pickup truck and made

the slow, slit-eyed, look-both-ways head turn that signals
absolute iniquity. He slid the beer onto the seat, slid
himself in behind the wheel and sat there, a look of pure
deliverance on his face. He looked up to see Peter offering
a knowing country wave as his bus passed by. Duck's look
of deliverance went away, replaced by dismay, and then
a forced nonchalance. Duck started the truck and drove
away, ever so stealthy, eyes on his rear-view mirror.

Farther down Main Street, Peter could see the lights
were on at the bank. The rest of Main Street was darkened
except for the window advertisements that never
switched off.

CHAPTER 19

MIKE RUTHERFORD

IN THE bank, inside his office, Mike was at his desk, slumped on his elbows, one hand with a phone to his ear, the other pulling at his hair. His voice breathed into the phone with wrath and determination in equal measure.

"Why am I out of the deal! You gave me until Monday . . . I told you I could get her to lease me the land . . . What do you mean a new man on the job? . . . Robley? Well, you'd better get your new man busy, because it's every man for himself from here on."

Mike slammed the phone down. He spoke to the air. "Dammit, Helen."

Mike's second-story office had a single window. It looked out the rear of the building above an alley. From it, he could see the intimate, leafy grid of streets on the south side of Volney falling away into the prairie. In the distance, he could see the highway under construction and Helen's adjoining land.

Mike Rutherford was not a greedy, or even selfish, man. His desire for Helen's property was inspired by genuine concern for the little town he loved. And he loved it deeply. Volney had saved him, at least that's how he saw it.

Mike returned from World War II having given no thought to what he might do after he arrived home. In this, he was not alone. In 1946, he was demobilized in Baltimore and found himself in the company of too many veterans who were lost and aimless, and looking for one more bar brawl.

Mike wasn't even sure where home was. At age 21, he had no family to speak of. But he had a friend. Carl Holland, who had been in Mike's unit, was eager to get home and take over his father's dairy. Carl was also ardent. A young woman awaited him – the love of his life, as he too frequently portrayed her – and they were ready for marriage and family.

Mike didn't have a planned future in the way that Carl did, but he shared Carl's impatience. Mike also had a car and a wad of cash he'd saved over the years. The two were soon motoring together cross country toward Volney. Along the way, Carl told Mike about the town, at one point relating that the Volney Grainworks and Feedstore was up for sale.

Mike had a working perception of what it took to run a retail operation, but he knew nothing about managing a set of grain towers in a farming community. Carl did, and by the time the pair slowed to 25 miles per hour and wheeled onto Volney's Main Street, Mike had a low-beam grasp of the business. The rest, he knew, he could and would learn.

He did learn. While Carl went on to operate Holland Dairy, Mike took over the newly named Rutherford Grainworks and Feedstore. Mike quickly earned a reputation for integrity among the farmers in the county. Rutherford was where you went for a square deal.

As his situation became more established, Mike became benevolent, anonymously so. More than one farmer was allowed credit during hard times and was sometimes forgiven the debt later.

Anonymous or not, word got around. Volney was, then and today, too small for a secret to survive. Mike's stature in Volney grew. Mike soon got a G.I. Bill college degree by studying nights. When he opened the Bank of Volney a year later, nobody was surprised. His reputation for honesty and fair play attracted depositors and loan applicants from the outset.

Mike came to view Volney as the place that delivered him from an aimless existence – that he was meant to be there. He was grateful for it. If Volney melted away after being bypassed, his meaning for existence would melt away with it.

It could almost be said that Mike Rutherford never made a serious mistake – "almost" being the key word. Mike was never a heavy drinker. He wasn't even what you would call a drinking man. He had been seriously pickled only once, and he'd been paying the tab for it for ten years.

The moment Mike laid eyes on Helen Bellamann, it was over for him. In everyone's eyes she was Volney's Most Eligible Girl – with the exception of the eyes of her flamboyant sister Lorelai, who claimed the title for herself.

Helen wasn't just the most eligible. In a way she was Volney personified. Her family founded Volney in 1859, with each succeeding generation adding another pillar for the community to lean on. As the oldest born of her generation, Helen had willingly shouldered what each previous generation of Bellamanns knew to be a responsibility of birth.

In Mike's eyes, she was his future. At first, he was tongue-tied in her presence, but a glance from her here, a touch on the wrist from her there, freed his tongue. Soon, they were inseparable. A year later, it was time for their wedding date to be announced. The wedding was to be in the spring.

When Helen went trousseau shopping in St. Louis, she went alone. She knew that her sister, Lorelai would just get in the way and shove extravagant, showy costumes her way. And she didn't want Mike to see what she would wear on their wedding weekend until she revealed it to him herself.

She purchased three dresses. For the first two she adhered to custom. She bought an elegant, understated dress for the rehearsal dinner. She bought an elegant, understated wedding gown. Both reached full length.

But she went outside herself for the dress she would wear when she departed Volney in a car with Mike for their honeymoon weekend. She had a dress made. Helen wasn't accustomed to spending money immoderately, but the last thing she wanted to be on her wedding night was moderate. She would make a gift of herself to Mike, and she would wrap the gift in unforgettable fashion.

The dress was pale yellow silk and just delicate enough. It was soft and feminine and showed off her figure. It was designed to reveal just enough to be alluring without becoming overly provocative. It had a fitted top with ever so soft pleating and a high neck – accentuated by lightweight silk roses – that also bared the shoulders. The roses were yellow, the color of love. Her slim waist would be cinched by a yellow silk bow above a flowing skirt hemmed just at the calf. There was also a bright yellow silk wrap made to cover her shoulders upon leaving for the honeymoon, something she could unwrap once alone in the car.

The dress was spectacular, and Helen was stunning in it. Helen was determined to keep it a secret.

The engagement party was on the lawn of Bellamann House. Everybody in town was invited because everybody would have come anyway. They ate finger food and drank punch while a fiddle and banjo group played in the background.

The trouble began when Calwood, Mokane, and Bloomfield each spiked the punch, not knowing the other two had. It wasn't long before the gracious garden party became seriously undomesticated. Townspeople – many of whom had never consumed alcohol before – became a little too enthusiastic, until high spirits fully took over and the fiddle and banjo group was pushed to the foreground and a spontaneous dance was born. Mike, who had hit the punch early and often, was in the riotous middle of it all.

Helen, inside the kitchen, missed all of this. She was

supervising, overly so, the production of little sandwiches and cakes for the finger food table, and punch for the punchbowl, and she was making sure the napkins were folded just so. She remained working in the kitchen until she rushed to the back side of the house, spurred by the sound of breaking glass.

It was at this moment that Lorelai came out the front door in Helen's hand-made yellow silk dress, without the wrap. Unseen by Helen, she waltzed Mike – boozy, affable, and clueless – off the dance floor and they disappeared into the night.

The next morning, Mike awoke alone in Round Hill Cemetery, up on top of the hill behind Volney, as first light creased the prairie horizon. He had no idea how he had gotten there. He raced straight to Bellamann House, hurdled the gate and side-stepped his way through overturned chairs and party debris. When he mounted the porch, he found the door locked.

He knocked, even though it was too early to arrive unannounced. He could hear steps in the foyer and then silence. He could make out Helen through the narrow stained-glass windows. He waved. She examined him silently and turned her back to the window.

Mike started to knock again but thought better of it. Whatever this was, another knock wasn't going to help.

It turned out nothing would help. Whatever Mike had done, he'd done it with, or to, Lorelai. Neither sister would speak of it, at least not directly. Mike received a one-sentence note from Helen at the bank Monday morning. There had been no announcement at the party. The wedding was off.

As much as Mike tried, he couldn't find a way to ask for forgiveness for something he didn't know he had done. He was just sorry. He groveled. He apologized for any transgression that came to his mind. Helen would have none of it. As long as Lorelai was around, communication between Mike and Helen was reduced to the slightest of polite and essential conversation – hers icy, his solicitous. Mike grew tongue-tied again, but there was no glance or touch on the wrist to free him.

Eventually, Lorelai departed for Kansas City and her first and second and third husbands. This brought about an opening and a stalemate. Helen and Mike would talk. They had to. It was a small town and much of life it in depended on them. The conversation would always be civilized but it would never be tender. It was a truce without a settlement.

They still loved each other. As the years passed, they both forgot that they both knew it.

And then, Lorelai returned.

Now, alone in his office, Mike turned away from the view out his window. He leaned on his desk, both arms straight, head dangling. He was absolutely disheartened. He muttered.

"Dammit, Helen."

CHAPTER 20

"YOU KNOW WHAT FREEDOM IS, AND YOU DON'T KNOW WHAT FREEDOM IS"

THE KITCHEN light was on at the Holland home. Brush and Carl were seated at the four-square table.

Carl sitting sideways to the table, arms folded, head cocked, pondered the sign that Brush had brought in and had leaned against the corner cabinet. It was the sign Brush had discovered in the barn. Carl spoke toward the sign.

"When I painted that sign, I didn't even know you would be a son. Your mom was pregnant at the time."

"It was your dream," said Brush. "I know it was. It had to be, or you wouldn't have painted it that way."

Carl unfolded his arms and scooted his chair to face the table. He leaned on his elbows to face Brush, who was leaning toward him in the same way.

"Son, I've had lots of dreams. Some, like you, came

true. Most, I just let slip away. Too many."

Silence overtook the room and lingered. The boy and the man both knew one of those dreams, the biggest dream, was Elizabeth Holland. Carl broke the silence.

"When I left here for basic training before the war, I was pretty nervous and shaky. I guess you're feeling some of that now."

Brush raised his eyes to protest. Carl stayed him with a look.

"Brush, I know war and school aren't the same. But when you think about it, they are kind of similar. When I turned out of our driveway those years ago, I only knew one thing – where I was going. One place. Basic training. I didn't know anything else. I didn't know what I would see after basic training, what I would have to do, who I would do it with. I didn't even know if I could do whatever it was I was supposed to do."

Carl paused and looked directly at Brush.

"And I didn't know if I would come back."

Brush shifted and turned his gaze away from his father. Carl went on.

"That's what's bothering you, isn't it? You're afraid you won't come back"

Brush slumped in his chair and spoke to his shoes.

"Well . . . yeah. I guess."

Carl pushed back his chair and went to the counter by the sink. He drew two tall glasses from the overhead cabinet, dropped in some ice and filled both glasses from the sun-tea jar on the counter. He returned to the table but didn't take his chair. He slid a glass to Brush and stood tall.

"Brush, you will never leave your home. You can't."

Brush looked up at his father, quizzical.

"I can't?"

"You can't. Your home. Our home. This prairie. Even the cows. You will take it, all of it, with you wherever you go for as long as you live. It's inside you. All of it. Some people might say I'm being corny, but I know it's true. It's how I felt when I was away during the war."

Brush grew thoughtful. He looked up toward his father.

"But I want to come back."

"You can do that too, Brush. Tell me why you are going to that school."

"To become a painter."

"To become a better painter. You're already a painter. You became a painter right here, without leaving home. Who says you can't continue to be a painter right here after school?"

"I don't know. It seems like painters are supposed to . . . "

"Stop right there, son. Supposed. Supposed. That's the problem in your mind. Here at the dairy, we do the things we are supposed to do. We have to or we'd spoil the milk. But what you'll be doing is different. If you want to be a great painter, and you are and will be a great painter, and I may be a hick with manure on his boots, but I know this – the last thing you should ever do is what other people tell you to do."

"Then, why am I going to school?"

"Because they can tell you how to do things you don't know. Not what. How."

Carl took a seat and sipped his tea, using the moment to put his thoughts together.

"Son, you know what freedom is and you don't know what freedom is."

This one stopped Brush mid-sip on his own tea. He looked over his glass at his father, who continued.

"Let me explain. You've had the run of your world since you were old enough to run. You could ride your bike into town by yourself. You could be gone all day on a summer day and nobody worried about it. Now you can drive and nobody asks where you are going or where you have been. As far as you're concerned, you own this prairie. That's knowing freedom."

Brush's eyes told Carl that the boy understood. Carl took another sip and went on.

"But here at the dairy, when are we free like that? How can we leave? Tell me, how many vacations did we take while you were growing up?"

"One."

"One. Two weeks, and I had to hire three neighbors to come here and keep the milking and delivery schedule so it didn't change, and they all said they didn't want to ever do it again."

"So, why do you do it? This life."

"Because I am free to choose. And I choose this. I didn't take over Holland Dairy after the war because dad wanted me to. I wanted to. I saw plenty of the world when I was a soldier. When that was over, I knew exactly the world I wanted to see. It was here."

"Why can't I just choose here now? Why Chicago?"

"Because you don't know where your gifts make you

free to go. Only when you know that can you truly be free to choose. How can you choose here if you don't know anything about what's out there? You're a painter. Even I know that the world headquarters of painting is New York and Paris. They will always be there. You need to understand that here will always be here, too."

Carl rose from his chair and turned back toward the kitchen counter. He spoke with his back to Brush.

"People say sobering up is hard to do, and I guess it is."

He turned around to Brush. He spoke with a confidence Brush hadn't heard in more than a year.

"But putting down the bottle was one of the easiest things I ever did. Why? Because I thought I was losing you, too."

The "too" hung in the air and both the boy and the man knew why. Brush looked up to answer.

"But now you want to lose me . . . well, not lose me, but you want me to go away."

Carl put down his tea and disappeared into the dining room. He reappeared with the suitcase Brush saw him scraping the night before. It now said "Chicago" in white lettering. Carl put the suitcase on the table.

"Son, you take a road, you can always turn around. You don't take a road, you can only wonder."

Carl softly pushed the suitcase toward his son.

"You don't want to stand in this kitchen twenty years from now and hear yourself say, 'I just let it slip away.'"

CHAPTER 21

"THE KID GROWS ON YOU"

THE LIGHT was on in Volney's only phone booth. Peter, in his blue cotton shirt, stretched the phone line so he could stand in the breeze outside the door. Spencer Grisaille was on the other end of the line. He had the look of a man who has just heard something jarring. He had heard Peter apologize. He had also heard that Brush was going to be at least a week late.

"You sound different," said Spencer. "You sound . . . normal."

"Well, I guess it's the country air," said Peter, ignoring the observation. "Look, I know tomorrow's the day for Brush . . . "

"You've already apologized once for that," said Spencer. "Don't do it again. I won't be able to sleep."

"This is going to take several more days, at least a week," said Peter, again ignoring the sarcasm.

"I'm not sending more money," said Spencer.

"I'm not asking for it," said Peter. "I just want your guarantee there will be a spot for Brush if he comes a week late."

"So, it's Brush now," said Spencer. "First name basis."

"The kid grows on you," said Peter. He paused to survey the empty Main Street of Volney. "The whole place does."

"There will be a spot for Brush Holland," said Spencer. "There was always a spot. Just do whatever it is you're doing and get it over with."

They both hung up. Peter stepped from the booth and breathed the Autumn air. Spencer studied his office, adjusted his cuffs, and took on a look of contemplation.

***

Above Peter, the crescent moon shone a little brighter over Volney.

"IT'S A GATHERING OF NUTS"

PAINT PROJECT HEADQUARTERS was as it always was first thing in the morning. It was swarming with townspeople in pink spattered painting clothes awaiting directions for the day, while balancing tools, coffee, and donuts.

Peter strode up to the table, still in his blue shirt, to see Lorelai and Lillian in a little argument. Lorelai looked hurt. "Well, I think it's a terrific name," she said.

"It sounds like somebody with nasal congestion," said Lillian.

When Lorelai spotted Peter, she bubbled over to him and launched into Bubble Machine Mode.

"Join us Sunday for The Big Pinknic!"

She bubbled down.

"Get it?" she said. "Pinknic. Picnic. Pink?"

Peter rewarded her with a smile. Lillian took note,

first of the shirt – it looked hand washed and un-ironed
– and then of the smile. It was a genuine smile. There
was none of the self-mockery that called all his previous
smiles into question. Then she noticed the absence of
his cape and hat. Peter had tossed them aside behind
the headquarters table. They had been there overnight,
maybe longer.

"Lorelai," he said. "Along with a fabulous set of
knockers, you've got marketing in your soul."

Lorelai bubbled back up at the praise, while Peter
canvassed Main Street. Helen could be seen walking
by the edge of the crowd, annoyed because she had to
navigate around it. Meanwhile, Mike came towards him
through the crowd the other way and came to the table.
He unrolled another map and spread it across the table.
This was a map of Volney, each building, with the ones
that were already painted colored in pink.

Both men leaned in, hands on the table, shoulders
hunched. That the map was thoroughly unnecessary
– you could look up and down the street and see all
you needed to see, and you could count the houses on
the streets behind it – didn't stop the two men from
surveying it in earnest.

"Look. We aren't even halfway," said Mike, sweeping
his arm across the map. "The highway opens in six days."

Peter stood erect, hand on chin, and studied the
map. Mike stiffened when Helen strode up behind him,
pausing while a man in paint clothes hauled a bucket in
front of her. She let him pass and moved along, her heels
clicking in disdain.

Calwood, Mokane, and Bloomfield grumbled in.

Calwood held a cigar in one hand and measured about half of it with the fingers of his other hand and held it up in front of Mokane.

"Now, a roll of dimes is about as big as this," he said. "And that's a hundred to a roll, right?"

"Sure! Dimes! In a pickup," said Mokane. "You can't just have a million dimes."

"Quarter after eight," said Bloomfield.

Peter and Mike exchanged glances over the map. Both knew the problem at hand without exchanging a word. The project was bigger and more complicated than either had imagined that first day in Lillian's café. Now, it was behind schedule. Far behind.

Both men also knew that doubt could kill the project. If they seemed irresolute or uncertain, the others would become hesitant. The project would quickly turn from a lark into a slog in townspeople's minds. Only about half the townspeople had joined in so far. It would be easy for the rest to walk away. The thing would crumble under its own weight.

Peter turned away from the map, put two fingers in his mouth and let out a piercing whistle, which brought a stop to everything, except Helen, who continued to walk away, unstartled. Peter held his hands high, preacher style, as the crowd moved his way and assembled before him. He addressed all.

"Volneyites! Or is it Volneyans?. . . People of Volney! We are leaking time! To your positions! Haste!"

He abruptly stopped. "No, wait!"

Peter could see Carl, Brush, and Susannah coming across Main Street toward the rear of the crowd. All three were pushing wheelbarrows laden with what turned out to be paint compressors. Carl looked a little sheepish. It was his first time back in Volney. Lillian followed Peter's eyes. She cried out.

"Carl!"

The townspeople turned around. They all spoke at once.

"Carl!"

Peter, seeing Brush, spoke under his breath. "Champ!"

The people of Volney surrounded Carl and welcomed him. The moment had the feel of a reunion, but there was more to it than that. Carl was his old self. Peter watched as, one by one, the people approached Carl and expressed a shared joy at his presence. He noticed a special glow about Lillian, whose eyes never left Carl.

The mini-drama had arrested Helen, now three doors away on the sidewalk. She watched in wonder. Her eyes traveled from Carl to Brush to Peter.

Peter Basque. Peter. Again, it crossed her mind that she really wanted to stop disliking him.

Peter pushed through the well-wishers and up to the wheelbarrows. "What have we here? Whatever they are, they're big."

"Paint sprayers and compressors," said Carl. He gestured toward Brush. "And a returning student."

Brush acknowledged this with a shrug and a half-smile. "We paint the barns with these, and we paint 'em fast," he said. "So, now I guess I'm a different kind of painter."

Now, the map actually did become necessary. Peter,

Mike, and Carl surrounded it.

"We're going to divide and conquer," said Peter. "We'll go into the houses now and finish Main Street last. We'll have a prep crew and a spray crew. How many compressors do we have?"

"Four," said Carl.

"How many people do we need to man them all?" said Peter.

"Minimum of two each, but two more on each would be fastest," said Carl.

"Okay, Carl assembles the paint crews," said Peter. "Everybody else is on the prep crew. Mike, that's your crew. Carl, what time can you get here in the mornings?"

"Nine, if Brush makes all the delivery runs," said Carl.

Peter, without checking to see if this was suitable to Brush, said, "Nine it is. Carl, the paint crew is yours to start whenever."

A strategy was quickly put in place. The prep crew would advance ahead of the paint crew. The prep crew was divided into two groups, chippers and maskers. First the chippers would scrape the old paint on the houses, followed by the maskers, who would tape plastic over the windows and doors.

As long as the prep crew stayed ahead of the spray crew, it would be possible to cover many houses each day. It would need to be all hands on deck. If all hands did indeed come on deck and if the paint crew/prep crew plan worked, the entire population of Volney would descend on buildings in a mass. When they left, the buildings would be painted.

More and more people volunteered on the spot to work in the afternoon heat. The crowd swarmed back into the hardware store and returned with plastic and tape of any available kind. Voices buzzed. Commands sang out. The air was charged with energy.

Mike looked up to see a man coming down Main Street. He wore the many-pocketed vest and dangle of cameras and lens attachments about the neck that is the universal look that says "photographer." The man spoke to no one in particular.

"Is this some kind of festival?"

"It's a gathering of nuts," said Calwood.

Mike went into Mayor Mode.

"Welcome to Volney," he said. "Mike Rutherford, mayor. How are you doing?"

"Just stopped for gas," said the Photographer.

"Keep it outside," said Bloomfield.

"I bet you're hungry," said Lillian.

"No time," said the Photographer. "Got a deadline."

"Then you're on business," said Mike.

"I'm doing a photo essay for the Globe Democrat. The towns along the new interstate," said the photographer.

Bedlam ensued.

Everybody started talking at once. Peter's voice arose above the crowd. "Duck!" Peter motioned toward the photographer. Duck looked over to Mike, who nodded his approval. Duck sauntered through the crowd and collared the photographer, who took one look at Duck and decided not to attempt escape.

Peter's voice arose again. "Pez!" Peter did a quick

mime of donning his cape and hat while pointing toward the Paint Project Headquarters table. Pez flatfooted to the table and returned with Peter's gaucho hat and cape. Peter threw them on as he strode toward the photographer, the crowd parting before him, many noticing the cape didn't work that well with the blue shirt. Helen hurried up behind Peter. She shouted over his shoulder.

"Duck, let that man go!"

Duck, seeing no directive otherwise from Mike or Peter, held his grip. Mike, still trying to maintain Mayor Mode, gave a sweep of his hand across the townscape.

"Perhaps you've overlooked some of our local gems. Please be . . ."

"Jesse James Rock!" said Duck into the wincing photographer's ear.

"We're painting the whole town the same color," said Mike. "But, I . . ."

Peter stayed him with his hand, swirling his cape skyward.

"We will throw the paint!" cried Peter. This one stopped the crowd. They had placed their confidence in Peter's directions, but even they had no idea how that would work.

Bloomfield shook a finger at the photographer.

"You can't paint the animals," he said.

Lillian came up to the photographer's side and whispered into his other ear. "It's no stupider than golf."

Peter, now fully in his old Olympian Mode, lofted a finger to the sky.

"A kinetic response to the intrusion of modernity."

"Do the other towns want the road moved, too?"

asked Susannah.

Helen shoved forward and faced the photographer. "Please excuse my friends. They're...'"

Again, Peter's voice crowded in.

"Visceral! Bloodlike upon the walls!"

Lorelai struck a modeling pose.

"I live here," she cooed.

"We have slain the past upon a secular altar," proclaimed Peter.

Lillian nudged herself in front of Helen and gave Duck a wink.

"Perhaps a walking tour," she said, and headed away toward the eastern end of town, the end that was already painted. Duck, trundling the photographer beside him, followed along, as did all but Helen, Peter and the three old codgers. Helen turned on Peter.

"Your little theatrics have an audience," she said. "I'm sure you're happy."

She huffed away without waiting for a reaction from Peter, which was good, because there wasn't one. Peter planted himself on Main Street and awaited the mob's return. When it arrived, with Duck still hauling the photographer, Peter swept around and led them away, Pied Piper style. The crowd shouted and pointed out highlights of Volney while the photographer struggled to shoot from within Duck's grasp.

Calwood, Mokane, and Bloomfield took to their usual bench and smoked cigars while awaiting another passing show.

After a few minutes, the mob returned without the photographer, but with Peter now using the photographer's camera. The mob shuffled on, now shouting instructions to Peter. Duck, hauling the Photographer, trailed behind.

Carl and Lillian stepped out of the crowd and stopped in front of her cafe. She had slipped her arm into his.

"Come on in," she said. "It'll be my treat. We have so much catching-up to do."

Carl hesitated and looked about, "Where's Brush?"

"He'll be fine," said Lillian, while lightly, but firmly pulling Carl towards the cafe door. "It will be like old times. You'll be my last customer of the morning. Then, who knows?"

With that she escorted Carl through her door.

At the bench, Calwood raised two hands and made the shape of a brick with his fingers.

"It's scientific," he said.

"Scientific?" said Mokane. "And I'm a cat!"

"You've got one on," said Bloomfield.

Mokane leaned into Bloomfield and bawled.

"Cat! Cat!"

Mokane turned back to Calwood and pointed at his air brick.

"The holes are drilled in, and any fool would know," he said.

"Nope," said Calwood. "They're molded in from the get-go."

"Let the cat go?" said Bloomfield.

"Then explain to me, Mr. Muttonhead Genius, how the mold makes the holes so they can get the brick off without breaking it"

"You can't paint the cats, too," said Bloomfield.

The trio was interrupted by the remnants of the mob passing by again. Lorelai led the way, posing pinup style, while Pez shot with the photographer's camera. They passed on, Duck following with the poor photographer still in his grasp. The rest of the mob dropped off, including Mike, who returned to the map at the Paint Project Headquarters. Peter was nowhere to be seen.

The codgers watched Lorelai waltz down the street.

"Now she could make your comb get red," said Calwood.

"Once burned, twice shy," said Mokane.

"Right, and you'd know," said Calwood.

"Not me, Mike Rutherford," said Mokane.

At the sound of his name, Mike looked up from the table and over toward the bench. The codgers, their backs to the sidewalk, were unaware of his presence.

"Helen will never sell him the land, and it's because of Lorelai," said Mokane.

"Helen can't sell it," said Calwood. "It's not hers to sell."

Now, the codgers had Mike's full attention.

Mokane put on his exasperated look. "Oh, and I suppose Helen lives in Bellamann House because she doesn't own that, either."

"No, she owns that," said Calwood.

"And just who, Mr. Scientific, owns the land under it?" said Mokane.

"Helen does, but Lorelai has the rights to half the farm. And that's the part that Mike wants."

The news struck Mike full force. A spark of a notion

followed by a parade of hope, dismay, and resentment crossed his face. Instantly and without prodding, a scheme began to form in his head, and it was a scheme he knew didn't belong there.

"I want some pie," said Bloomfield.

"Helen's house. Lorelai's land. it makes no sense," said Mokane.

"Fifty, with coffee at Lillian's," said Bloomfield.

"It did to Cyrus Bellamann," said Calwood. "He said, 'I'm not leaving that child anything she can burn down.' Helen got the house and the land north of town. Lorelai got that land south of town that Mike wants. What time is it?"

A pink squirrel scampered across the sidewalk in front of them. Calwood watched in satisfaction.

"Oh my God," said Mokane.

Calwood stood up and tilted his boater to a dressy angle. "C'mon, we can be the last customers of the morning at Lillian's."

The trio mumbled away and through the cafe door. Mike's expression was a riot of conflicts. He fished the plans for his traveler's plaza from the pile on the table. He unrolled it and scanned it for the millionth time. His expression became resolved. He rolled up the plan and tucked it under his arm.

He spoke to the air, his expression fixed. "If that's the way she wants it."

He looked back down at the drawing on the table, his expression suddenly lacking all resolution.

"Dammit, Helen."

When Mike walked away, the scene in front of Paint

Project Headquarters became empty. The plop plop of flat-footed steps signaled the approach of Pez, who placed the photographer's camera and vest on the Paint Project Headquarters table and departed.

Another sound of footsteps approached through the quiet. The bedraggled photographer, alone, stopped and looked both ways. He removed his hat and pulled a kerchief from his pocket. He swiped the kerchief across his forehead and gathered up his camera and vest. He paused, furtive, and eyed all directions again before hurrying away.

CHAPTER 23

FOLDING THE ACT

PETER BASQUE stood alone in his bus, a dram of Irish whiskey in his hand as night overtook Volney. He eyed his party-worn couch. There, draped across it, was his cape. His hat sat atop the arm of the couch. At first glance, it had the effect of a person lying in the couch, and Peter regarded it as if it was a person.

Earlier that day, he had been carried by the moment when he donned the hat and cape, swirled into his Olympian manner, and flourished his baroque tongue before the photographer. He was still on Main Street hustling the photographer along with the crowd when the moment passed and stopped him in his tracks. He let the crowd go ahead of him and quietly escaped.

He couldn't get the hat and cape off fast enough.

He hadn't worn the hat and cape since the day of his haircut at the Big Three. The Big Three. He caught a reflection of himself in the side window glass. Why had he done that? He knew deep down that even before the Big Three he had sensed the costume was out of place in Volney because that's what it was, a costume, something he never considered it to be before. It had been a part of him. It was him. At least that's what he thought until his second day in Volney, when he noticed he couldn't bring himself to wear it in the presence of Brush's paintings.

Peter didn't like what he was feeling, even as the feeling gave him an untranslatable buoyancy. It was too new. Too uncharted. He sipped his dram.

He regarded the costume, flat and fallen on the couch before him. For a long moment, he was motionless. Abruptly, he looked up, drained his dram, placed his glass on the bar, and lifted the cape. He unhurriedly folded it up and carried it, and his hat, through the door to the back of the bus. After a moment, he re-emerged without both.

Peter Basque acknowledged to himself that he had folded The Act.

***

The crescent moon shone a little brighter that night over Volney.

CHAPTER 24

THE PAINTING OF VOLNEY

IT TOOK four days to paint every house in Volney. After a first morning of fits and starts, the project settled into a remarkably efficient routine. The prep crews led the way and the spray teams followed. All of Volney – men and women, young and old, black and white – stepped up for the job, mornings, afternoons, and evenings.

Word traveled fast about the revived project. After the first day, farmers driving tractors with front end loaders arrived in town. They raised and lowered small groups of chippers and maskers and spray painters. Ladders were cast aside. Things moved even faster.

The atmosphere grew festive on the second day when a fiddler and banjo player showed up, there to serenade the workers. The next day there were two fiddlers, a guitarist and a bass player. On the final day a woman arrived carrying a flute. Somehow, the musicians made a flute work in bluegrass.

The mood was convivial and there was a brisk energy to it all as the people of Volney moved from house to house. The Ladies Auxiliary, led by Lillian, set up long tables in the shade and served up a robust lunch every noon, and iced tea and cakes later in the day.

Susannah organized the children into cleanup crews. They followed the final spray teams and tidied up after them. She made a game of it. Every child wanted in.

Peter no longer commanded. He put away his movie-director routine and let the teams organize themselves. He was here and there, though, and he created a new, smaller team for touch-up painting. This became the last crew to pass before the children cleaned up.

If Peter wasn't onsite, Lorelai was in charge, mostly of the touch-up crew, but luckily, nobody paid her much attention. Peter already wanted improvements, especially a paler shade of pink for trim. They would have to wait.

His camera never left his hand.

Again and again, Peter was struck by this thing he'd created. As the teams and crews moved around and over the buildings and houses, he could see that people wanted to be there. Even at the end of a long day, they lingered at the final work site. The bluegrass band lingered, too.

Peter saw people who had lived close to their neighbors all their lives, but with those lives acted out in parallel lines. Now, confronting a powerful and unwanted threat, those lines were entangled, and in a delightful and valuable way.

He could also see that the devotion of the people of Volney to the project was wholehearted and genuine.

Peter could feel it, which made him cringe at the thought of himself in cape and gaucho hat at that first town meeting.

He heard himself proclaiming "From many, adjoined yet inchoate, we become one!"

Now, and against all odds, it was coming true, but what did it mean for him? He winced inwardly at the inflated, counterfeit Olympian poses that had made him amusing and notorious in art circles but rang so false here. Had he been mocking these people? These good people?

Had all of it, really, just been classic Peter Basque rubbish? The question spun without rest in his mind along with other questions. If so, what was this project now? And what was he?

Peter Basque had always flattered himself with the notion of himself as a maverick, an individualist free roaming a straitjacket world. But he was perceptive enough to know that maverick can be just another word for outsider, and on those rare moments when he stopped to consider himself in a straightforward way, he knew that's what he was. A loner, and reluctantly so.

He had never really been a part of any group, social or otherwise. He had loathed the cliques and cabals of the art world even as he used them for his own purposes, and even as he knew that his loathing grew from his understanding that he would never be fully accepted into one. For the same reason, he had never even considered the leagues and clubs and congregations that glue communities together.

He knew there was something about Peter Basque

that kept him at arm's length from humankind, and he was pretty sure that something was Peter Basque. He usually needed at least one drink just to be in the company of others. It was the only way he could get past the mediocrity. Not that he was some kind of genius, or that he considered himself one.

The problem was that his mind was always on. An insight here, a discernment there connected lightning quick threads of perception in him that seemed contrary, but were reconcilable if you put your mind to understanding it, or him. These surfaced in his conversation, which made him exhausting to be around, and he knew it.

He also knew from long experience that if he opened the minds of others, he would usually find a narrow range of obsessions, which signaled it was time for another drink.

In time, he faced a choice. Fix his condition or become a reception-wine sot. He addressed the choice by reversing the situation. He wouldn't let the world hold him at arm's length, he would stiff arm the world first. He did it with The Act – the cape and gaucho hat, the Olympian manner, the baroque flourishes of the tongue, and finally, the insufferable red splotch paintings.

The first group of paintings found a home in a Manhattan gallery. The outcome was bittersweet. The critics warmed to him. That was the sweet part. One declared Peter to be "the man who punctuated Jackson Pollock," and the table was forever set that way. That was the bitter part.

He would always be seen in the context of another

artist, and in that context he was second rate. He would always be the guy in the background, the second tier, the also ran. The one who wasn't original. That other guy.

Peter had always been struck by the banality of art critics. They were people with vocabularies that exceeded their perception. They were people who could not discern between novelty and ingenuity. They were people who needed other people's work in order to be somebody themselves, which made them people who are forever unsure, which made them vulnerable to folly.

They didn't see, they couldn't see, the intelligence underneath the restless surfaces of his paintings. There was a system at work in his paintings. To plan his paintings, and he did plan them, Peter simplified the compositions of the Old Masters into framework skeletons for his own paintings. His paintings were organized even as they appeared wanton. There was madness, but there was a method. Yes, there was a Rembrandt beneath the Basque. You just had to know it was there first, and Peter couldn't bring himself to point out what he considered to be obvious.

But he had found something he could turn out and sell, which he did in excess, each painting making the previous one less valuable, until The Act became a trap, a lifelong hustle for just enough money.

And he, forever on stage, just wanting to be left alone.

Now, he found himself in a position he'd never known or wanted. Peter Basque had become a team player. To his surprise, he was good at it. He had a stake in the outcome of Volney's eleventh-hour bid for survival.

Again, to his surprise, he wanted in on that stake.

He heard echoes of himself again – "We have slain the past on a secular altar." It was standard Peter Basque hot air when he proclaimed it on the street. Now, he saw truth in it. He could look at Susannah and share her resentment about the unpreventable interstate highway. There was a wisdom in her notion that he'd considered laughable before.

And, for him, there was one more surprise. The paint job was working. It looked good, better than good. It was splendid, and it was a sublime answer to the antiseptic and disenchanting interstate.

But he was too involved in the project to notice the captivating effect, especially at sunrise and sunset, of the evolving paint job. There was the unexpected pink, but there was also something elevating about letting your eyes travel over house after house, shed after shed. fence after fence, all different, but all the same, all composed and serene, like after a snowfall.

All but one. Bellamann House, towering and unyielding, remained as it was, which Peter constantly kept in mind. Peter glanced over his shoulder. He could see the tower from where he stood. You could see the tower wherever you stood in Volney.

It was the only thing wrong in a picture so right.

✳✳✳

By the time all the houses of Volney, except Bellamann House, were fully painted, a quarter moon had passed.

195

CHAPTER 25

THE PAINT FIGHT

SATURDAY. The painting of Volney would be complete by the end of the day. Peter knew this. He had already told Lorelai that it would be right on time for tomorrow's Sunday Pinknic celebration.

The morning shadows cooled him as he sat on the table of Paint Project Headquarters, legs dangling, ready to jump into work. He had sized up downtown Volney. Only the western end remained unpainted – Big Three Barber Shop, Post Office, McIntire Grocery, Tucker's Mercantile, and the Rutherford Grainworks.

Remarkably, Mike had wangled an out of service ladder truck, and two firemen who knew how to operate it, from the St. Louis Fire Department for the day. The truck was already parked near Peter's bus in the gravel around Rutherford Grainworks.

Mike and Peter had decided to delay painting the awning poles, lampposts, and fire hydrants until Monday morning when the scene would be clear. Duck and Pez were slated for the job. Main Street was blocked and detour signs set up. The highway traffic would divert to the parallel residential street on the north side from one end of town to the other.

When the people of Volney were assembled in front of Paint Project Headquarters, Peter addressed them by saying nothing. He spread his arms and indicated the tools and supplies spread before him. The self-organizing teams – now thoroughly experienced – went into action.

The spray teams would attend to the towers first. The towers weren't chipped and scraped. The paint was just laid on. Meanwhile the chip and scrape crews, and the masking crews launched into prepping the buildings on Main Street while the spray guns were busy at the towers.

The ladder truck made quick work of the tower job. The towers were lined up close together, almost adjoining, enough that two towers could be sprayed at the same time from one ladder. Carl's industrial-scale guns had the reach. All four towers were fully pink by the time the teams broke for lunch, this time served on the sidewalk outside Lillian's cafe.

Afterwards, the painters rested. Lillian came through the door with a large pitcher of lemonade and waded through beseeching hands holding glasses aloft, ignoring all until she reached Carl and poured him a glass.

Spirits were high, and there was a new aura of optimism among the workers. The feeling of optimism was elevated by the U.S. 40 passersby who stopped at the detour sign on Main Street.

For many drivers, the detour was expected. The

paint crews had been at it for ten days. The work had sometimes closed one lane and slowed the through traffic to a crawl, especially when Pez planted himself on the mid-stripe and brandished a "slow" sign.

The early response was predictable. There was honking and door slapping and the occasional epithet. Now, as the project neared completion, the reaction from passersby was new and welcome. The honking and epithets went away, replaced by expressions of curiosity and wonder. Drivers slowed on their own. Many stopped and parked. They all wanted to know: what was this marvelous thing?

Peter's scheme, which was now the entire town's scheme, seemed to be working. Hope gave way to confidence.

Confidence gave way to hijinks.

Carl, Mike, Mattingly, and Frank fired up sprayers and turned them on the McIntire Grocery facade, spraying from the hip and shouting "Take that!" like they were letting the bad guys have it.

Peter, brandishing a paint brush like a sword, led a crew of touch up painters in what resembled an assault on a castle. They charged Tucker's Mercantile, throwing up ladders and scaling the walls.

Calwood, Mokane, and Bloomfield held brushes like they were cowboys about to draw as they ambled up to their bench. They yanked their guns and let the bench have it.

Lorelai, using a tiny, watercolor-sized brush, dabbed paint on the trim of the post office facade as she arabesqued and pirouetted.

Carl, who had moved on to spray the Big Three facade, saw Lillian heading his way, swiveled around to greet her, sprayer still on, and accidently doused Duck head to toe.

Outside of town, Brush and Susannah put the finishing touches on the Symington Produce stand and headed back toward Main Street, not knowing they were just in time.

Hijinks gave way to mayhem.

Nobody ever found out who started it, but it began when a voice rose over the crowd in imitation of Peter. "We shall throw the paint!" After which, a gob of pink smacked Peter in the back, which sent Carl into a fit of laughter.

Peter retaliated by lobbing a glob of paint at Carl. It missed and hit Lorelai, who grabbed a large, loaded brush and reared back to return fire, which launched a glob of paint backwards, which hit Lillian.

Lillian grabbed a paint gun and let Lorelai have it, in the process saturating about half a dozen other people, which spread the paint fight onto Main Street, engulfing all the townspeople. Flying paint filled the air, while Calwood, Mokane, and Bloomfield moseyed through the fight scene with paint rollers, swiping wide swaths on the behinds of women.

Brush and Susannah, returning from the produce stand, walked into the fray. Out of nowhere, both received a glob of paint in the kisser. They regarded each other and began to fingerpaint each other's faces.

Lillian hustled up behind Peter, now a spraying maniac, ready to dump a bucket of paint on his head.

Mike and Carl came up behind Lillian. Mike tapped her shoulder and tossed a paint-soaked cloth in the air. She turned and gave Carl a warm smile as the paint cloth landed on her head, and Peter escaped.

Peter found himself in the center of Main Street as the paint fight ran out of steam. He rotated to take in the view. Helen, stony and unamused, stood at the detour sign on the west end of town, making sure no traffic came through. Pez, untouched by paint, had done the same on the other end of Main Street, one hand offering his candy dispenser. The people who stopped had gotten out of their cars. They looked on in a mix of delight and consternation.

When Peter's eyes returned to the scene around him, he saw the paint daubed people of Volney slowly stepping his way in mock menace, buckets and rags in hand. He went into his Olympian pose and faced the enemy as the crowd descended upon him and drenched him in paint.

A cheer went up as buckets, brushes, and paint cloths were tossed in the air. Peter found himself cheering with them.

It was done, all but a few signs and posts and fire hydrants, and later the fake sheriff's car at the edge of town, which people argued would defeat its purpose.

It was done. His impossible, nonsensical project had become theirs. They made it possible. They made it sensible.

A warmth crept inside Peter as his eyes traveled over the people of Volney, all exhausted by celebration and a job well done.

He had cheered with them, but now he was quickly

sobered. He was surrounded by affection and had no idea
how to bear it.

CHAPTER 26

INTERRUPTED MELODY

THE GOLDEN hour of evening exhaled as Mike Rutherford strode down Bellamann Street. He was cleaned up from the morning paint fight and heading home. He had a melancholy air despite the revelry earlier in the day. The nearing sunset was a reminder that the late summer days were ending earlier.

He couldn't shake a feeling of loss that he couldn't put into words. Time was passing – another day, another season, another year – and he wasn't moving forward. But to where would he move if he could?

He looked up from his feet to see the answer. He was passing Bellamann House. He stopped. Bellamann House was more or less on his way home. In a very small town everywhere is more or less on the way home, but this was the route Mike always took. He usually lingered in front of the house if he thought he was unobserved. He slowed his pace and kept walking if he thought eyes were upon him.

Of course, to be unobserved on the streets of a very small town is a rare thing. The sight of Mike in front of Bellamann House was a source of yet another kind of wry, low-beam amusement at Mike's expense. The people of Volney knew why he was there.

Still, he lingered. Perhaps Helen would appear on the porch. A wave of the hand would lead to a conversation. A conversation would lead to a tender moment, a touch on the wrist. A tender moment would lead to a resolution and a life that could begin anew.

Inside Bellamann House, Helen entered the parlor and made for the piano. It was a genuine old-fashioned parlor, formal and informal at the same time. Everything in the room was ornamental in some way – including an antique cabinet radio and an antique camelback sofa – except the piano. It was a new and shiny baby grand, and it meant business.

Helen scooted the piano bench to the keyboard, paused, scooted it back, stood up and lifted the lid on the bench. She shuffled through some sheet music, withdrew some and scooted herself back to the keyboard. A sheet fell into her hand. There was a hand-written note on it. "Always play this for us – Mike." She held the sheet in her fingers for a moment. Her expression hardened. She started to put the sheet away. She looked at it again. She softened. She placed the music above the keyboard and her fingers traveled to the keys.

Outside on the sidewalk, Mike had lingered long enough. Helen had not appeared on the porch, and he began to feel absurd standing there and longing for a magical coincidence. As he stepped away, he was arrested by the sound of the piano coming from the house. It was their tune. It was their melody. The sound engulfed him, and it drew him toward the door.

He took a step, hesitated, and listened. He took another step. Another stop. Another step. He stopped at the gate. It was now or never.

He passed the little gate and navigated the serpentine walk, eyes never leaving the door. He stepped silently onto the porch and approached the door. He paused again and raised his hand to the knocker. There he paused and wavered, his self-possession pocketed.

In the parlor, Helen played elegantly and without hesitation. Her expression took on a faraway aspect. She didn't need the sheet music. She was intimate with the melody, and it flowed from her hands.

She didn't see Lorelai enter the room behind her, gossip magazine in hand. She didn't see or hear Lorelai flop on the sofa. She did hear it when Lorelai flipped on the radio. Helen, her back to Lorelai, pulled her hands from the keyboard and once again summoned her patience.

Helen silently rose from the piano bench and left the room.

Mike, in the silence out on the porch, lowered his hand and withdrew from the door.

CHAPTER 27

SKETCHBOOKS

THERE WAS one light on at the Symington home. The house was small and, like most farmhouses, unpretentious. It seemed even smaller in the night. If the house had an identifiable style, it would be Cape Cod without the half story on top. Susannah's father built it himself.

Like Brush, Susannah was an only child. Unlike Brush, Susannah's parents were much older. She had been a surprise to a couple in their mid-fifties who had long ago accepted they would be childless. They were now semi-retired and, although caring parents, granted Susannah a great deal of freedom. They were, they said, too old to keep up.

The Symingtons no longer worked the farm. The land was leased to neighboring farmers, all but two and half acres that were devoted to a vegetable garden, plus another acre of apple and peach trees, pear trees, and berry bushes. There was also a grape arbor and an adjoining greenhouse.

Her parents worked the garden for a couple of hours in the morning cool. The rest was up to Susannah, including the operation of the Symington Produce stand, where depending on the season, you could find strawberries, raspberries, blackberries, peaches, apples, and pears in the fruit section. There would also be lettuce, peas, tomatoes, squash, cucumbers, peppers, green beans, carrots, and pumpkins. Susannah grew herbs and flowers in the greenhouse. She also bought produce from neighboring farmers.

For the past year, her days had been long, especially in the summer months when the produce stand was open. She put in a couple of early morning hours at Holland Dairy, worked the breakfast shift at Lillian's cafe, opened up Symington Produce for the rest of the day, and joined Brush in his studio at night. She didn't consider her work life a burden. It was her life as she knew it should be.

The bulk of her obligations – the produce stand – she knew to be hers alone. Her parents didn't need the money, but they also had no other money to give to Susannah, and so, the garden and the produce stand were hers.

The one light from the Symington home came from Susannah's bedroom, where she sat cross-legged on her bed, surrounded by sketchbooks. She was the only one awake.

She went through the sketchbooks, unhurried. Turning each page as though it was precious, which each was to her. The sketchbooks told the story of her life as drawn by Brush. Crayon drawings of her as a child were followed by pencil sketches, then more sophisticated pen and inks, chalks and watercolors.

She smiled here, laughed there, and was swept away into fond memories. These images were echoes of their days together.

She stopped at one page and let the moment hang in the air. The page was more care worn than the others. She had stopped there often. It was a portrait of her in late adolescence. It was warmer and more intimate than the others. It marked the day that Brush began to see her as a woman.

Susannah eyed the drawing as though it were speaking to her, which, in a way, it did. She didn't see the drawing as a representation of herself. She knew it to be Brush's representation of her as part of himself. She lingered long before closing the sketchbook. Peace and disquiet overtook her in equal measure.

She cleared her bed and turned out the light.

***

Across the night, the waxing moon spread a luminous light over Volney.

CHAPTER 28

"YOU HANDED BACK BEAUTY"

THE ATMOSPHERE in Brush's studio barn had never been so relaxed. Another shipping box was complete. It was only a matter of sliding another painting through the side, which Brush and Peter, working silently, accomplished smoothly. Peter handed Brush screws and a driver. Brush answered with a long, questioning look. Peter, balancing the shipping box on its side, responded.

"You wish to speak."

Flashes of doubt and anxiety had passed over Brush, uninvited, since the day he agreed to go to Chicago. Sometimes they were flashes of dread. Now, he was having a flash. He tried to hide it and failed.

"What am I getting into?"

Peter put down his screwdriver, shifted the shipping box a little and leaned it against a post, once again causing Brush to note the great care that Peter used when handling the paintings. Peter stepped away and strode to a small cluster of hay bales. He sat on one and indicated another one nearby. Brush took a seat. As he spoke, there was warmth and respect in Peter's voice, something that Brush observed was always there when Peter was in his studio barn.

"You will have only one difficulty at this school, any school. You must learn it all but choose what not to use."

Peter could see Brush trying to order that one in his brain. He continued.

"Art is mostly just a matter of confidence, kid. You just need the chops to back it up."

"Chops."

"Skill. You have it in spades."

"I do?"

Peter gave Brush a long, penetrating look, enough to make the boy squirm a bit.

"Are you bullshitting me? I need to know."

Brush returned Peter's gaze, his question still there. Peter looked away.

"My God, you really don't know."

Peter came to his feet and motioned for Brush to stay seated.

"Chops, kid. Skill. Talent. But you've got more."

He held his eyes on Brush until the boy looked back into them.

"When you were going through the worst of it. Your mother. Your father . . ."

Brush looked away. Peter pressed on.

"When you were going through the worst of it, your paintings got better."

Brush looked back to him with a shock of recognition. Peter observed the shock and continued.

"Why?"

"I . . . I don't know."

Peter took on a new tone. It was like he was delivering a lecture he'd long rehearsed.

"Too many painters, way too many, think they are worthy of putting themselves on canvas."

He looked at Brush, who looked back to say he needed clarification on that one.

"They come in two types. The ones who think their opinions matter and the ones who think their feelings matter. Hard to say which is worse. In both cases, their assurance is overblown, and the art they make has the stamp of self-indulgence. What you get is the weakness of manifestos done by artists, if that's the word you want to use, who consider themselves special, or worse, the muddle that comes because you, the viewer, can't penetrate what they think or feel. Look at us. Your opinion, my opinion, have no more substance than anyone else on the street just because we have a brush and a canvas and an audience. Same with our feelings. Bawling out loud with a brush. Who wants that? Who needs it?"

Peter's eyes rose. He spoke to the ceiling.

"It all comes down to what you worship, kid. And if what you worship is yourself, you'll be just another painter producing an endless string of self-portraits turned inside out, and lifeless on arrival. You will be tossed aside by history even before you die."

Now, his eyes returned to Brush's eyes.

"You will not be one of those, kid. When your world was ruined, when you had every motive to turn yourself inside out, you went deep, and you found something other than yourself. The world handed you ugly. You handed back beauty. You're a painter, kid."

Peter's tone changed again. He spoke like a coach.

"Take your work seriously. Don't take yourself seriously. Look, just be yourself and everything will work out. You will be told that this or that is fashionable. It could be a color palette or a style or a certain subject matter. Ignore it. Ignore it all or you will spend your years chasing fads. You must be a maker of fashion. You can't do that without confidence."

Peter was pacing. His steps quickened.

"They will introduce you to theories but knowing a new theory doesn't mean your old fundamentals are wrong."

"Fundamentals."

"Yours are innate, and that's the only kind. Composition and color are unteachable, but they teach it anyway. You're already the next Frederic Church, kid. Once you get the hang of atmospherics, you'll be in your own league."

"Atmospherics?"

Peter, hands on hips, cocked his head and perused the boy.

"You've seen hundreds of masterpieces in photographs, but never in person, right?

The observation was correct, which astounded Brush. He nodded in agreement. Peter began to move about, acting out what he was saying.

"Go and see them. Push the tourists aside and peer into the background of the Mona Lisa. The mountains. The little bridge. You'll see what I mean. Or stand at the foot of a Turner – Rain, Steam, and Speed – or back twenty feet away from a Monet."

Peter's arms flew wide. He proclaimed to the ceiling. "Air! Light! Distance! Magic!"

Brush shifted on his bale. "I just try to make things . . ."

"Perfect. Right. You've told me already. And you are hell on any artist who isn't."

The comment baffled the boy. Peter eyed him.

"You know, the print at Lillian's."

It surprised Brush that Peter even remembered the encounter. Brush watched him with new regard as Peter returned to his hay bale. Peter resumed.

"Speaking of Turner, what's next for you?"

"Next?"

Peter went to mock hypnotist mode, tickling the air with his fingers. "Subject matter. Pictures that give birth to a story. You're done with landscapes for now. You don't care if you ever paint another one, even though you know you will return to them someday. How am I doing?"

Brush, again astonished, nodded in agreement. Peter continued. "You are so ready to go, kid. The only thing that can hurt you right now is a bad teacher."

"How will I know the difference?"

Peter rose again, all pretense gone, and walked in a little circle, occasionally gesturing toward Brush as he spoke.

"Not by their work. All great artists are good

teachers. All good teachers are not great artists. You must be honest with yourself without being precious. Don't let anyone, and by that I mean anyone, force a method on you. Any teacher who attempts to alter your brush handling should be taken out and shot. At the same time, accept that your teachers are there to raise your game so you can play in the big arena. In the end, you are your own judge and jury. Just make sure of one thing. Nothing leaves your studio until it's a Brush Holland."

Brush felt as though Peter had opened an inner door. He wanted to know more.

"Was that the way it was for you?"

Peter stopped circling. He looked into the distance.

"In a way, yes."

One question had pestered Brush since he met Peter. This seemed like the time to pose it.

"Why are you doing this?"

Peter became evasive. He knew deep down he couldn't reveal the deal he'd made with Spenser. It seemed so impersonal now, and so far beneath the feelings Brush's paintings had arisen in him. It had the stench of a betrayal, even though there wasn't one. He answered in something of a mumble. "Let's just say it's for art's sake."

Brush let the question drop, but still had one more. Peter could read it in the boy's eyes.

"Another question?"

"Why did you stop painting?"

Instantly Brush wished he could take the question back. He could see it jolted Peter and he could see the question went deep. Brush struggled to cover the moment.

"I mean, not stopped, you didn't stop, but . . ."

Peter stayed him with his hand. He walked over to the newly filled shipping box and retrieved his screwdriver. Brush did the same. Peter raised his screwdriver and pointed it toward the boy.

"I turn my screws, kid. You turn yours."

The two, once again silent, went back to work. When Brush finished his final screw, he rose up and announced, "We're done!"

Peter pointed to the final large canvas still hanging. It was Brush's only portrait. It depicted Susannah, windblown and winsome on the prairie. "One more."

Brush gazed at the portrait. "No, not that one."

Peter's eyes went from Brush's eyes to the portrait and back. He spoke to the air.

"First love. That which stands between a man and second love."

The sound of the sliding door broke the moment. It was Carl. He strode up to Peter and Brush, took in the completed shipping box, and clapped his hands together. "Looks like we're done!"

Peter gestured toward the box. "To the trailer with this treasure, my good man."

CHAPTER 29

LORELAI BELLAMANN

LORELAI BELLAMANN had a twofer. There was a party that night. That was one. The party was her idea. That was two. But she needed a three. She needed her sister to attend. This would not be an easy thing to make happen.

Luckily for Lorelai, she had been placed in charge of the party. This would normally be a job for Lillian and Susannah, but those two were busy, although they ended up busier because Lorelai, acting as director of the event, asked them to do all the jobs they would have done anyway.

It wasn't that Lorelai just had to see Helen at the party. It was something deeper rooted. Lorelai enjoyed persuading Helen into doing things she didn't want to do. Helen was older and wiser than Lorelai. Everyone knew it, including Lorelai, but Helen wasn't as artful or sly as her little sister.

Successfully manipulating Helen was a small, wicked pleasure for Lorelai. That was all the motive Lorelai needed.

Lorelai had been in competition with Helen so long, she didn't even understand it to be a competition. The problem with Helen was that she wasn't ugly. To Lorelai, this wasn't fair. Ever since she could remember, her older sister had been better at everything. Better at school. Better in the kitchen. Better working the land. Better in business. Better with other people.

But it wasn't all Helen. Early in her youth Lorelai gave up trying to be accomplished, much less as accomplished as Helen. Lorelai got along by using her looks, so it annoyed her deeply that Helen was good looking, too. This wasn't fair.

As they grew into womanhood, Lorelai became more and more extravagant with her appearance even as Helen muted hers, which annoyed Lorelai even more. Her sister could look good without trying. Painfully unfair.

And so, the competition became day to day, moment to moment, always there in its small, petty way. For Lorelai it became a reflex to discover and then exploit any opportunity to top her sister. It became so ingrained that the reflex remained even when they lived 150 miles apart. In many ways it was an imaginary competition. There were two people, but there was only one player. Helen didn't even know there was a competition.

Over time it robbed Lorelai of her nobility. Her charm became false. Her nature became mercenary. This was sad, because even she knew there was a good little girl somewhere inside her, but that person had been

closeted too long to be recognizable. What remained
was an overweening showoff. It made her unattractive
even as she labored to become more enticing. It was a
concocted front and she never attempted to put her real
self, whoever that was, ahead of it.

The front was protected by her Bubble Machine
persona. She could turn it on at a moment's notice,
creating a light wall that was transparent and
impenetrable at the same time. It was a natural reaction
like you see in nature, and could go either way –
camouflage against threats or display to attract mates.

Now, the mercenary spirit was loose in Lorelai.

The last thing Helen wanted to do was attend the
Pinknic, so getting her there was the first thing on
Lorelai's mind. In a rush of inspiration that Lorelai took
for genius, she decided the Pinknic celebration would
also be a fundraiser for the Volney Historical Society, of
which Helen was president.

Lorelai didn't consult anyone about this decision, but
when the announcements went out, everyone in town
thought she had. It seemed like the kind of decision a
committee would make, and it also seemed appropriate.

The Volney Historical Society consisted of two rooms
– a big one and a small one – off the interior of the Post
Office. The big room was for exhibits. There were pioneer
rifles and tools, and antique chests and cupboards that
functioned as displays for photos and household items.
There was a small section devoted to the Civil War.

There were small pieces of farm equipment from
the 1800s – including blacksmithing tools, a yoke and a
saddle – and a spinning wheel. There was a mannequin

that featured women's dresses from a century past, a project of the Singer Sewing League, a group of women who repaired or remade historic patterns. The dress on the mannequin changed often. It always brought in an audience.

The room was centered by a magnificent, five-foot tall scale model of Bellamann House, fully furnished. People said looking into the doll house – that's what they called it – was just like standing in one of the real rooms.

The exhibits had a nice flow of visitors. It was something to drop in on when you went to the Post Office, plus the Historical Society members took care to update the old displays and add new ones to keep it fresh.

The small room was occupied by a cramped meeting table surrounded by shelves overstuffed with archives, books, photo albums, and odd small things nobody knew what to do with but couldn't bring themselves to throw away. Other than Bellamann House, Helen lived in that room. It may have been a historical society, but it was mostly Helen acting solo.

The people of Volney were proud of the exhibits and the Historical Society, but very few of them had time to devote to either. So, it was Helen and any assistants she could round up, plus the occasional high-school student volunteer.

Lorelai knew Helen could not resist attending a fundraiser for her historical society, and Lorelai was right. Like everyone else in Volney, Helen never guessed the fundraiser scheme was cooked up by Lorelai.

It was also assumed by everyone, including Helen, that she would speak at the Pinknic she loathed.

CHAPTER 30

THE PINKNIC

THE ONE task Lorelai did not delegate was the preparation of the Pinknic banner, and there it was, draped along the picket fence bordering Jesse James Rock Park & Fairgrounds and Duck Pond. It gleamed, loud, sparkly, and pink in the early sunset as the people of Volney passed by, plus two couples from Robley.

The Pinknic was a covered dish supper. The Robley people were cordially accepted, but word traveled quickly that they did not bring a dish.

The Robley people did bring their own chairs, like everyone else. They arrived to see a long table set up in the shade, Susannah in charge. Townspeople brought their preparations to her. She placed them in arrangements on the table. The desserts were at the far end, where several Holland Dairy ice cream churns were being worked.

Lillian stood sentry by the punch bowl, keeping a

keen eye out for Calwood, Mokane, and Bloomfield.

A small, two-step up bandstand had been erected in front of Jesse James Rock. The fiddle and banjo group that formed during the painting project, including the flutist, was already playing there.

The day's heat had broken, and the night promised to be cool enough for early September. The music was backdrop to easy chatter and an atmosphere of fulfillment. The people of Volney acknowledged each other for a job well done while chowing down on fried chicken, sliced ham, baked beans, cornbread, potato salads, bean salads, slaw, deviled eggs, and bright red gelatines with embedded fruit. All this before they returned for the pies, cakes and ice cream.

When dusk grayed the horizon, the citronella torches came out and the paper plates were put away. Susannah and some helpers tidied up the long table to make room for even more ice cream. Soon, sugar-charged children chased fireflies, while teenagers faded out of the torchlight and into the shadows, and it was time for the dance.

The fiddle and banjo group – now joined by a ukelele player – picked up the tempo. After a few daring couples broke the ice, the grass dance floor in front of the bandstand began to fill.

Peter, who had slipped in while the supper was closing down, stood unnoticed at the edge of the crowd. He was in a yellow version of the blue shirt Lillian had given him. He also had a green one back in the bus.

This was one of his favorite times of day. The light changed. For a brief moment, the yellows and oranges of sunset went away, leaving blues and greens and violets. With the color change, the view of each item in his field of vision sharpened into focus, detailing leaves and blades of grass, plus gray tones and textures in stones. It was as though the landscape was revealing its secrets before it accepted the darkness that would conceal them.

He watched as Carl and Lillian worked out a two-step, Lillian holding him a little too close. He couldn't resist a grin when Lorelai dragged an openly reluctant Mike onto the dance floor and proceeded to lead him. He felt Helen come up to his side before he saw her.

Peter didn't know what to expect from Helen. He did know she was inflexibly opposed to his paint project, even as it was complete, except for her house, so he was surprised first that she was there at all, and second by the softness in her voice. She actually sounded friendly.

"Working the fringe here?" she said. "Nice shirt."

Peter scanned the scene in the torchlight before him. He spoke softly, almost to himself.

"This place suits me."

Peter could sense that Helen wanted a conversation. He invited it with a look. She answered.

"When you first came here I thought . . . "

"Fraud? Scoundrel? Picaroon?"

Helen answered him with a look that said "yes" to all three. She continued.

"But you've made people happy. You've united the town. And you've brought back Carl. And Brush . . ."

Peter stopped her with a cocked eye. "Let me paint Bellamann House and I'll be four for four."

Helen stiffened and turned away. Peter intercepted

her by lightly taking her arm. She went along, only slightly flummoxed, as he led her toward the dance floor, where the band was playing a waltz.

Peter Basque knew his way around a dance floor, even a grass one. He had self-consciously perfected this over the years. At first, it had been part of The Act. He observed that many men were timid or wooden on the dance floor simply because they didn't know what they were doing. He knew he could stand out simply by being practiced and confident. He became good enough that he could lead any woman in any dance, even if she did not know the steps.

He discovered that he liked dancing itself. He had a natural rhythm and was unusually fit and athletic for a man with a rare talent for dissipation. The dance floor became one of the few places his relentless mind and his mouth could shut down.

Out on the grass, he twirled Helen into an easy waltz. It turned out she was an accomplished dancer, too. Neither noticed as the other dancers gradually drew away, leaving them alone on the grass with the people of Volney in audience. They circled the dance floor, gently swirling with the music. They may have been antagonists in all else, but as dancers they were a rare match. They looked as though they had danced together for years. Helen was transported and didn't try to hide it.

On the edge of the crowd, Mike looked on and wilted. He was witnessing something he never thought he would see – another man with Helen. Throughout their long estrangement, Mike had held fast to the notion that their condition was temporary. Helen would come around and he would be there when she did. As the people of Volney put it, they were the couple who just weren't together yet.

Mike had been Peter's ally all along and he had watched in fascination at Peter's persuasive powers and in envy at the way Peter drew people to him. Now, he watched in despair as Peter's magnetism pulled Helen into his orb. Mike and Helen had danced, too, but Mike knew he never moved her in the way Peter did.

Mike turned away and melted into the darkness.

A feedback shriek from a sound system interrupted the band and broke the dance. The "system" was a thoroughly unnecessary speaker about the size of a bread box, attached to a microphone which Lorelai brandished in full Bubble Machine glee. Peter and Helen separated, she becoming instantly abashed. He offered her an airy salute. "By God, there is a woman underneath all that."

Helen rolled her eyes and turned to see they were alone on the dance floor, and before a full audience. She scurried away, eyes to the grass, as the speaker squawked again. All eyes turned to the bandstand as Pez solemnly strode to the ground before it, executed a military-grade parade left and presented his candy dispenser to the crowd. All, with the exception of the Robley foursome, responded at once. "No thanks, Pez!"

Lorelai, who had been restlessly patient as Pez stole the limelight, went back into Bubble Machine Mode and let her voice rise over the assembly.

"I went out to the new Interstate today, and do you know what I saw when I looked back?"

The assembled people of Volney, now including the

foursome from Robley, answered as one. "What?"

Lorelai was effervescent. The crowd was with her!

"A town that says, 'Come and smile with me!" she shouted into a wall of enthusiastic applause and whistles and attaboys.

Lillian came forward and took the microphone, tugging twice to release it from Lorelai's grip.

As Lorelai pouted, Lillian shouted into the mic, "We've done it! All of us!"

Another round of applause and attaboys followed. Lillian had more. "I'd like to toast the man responsible . . . "

She paused, lowered the mic, and pointed toward the grass in front of the bandstand. Duck and Pez appeared in the light, gingerly inching toward the spot Lillian indicated. They carried a table laden with a pyramid of champagne glasses arranged in such a way that all glasses could be filled by pouring only into the top glass. When they came into view a shower of oohs and aahs flowed from the crowd, followed by a hum of astonished approval.

The air was charged with anticipation and suspense. There was an open and unspoken question. Would Duck and Pez get the table planted without toppling the glass pyramid? A wobble here, a misstep there, brought pants of anxiety from the crowd. Duck walked backwards, eyes over his shoulder, wary. Pez, solemn in the moment, moved forward, flatfooted.

Time was suspended until Duck and Pez inched it to the spot before the grandstand and ever so cautiously maneuvered the table toward the ground. Silence overtook the park as the table went into place, and the glass tower quivered and tinkled and finally came to rest without so much as a bobble. Duck and Pez broke from the table, both in a full sweat, to an avalanche of applause as Lillian poured in the first bottle and turned the pyramid into a fountain. And then, more bottles.

When the glass pyramid was full, Lillian took up the top champagne flute while the rest of the crowd came forward to get theirs. She raised her flute and spoke triumphantly into the mic. "I'd like to toast the man responsible."

She tapped Pez, who was now standing before her on the ground. Pez gestured toward Peter with a raised flute. Peter looked all around to see flutes raised toward him in salute. He approached the bandstand, somehow managing to conceal the fact that he was overcome with a sentiment he didn't recognize. He took the flute from Pez and the mic from Lillian and turned to the people of Volney. His gaze swept over them.

For a moment, Peter didn't speak, because he couldn't. The warmth that had spread over him the day before in the aftermath of the paint fight, had returned. Now, though, he was expected to speak. He feared choking up, another entirely new sensation for him. He had to recharge some part of his old self in order to swing into action. He did.

"You're all fired," he said, and drained his glass to affectionate boos and jeers from the crowd. He took a deep bow and returned the mic to Lillian as Lorelai danced onto the stage toting a lawn chair and a shopping bag from a store in Kansas City that she was sure no other woman in Volney had ever entered. She planted the chair and bag, store logo side outward, and swiped the mic out of Lillian's hand.

"My turn!" she piped out using her ukelele voice. Her eyes scanned the crowd until they rested on Brush. She patted the chair and beckoned. "Sit right here, Mr. Windy City!"

Brush and Susannah exchanged glances. He hesitated. The crowd encouraged him until he could no longer refuse. He broke from Susannah and made his way to the bandstand. When he neared the chair, Lorelai spun him around and pushed him into it. She moved behind the chair, standing while keeping one hand on his shoulder. It was time for her big moment. She spoke for the crowd, but toward him.

"Now, about Chicago. It's not like Volney. Nobody knows you. You have to find your own special way to stand out."

She drew a black beret from the shopping bag and tugged it onto Brush's head with one hand. She stood back and admired it, then made an adjustment before presenting Brush's new look to the crowd. This elicited silence followed by a smattering of applause that was tentative, but enough for Lorelai. She turned back to the mic and pointed toward the beret.

"And this says it all! It's best at a rakish angle." She adjusted the angle downward. "Perfect! Now everyone in Chicago will know you're an artist!"

She abandoned her proclamation mode and became reflective, still speaking into the mic.

"Clothing is so important, Brush. It's so sad that

some people go through their entire lives and never get a chance to cut a dramatic figure. If you can create a sense of style – and I do mean create, Mr. Artist – it can be so rewarding for other people to enjoy. And it helps them so to have us to emulate."

She leaned in at his side, pendant cleavage at his eye level. "It's so easy for me to picture you, virile and strong at the center of the social whirl." Her eyes drifted up to Susannah, while her cleavage stayed put. "Ooh, he'll be so hard to share."

Susannah looked mortified and apprehensive at the same time. Lorelai's eyes went back to Brush. She rose from his shoulder and placed her hand gently on his neck and began gently stroking up and down.

"The excitement goes where we go, no? Oh, the stir you will make! Men your age are so delightful. You haven't developed your capacity to disappoint. Now, you must calculate. If you get confused, speak in riddles. Never ignore a challenger. That's the same as attention. Be an hors d'eouvre, never an entree. And remember, the flower is the sex organ of the plant. Good luck!"

She kissed him on the cheek and presented Brush, bugeyed in beret and lipstick stain, to the people of Volney. He was dizzy with embarrassment.

Brush was brought back to the moment by the sounds of a minor commotion at the back of the crowd. He looked out as the crowd parted to see Elizabeth Holland approaching the bandstand, her step an easy swing, as confident as it was defiant.

"Mom!"

How much can you pack into a single word? For

Brush it was joy and dread, relief and dismay, welcome and unease. And shock. The park became deathly silent.

"Hello, Brush." Elizabeth spoke on arrival in an even voice, with suggestions of a remnant warmth which departed when she acknowledged her husband. "Carl."

His eyes held hers for a moment and then dropped to the ground. Lillian, who had moved up beside Carl, clutched him in a sheltering way, her eyes, steady and cold, holding Elizabeth's eyes.

"I thought you'd be the one," said Elizabeth. Lillian's glare heated as she held Elizabeth's fixed eye.

Brush watched his mother. Her eyes scared him, but his fear was not for himself. He could gauge her return. He feared his father could not. Brush's mind juggled competing thoughts. He knew who she was, but he didn't recognize her. Or was it vice versa? He couldn't compress the two into one. Something else arose. Pity. Pity for a woman who had made herself a stranger to herself. And then fear. Fear for what might happen next. And then anger. Anger that it might happen at all.

Helen stepped into the light. "What do you want, Elizabeth?"

Elizabeth produced a newspaper page. "I just had to see this for myself." She showed the page to the crowd. There was a large photo of Peter in hat and cape, and Carl, spray guns in hand, standing on Main Street. She addressed the crowd.

"Would you like to hear what the art critic at The Globe Democrat has to say about this? Yes, you would."

She reached up and yanked the mic from Lorelai and began to read.

"D-list celebrity Peter Basque has finally driven his Traveling Roadshow down the dead end where it belongs. The man who took the expression out of expressionism somehow maneuvered the gullible citizenry of a Missouri backwater to paint the entire village pink. Oh, the humanity. The good people of Bumpkinville may think they are participating in an artistic statement, but we're told that Basque swapped the whole stunt for a shot at a retrospective at the Art Institute of Chicago. The joke's on . . ."

Helen grabbed the mic.

"I think you've accomplished what you came to do," she said in a tone that was as much statement as warning. For a moment, Elizabeth braced for a confrontation. She took another look at Helen and decided to let the moment pass.

Elizabeth dropped the paper and laid her vacant eye on Carl. "Still going nowhere," she said, and stepped past him without acknowledging Brush. The crowd parted as she walked away. She stopped when she came to Duck and Pez. For the first time, she spoke with genuine warmth.

"Duck, Pez."

Duck returned a hesitant smile. Pez raised his arm to offer her his candy dispenser, then thought better of it and returned his arm to his side. A flash of hurt crossed Elizabeth's eyes. She recovered and walked away into the dark.

Susannah watched Brush as his eyes followed his mother. Lillian quietly embraced Carl, whose expression remained unmoved.

Nobody said anything because there was nothing that could be said. After a too-long moment, the crowd silently dispersed. Brush hurried off the bandstand, tossing his beret into the dark. Susannah trailed him until she let him go. Lillian held Carl as he turned to go. Carl gently pulled her hand away. He, too, went away into the dark. Lillian trailed until she, too, let him go.

Now, it was only Helen and Peter. Helen stepped toward him.

"Peter . . ."

"No."

Peter walked away into the dark. Helen let her eyes sweep the scene. She silently put out the torches and left the park.

CHAPTER 31

TURNING AWAY POINTS

MIKE RUTHERFORD stood alone on the overpass of the empty stretch of concrete that would soon be an interstate highway. He scanned the nearby pasture in the dark. He began to trace an outline in the dust with his toe. It was the shape of his traveler's plaza. He looked down on it and scuffed the outline away as he spoke.

"Dammit, Helen."

***

In his bedroom, Brush opened the top drawer to his chest and pulled out a small case. He extracted a ring box from the case and opened it to reveal a wedding ring. He closed the box. He gathered up the brochure and folder and manila envelope from the Art Institute. He dropped them in a trash can. To the right of the chest, he observed an easel with a canvas, almost finished. The painting was small and intimate. It depicted a young man struggling against a fierce prairie headwind. He had painted it in his room, out of sight of all, including Susannah. He strode to the easel, grasped the canvas and hurled it against the wall.

In the hallway outside, Carl was approaching Brush's room when he heard the thud of the canvas on the wall. Carl approached the room noiselessly. He peered through the crack between the door and the frame to see the Art Institute folder in the trash can.

Carl left the hallway without being noticed. He crept downstairs to the kitchen, where he leaned on the counter and slowly opened a cabinet door to reveal a bottle of bourbon. He hefted the bottle in his hand and looked at in long and hard. His eyes traveled to the chair on the porch and then back to the kitchen. He waited for the familiar tingle. His eyes caught a reflection of himself, distorted on the metal of the toaster on the counter. He examined the reflection, moving his head from side to side to watch the distortion shift and change. The tingle never arrived. He looked at the bottle in his hand, and replaced it in the cabinet.

***

Susannah, in her bedroom, held two pencil sketches done by Brush. One was of her. The other was a smiling self-portrait. She arranged them on her dresser, she to the left, he to the right, and placed a pencil between them. She spun the pencil. It stopped with the sharpened point in the direction of her drawing. She spun again. Same

237

result. She spun the pencil a third time. It slowed as it
neared the drawing of Brush, paused there, and then
wobbled off the dresser.

She regarded the pencil for a minute, then picked it
up. She pulled some paper out of her dresser drawer and
began writing as she sobbed.

***

Peter, inside his darkened bus, slumped in the swivel
chair closest to the party bar. He dangled a highball glass.
Irish whiskey, straight, was his preferred spirit when he
had nothing to say and no one to say it to. He could let
his thoughts in, undiluted like the whiskey, just to see
where they would go. When the thoughts arrived, they
came with gray flashes of remorse, something entirely
new to Peter Basque.

***

The rising moon pushed away the dark and cast a
lustre of silver over Volney. Tomorrow would bring a full
moon.

CHAPTER 32

THE DEED

THE STUDY in the Bellamann house, was a medium-sized room with a wide, arched entrance way that opened off the first-floor hall. It was an essay in color, especially in the morning. It was lit by a floor-to-ceiling stained-glass window facing the eastern sun. An antique Persian rug centered the room beneath an oval mahogany table topped by a standing Tiffany lamp. To the right was an antique roll-top desk that had been the nerve center of family business for generations. Otherwise, the room was lined floor-to-ceiling with mahogany bookshelves. The books, many leatherbound, all without dust jackets, reflected heavy greens and dark blues, but mostly maroons.

It was early morning. The combination of colors enveloped the room in warm, reassuring auburn hues. It was a good place to stop and think, which was exactly what Lorelai Bellamann, alone in the room, was not doing. She muttered to herself as she bent over the rolltop and rifled the drawers.

"No, I don't have the slightest idea. No! I've never read any of the papers. Well, why on earth should I? Now don't you dammit me Mike Rutherford. Save that for Helen."

Lorelai did not know how to be discreet, but she did know how to be sneaky, so as she searched from drawer to drawer, she attempted to leave each as it was. Still, there was urgency in the air as she combed and sifted her way through envelopes and folders. Lorelai was in a hurry and each passing moment hurried her more.

And then, "Got it!"

She slid a long slender green legal envelope from a folder as Helen entered the study, unobserved. Helen was taken aback. She had never seen Lorelai so much as touch the desk, much less show any interest in its contents.

"May I help you?"

Lorelai sprang up, knocking a container of pens off the desk. Helen's eyes traveled to the floor, which gave time for Lorelai, her back still facing Helen, to shove the envelope down the front of her blouse. Helen gestured to the pens on the floor.

"Shall I get those for you?"

Lorelai turned Helen's way, cautiously, eyes still checking her blouse.

"No, that's alright. I'll get them."

"It will be faster if we both do it."

Helen bent to the floor and set about ordering the pens and pencils. Lorelai made no move to assist. Helen arose with the pen container intact and offered it to her sister.

"None of them work," shrugged Lorelai.

Helen reached into her pocket and offered her own pen, which Lorelai ignored.

"Perhaps I can help you," said Helen. "What is it you seek?" Her eyes scanned the desk, which, despite Lorelai's efforts, was not as tidy as usual. "Then again, perhaps you've found it."

"No, just here for coffee," said Lorelai, just barely succeeding to seem bubbly as usual. Helen glanced over the desktop and the oval table and took in the absence of a coffee cup.

Helen did not reflexively distrust her sister, although she knew she should. Lorelai's prevarications seemed harmless enough. As the people of Volney put it, Lorelai would rather climb a tree and tell you a fib than stand on the ground and tell you the truth. Her countless small lies never seemed to add up to a big one. And she was family. Lorelai won all ties in a contest of truths.

But Helen did have instincts and her truth antennae were rising.

"Where's your cup?"

Lorelai managed to seem self-astonished. "Oh, my! Now, where did I put it?"

"I'll get some," said Helen and she headed out of the room and toward the kitchen. Lorelai squirmed the envelope further down her blouse until she was sure it was fully concealed, then turned to the desktop and re-ordered it. At the sound of Helen's approaching footsteps, she closed the rolltop and leaned against it.

Helen entered the study with two cups of coffee. She

placed one for Lorelai on the oval table. Lorelai watched Helen warily examine the now shipshape rolltop. Lorelai could sense Helen's truth antennae in the room. It was time for a diversion. She patted the rolltop.

"Papa's holdings are in such good hands with you," she said as she moved toward the oval table and her coffee. "I'm so impulsive and you're so level-headed. Why I don't think you've let your emotions control you . . . except, of course, for your hand-made couture dress. So expensive!"

Lorelai brought her coffee to her lips and eyed Helen's growing discomfort. The diversion was working. "You threw it away. The dress. It could have been repaired. That's so unlike you!"

Lorelai took a tiny sip from her cup and looked away, speaking to the room with unhidden stagecraft. "I'm so glad you've forgiven me for that."

Helen ignored the theater. "It was for the better, Lorelai."

"I don't know what I was thinking. I just had to wear it!"

"Water under the bridge, Lorelai."

"I was just going to test wear it. What is it about me? I see something that's yours and . . . how was I supposed to know that Mike Rutherford would . . ."

"Ten years ago, Lorelai."

"Funny, isn't it? Nothing has really changed. You never married. Mike never married. And here I am back in Bellamann House, still looking for the number one catch in Volney."

"I wouldn't know who that might be."

"It can be so hard for a divorcee. You have to start over. Rebuild your social life . . ."

"I'm sure . . ."

"Of course, you wouldn't know. You haven't taken the plunge. And Papa so wanted you to marry Mike. Helen and Mike. Who could possibly imagine that now? What you need is more experience. Men are too eager or too cautious.

"You're right. I wouldn't know."

"That's what I mean. Take businessmen. Bankers! They can be cautious. You have to offer them a challenge, but they have to think it's their idea. Now, who do I know at the bank? Sometimes he is just so . . . eager"

Helen planted her coffee cup on the oval table, a little too firmly. "I have things to attend to," she said.

Lorelai flitted past her, words trailing as she left the room "So do I! Maybe I'll go to the bank."

Helen's noble dancer posture went slack when Lorelai went out of view. Her shoulders sagged. Her face became unreadable, her eyes a thousand miles away until they traveled to the pendant she always wore. She grew tender as she clasped the pendant with her fingertips. She opened it and extracted an engagement ring. She slid it onto her finger and held it before her eyes. A tear ran down her cheek.

CHAPTER 33

"MEET ROBERT GARRETT"

THE MORNING cool still lingered as Brush approached Peter's bus. He rapped on the metal door. No response. He pushed on the door. It folded away. Brush stuck his head in.

"Peter?"

No response.

"Mr. Basque?"

No response.

Brush climbed the steps and entered the bus. Peter was still in the swivel chair, still with an empty stare, and still holding a high-ball glass, it, too, now empty. Peter didn't acknowledge the boy. Brush broke the moment.

"I need to ask you a question."

There wasn't the usual awe in Brush's voice, the combination of wonder and apprehension that Peter evoked. It was replaced by a tone of resolve.

Peter did not respond. Brush broke the moment

again.

"Was any of this about me?"

Peter's eyes stayed fixed to the floor between his feet. Brush broke the moment again. This time there was an added tone of annoyance in his voice.

"You can't answer me," he said. "So, it's true. You did this, all of this, for yourself. You don't care about me. You don't care about Volney."

Brush turned toward the door. "I'm not going to Chicago."

Peter spoke toward the floor. "And you will never return."

This halted Brush. He turned around. "What?"

Peter's head came up and his eyes moved from the floor. "The aw-shucks farm boy abjures his palette to toil in the fields."

"I don't know what abjures means, but I can guess. How about we just talk normal?"

"And this girl."

"Susannah?"

"You will renounce her, too."

"That's not true."

Peter put his highball glass on the floor and pushed himself up from the chair. He came face to face with Brush.

"You will forsake her for a chimera."

"I know what a chimera is."

"Vapor beyond your fingertips. Ridiculous, you yearn and claw. Too late, it concedes. You grasp your delusion and you gaze upon it and the truth mocks you. Hideous laughter and false affection. Your hands are cold."

Peter moved even closer, his eyes never leaving Brush's.

"In years to come you will lie awake, pursued by your folly. Then happenstance triggers it! A scent, a hint of music, and she returns. Tender blessings drape gentle upon you, and you sink into her. Gossamer! But the truth trumpets your true choice! You start and she is gone and the chill creeps back to gnaw at you on sunless days when all your songbirds turn into crows."

Peter fell back into the chair. His eyes returned to the floor. Brush considered him as silence emptied the bus. The two remained motionless, the boy standing, the man sitting, in a wordless showdown. Again, Brush broke the moment.

"You know what? I don't think you're talking about me."

"Brace yourself for a lonely existence, kid."

Brush headed away to the door. Peter halted him at the steps.

"Stay, I have something to show you."

Brush descended a step toward the door.

"Stay, son. Please."

Peter had never addressed Brush in such an intimate way. All the bombast, all the mesmerizing, all the extravagance, all of it was gone from his voice. Brush looked back to see Peter. Brush did not know what The Act was, but he could see it was over. He came back toward Peter, who rose from the chair and ushered him through the middle door and into the back of the bus.

The room was a portable art studio, centered by a canvas director's chair. To one side, the room was in

disarray – a pile and jumble of oversized expressionist
red-splotch paintings. The other half was orderly,
arranged with vertical slots that held medium-sized
canvasses, maybe three feet wide, painted in naturalistic
landscapes. There was an unfinished landscape on an
easel. It depicted the prairie around Volney.

The scene mystified Brush and left him speechless.
Peter walked to the storage slots and slid a canvas out. It
was the original to the print that Lillian had hung in the
cafe.

"Lillian was right," said Peter. "This is my best-seller."

Brush was still mystified, but at least here was a clue.
He pointed to the canvas in Peter's hands. "That's the
painting by . . ."

"Robert Garrett," said Peter.

"Where is he?"

"He's right here."

"You're Robert Garrett. You?"

"If I had any friends, they'd call me Bob," he said.

"I don't get it," said Brush. "What is it you think you
are doing?"

Peter replaced the painting from Lillian's and spoke
as he went about the room, picking up red-splotch
canvasses here and there and glancing them over.

"Painting is the cruelest profession, kid. You want
the world, then one day you find yourself accepting a
smaller arena. Then, later, you face the real question,
ugly in its clarity. Have I spent a lifetime denying my
own mediocrity? Mediocrity, worse than foul. Colorless,
odorless, tasteless. Well, I wasn't going to wait around. If
fame was to be mine, I didn't want to be dead first. And

so, Peter Basque, poseur, was born. He's done well, too, just not lately."

"Is your name Peter Basque?"

"Yes. Robert Garrett is an alias. Think of it as a stage name."

"But Peter Basque isn't really nuts. He's really Robert Garrett, who's normal."

Peter pulled another landscape from a slot. He now held a landscape in one hand and balanced a red-splotch canvas with the other. He nodded toward the landscape.

"Robert Garrett paints landscapes and sends his originals to a publisher in Milwaukee who prints them up by the thousands and sells them for a song."

He nodded toward the red-splotch canvas.

"Peter Basque mounts bombastic shows and attends receptions where he is hailed as an oracle. People who never missed a meal adopt his tortured soul. One's a living. The other's a life. One is bread, the other, wine."

He stepped back and thrust both canvasses in front of him.

"With Robert Garrett, they buy the painting they love. With Peter Basque, they love the painter they've bought."

Peter did not know what to expect at the end of this revelation. He certainly did not expect the reception he got, which was silence. He watched as Brush shifted into the same tone and stance that he assumed when they discussed the print at Lillian's. For the first time, Peter felt disadvantaged in the presence of the boy. Brush broke the silence.

"Which is better?"

"Depends on what I feel like drinking."

"No. I mean, which is the better artist?"

Brush detected an uncertain flinch cross Peter's face, a reaction that Peter attempted to conceal by busying himself with the two canvasses. He replaced them and took a seat in the director's chair. He looked at Brush and he looked away. Peter had no answer. Once again, silence took the room. This elicited another emotion toward Peter that was new to Brush. Wrath. Brush broke the silence.

"Look at you. You want me to become you. A two-faced fraud who can't make an honest living."

"The son must slay the father."

"Oh, stuff it."

"I may not be honest, but the money is."

"Fraud. You can't draw the human form."

"How do you know?"

Brush swept the room with his arm, singling out the canvasses on both sides.

"Look at these. All of these. You never paint people in your landscapes."

"Neither did Cezanne."

"He painted portraits. Let's see yours. You're afraid to paint one single human being. You're afraid of people."

Brush pulled a sketchbook from his back pocket and pencil from his shirt pocket. He tossed them into Peter's lap.

"Here. Give me one in ten strokes. Draw me. Draw yourself."

Peter picked up the pencil and left the sketchbook unopened. He eyed the pencil. "So, now you're the teacher." He tossed the pencil aside.

Brush went into a remarkably accurate imitation of Peter. "'I don't have time for some random walk to self-discovery here, if that's okay.' You said art is a matter of confidence, but somewhere along the line you chickened out and made two bad artists out of one good one. How am I doing?"

No response.

"What was it you said? Nothing leaves your studio until it's a . . . a who? A Basque? A Garrett? Well, we don't know, do we? And that's the bullshit part. How do we know this? You've got thousands of little cries for help hanging all over the country and you don't even know who's doing the crying. You said the only thing that can hurt me right now is a bad teacher. Lucky me, I get Zorro. At least you've made it easy to choose what not to use."

Brush moved to a paint stand beside the easel. He found a tube of red, opened it and squeezed some onto his palm. He stood beside the painting on the easel and addressed Peter.

"Mr. Garrett. . ." He smeared the paint on the unfinished landscape. "Meet Peter Basque."

Brush tossed the paint tube to the floor. He grabbed a shop towel from the paint stand and wiped his hands. "Mr. Basque." He dropped the towel to the floor. "Go paint on velvet."

Peter observed all of this without emotion.

"So you are that good," he said. "That you can judge me."

Brush again mimicked Peter. "'Oh, no. In the end, you are your own judge and jury. But, hey, in order to do that, you must be honest with yourself without being precious.' Did I quote you right?"

Brush headed toward the door. He stopped at the door and swung his arm toward the red-splotch abstracts. "I shovel that stuff out of our barn."

He moved to leave and paused again. "You never told me. It's true, isn't it. You traded this whole . . . this whole thing so you could have an art show you don't deserve."

Peter looked him straight in the eyes. "I deliver you, I get a show, but that's all shot to Hell, now." He offered a wave of dismissal. "But you can still go. Go. Go be a bigtime artist."

Brush opened both arms and assessed the room. "And maybe someday have all this? No thanks."

And he was gone.

Peter came up from his chair and walked to the easel. He touched the red paint that Brush had smeared and moved it around bit with his finger. He heard a scraping sound and looked through the door to see a pink squirrel inside his bus. He released a huge sigh and let his hand fall, making a bigger smear across the canvas.

CHAPTER 34

FOLLOWING ORDERS

IT WAS nearing noon.

The air was charged with tension in Mike Rutherford's office. The strain was palpable. Mike, standing behind his desk, was on the phone. Duck, propped on a step ladder outside the window, and doing touch-up painting, could feel the tension.

Mike, hunched and whispered into the phone. "Are you sure . . . Lorelai, stop talking . . . are you sure you have the correct envelope? . . .Green . . . Because I'm a banker, that's how."

He covered the mouthpiece and addressed Duck. "Yes, paint the shutters. The touch-up crew missed them."

Mike put the phone back to his ear, listened and whispered. "On the cover."

He covered the mouthpiece and addressed Duck. "Just do what you've done to the other buildings."

Duck descended the ladder and disappeared from

the window as Mike shouted into the phone.

"No! Not that color!"

Duck reappeared at the window, very confused. Mike saw Duck and addressed him. "What!"

Duck shrugged and descended again, Mike put the phone back to his ear. He shouted again. "Green! . . . Yes!"

Mike looked back up to see Duck, again returned to the window, now very confused. He addressed Duck. "What?"

Mike put the phone back to his ear and whispered. "Yes. Read it . . . No."

Mike saw Duck still at the window and addressed him. "What? What?"

Duck began to speak. Mike halted him with his hand.

"Duck, I don't have time for this. Just, just do it."

Duck nodded, now very, very confused, and descended out of sight as Mike whispered into the phone. "Yes. Yes. Read that part."

He was silent for a moment, then shouted, "Stop!"

Mike whispered into the phone as Duck came back to the window and looked probingly at Mike. "That's it. Deed of trust."

Mike covered the mouthpiece and addressed Duck, tension rising. "What, dammit!"

Duck, bugeyed, descended from view as Mike, in full exasperation, shouted into the phone, "Wait! Wait! . . . Just bring the stuff to me. I'll do it."

Duck returned to the window. He leaned into the room and placed his paint bucket and brush on the floor as Mike watched him in furrowed brow. Mike covered the phone's mouthpiece and addressed Duck. "What are you doing?"

Duck answered with a shrug as Mike returned to the phone and whispered, "What?"

Duck leaned down to retrieve the bucket and brush as Mike shouted into the phone, "No! Don't do that!"

Duck stopped dead, arms still reaching out. Mike covered the mouthpiece and addressed him. "Nevermind. I'll catch you in a minute. Just finish up out there."

Duck remained in place, motionless. Mike stared at him, brow again furrowed. "What? What? What? What!"

Duck extended in slow motion for the bucket and brush, never taking his eyes off Mike. Duck finally lunged for the bucket and brush. He gripped both, checking Mike's reaction. None. Duck ever so slowly withdrew, passing through the window with his bucket and brush, eyes still on Mike, until he sank from view down the ladder.

Mike, now alone, continued to whisper.

"I need that one. . . It's the deed for your father's land. You need to sign what I have. That's the contract for the sale of the land to me . . . We both do . . . The sooner the better . . . No. Not there! . . . Just come here . . . Lorelai, I don't think that's a good idea. Can't we just . . . but this is business . . . It's not supposed to be fun. No! I'm not being . . . yes! I really want . . . what? Are you serious? Alright. Okay. What do you mean just like the old days. What old days? . . . Clickers? . . . No! Why clickers? . . . Okay. Whatever . . . No! I'm not going to wear that! . . . No, I'm not going to say goodbye on the phone that way."

Mike hung up the phone a little too hard and turned

to his file cabinet, muttering. "Dammit, Lorelai."

He strode to the window and leaned out and shouted, "Duck!"

Mike returned to the cabinet and muttered, "Contracts. Contracts. Who does the filing around here?"

He spoke with his back to the room as Duck appeared at the window behind him.

"Duck, when you finish what you're doing, go paint one of the fire hydrants on Main Street, but just do one. One. Helen may hate the idea, but she wants to look at it before you continue. Got it?"

Duck saluted, unseen by Mike, and withdrew. Mike went to the door, opened it, and shouted, "Pez!"

He returned to the cabinet, his back to the room. Pez entered with his characteristic thumping footsteps and offered candy. Mike didn't turn around. "No thanks, Pez."

Pez returned the candy dispenser to his pocket. He stood at attention. Mike, his back to Pez, addressed him.

"You know those little cricket toys at the Five and Dime? Click click? Click click?"

Pez affirmed, unseen by Mike, who continued, "Go get two."

Mike, hunched over the file drawer, muttered to himself, "I can't believe I'm doing this."

He turned and spoke. "Put it on your bill. Go to Bellamann House. Give one to Lorelai. She'll give you an envelope. Tell her, nine o'clock at the cemetery and make sure you say 'just like the old days – XXXX Mike."

Pez gave Mike a look that said, "How?" Mike took in Pez's look and said, "Okay, I'll write you a note." He scribbled out the note as he hunched again and muttered to himself. "What good old days? Just one bad one."

He returned to Pez and handed him the note.

"Remember the envelope," he said. "Long, thin, green. Bring it to me. Now, hustle."

Pez headed out the door while Mike returned to the cabinet, his back to the room. He looked up and shouted, "Hey! Come back!"

Duck appeared at the window. Mike didn't turn around. He spoke to the wall before him. "I want you to keep this a secret."

Duck remained at the window, fully perplexed. Pez entered through the door. Mike turned and spoke to the room. "Got it?"

Mike turned to see Duck. "What now, Duck?"

Duck saluted and descended. Pez saluted and departed, as Mike returned to the cabinet. He raised and shouted to the wall again. "Hey!"

Pez entered the room. Mike spoke with his back to Pez. "Changed my mind. Do every one on Main Street. We can't do this one at a time."

Pez saluted and exited as Duck reappeared at the window while Mike pulled a contract from the file and turned. He looked at Duck. "Got it?"

Duck, profoundly unsure, nodded "yes." Pez re-entered, pointed to Duck and made the clicking sound.

"Him?" said Mike. "Are you nuts? No!"

Mike turned his attention to the contract. Duck and Pez did not move. Mike looked up to see them and spoke in pure aggravation. "What, dammit?"

Duck and Pez saluted and slowly melted away. Mike gripped the contract, wrinkling it.

"Dammit, Helen."

***

There weren't many people on Main Street in the
heat of the day when Duck, in full Double Secret Agent
Mode and laden with a paint can, plus a brush, and a
sheet, stole up the alley and hugged the shadows. He eyed
the street up and down. The coast was clear. He emerged
on the street with an air of forced nonchalance. When he
neared a fire hydrant, he paused and let his eyes slide in
all directions before swooping down on the hydrant and
covering it, and himself, with the sheet.

After some time passed, he flipped the sheet away
and, once again nonchalant, whistled away, leaving a
green hydrant.

***

There was enough late afternoon shade in the Jesse
James Rock Park & Fairgrounds and Duck Pond to
cool most of the park. Helen Bellamann was using the
opportunity to tidy up the remnants of the Pinknic. This
was something that the people of Volney normally did
themselves, but nobody wanted to return to the park that
day. The night before had ended too cruelly.

She glanced up from an errant paper plate to see
Peter outside his bus in the Rutherford Grainworks gravel
tract next door. She watched as he uncoupled his trailer,
went into the bus, and reemerged with a piece of paper.
He taped the paper to the side of the trailer and returned

to his bus.

Helen stopped what she was doing and walked out of the shade and over to the trailer, pausing to read what was on the paper. She ripped it off the trailer as Peter's bus started up. She hurried to the driver's side window, waving the piece of paper. Peter slid his window open. He said nothing. She said nothing.

Peter started to ease the bus forward. Helen hurried to stand before it, blocking him. Peter backed up the bus to go around her. She again maneuvered to block the bus, this time with hands on hips and a look that said, "Try me."

The silent faceoff lingered until Peter shut off the motor and came out the door. He and Helen stood in confrontation. Peter's gaze traveled up and down in a full circle, beginning and ending with Helen's eyes. He offered an airy salute. "Farewell, thou art too dear for my possessing. And like enough. . ."

"Oh, stuff it."

Peter did, indeed, stuff it away. He eyed Helen. And spoke in a voice that tried to hide that he cared about the moment.

"Second time I've heard that today."

Helen brandished the note, angry and dismissive at the same time. She read it aloud. "Property of Brush Holland."

"And it is thus."

"Those paintings are the property of the world."

"The world will have to wait. He won't go. And it's tomorrow or never. He doesn't believe in me anymore."

"Brush's work. Brush. He's a gift. And it's your job to

. . ."

"My job. . ."

". . .to present him to the world.

"My job."

"Oh, yes. You came here. You created the expectation. You made it seem possible. You changed him. And now . . ."

"And now the queen of missed opportunities says I can't clinch the main chance."

"You must finish the job you came to do. And that wasn't fair."

"I know."

"You know it wasn't fair or you know you must finish it?"

Peter turned away. He couldn't hide that he was cornered. Helen, a bit more forcefully than she intended, spun him around and turned him toward Main Street, all of it visible and retreating in perspective. She spoke from behind him.

"All this." Her hand swept the town. "Why? It has nothing to do with your purpose in coming here. You could have left with Brush two weeks ago. Job done. Back to wherever it is you go to do whatever it is you do and to being whoever it is you are. Why, Peter?"

Peter's eyes took in the town. Even he couldn't contain the impossible memories he'd made in such a short time. Helen spun him back to face her.

"Peter, you think I don't know you, but I do. I know you don't want to go back there. You don't want to do what you did. You don't want to be that person anymore."

For a moment, Peter wished he hadn't quit cigarettes.

Lighting one up would give him a break to gather his thoughts, one of his favorite feints. Instead, he faked indifference.

"Of late, I seem to be the focus of intense analysis. This is my second session today."

Helen ignored him. Her voice took on a beseeching tone. "One more day. For Brush. Don't make me beg."

Pez, grave and secretive, approached them and broke the moment. He didn't offer candy, which surprised them both, and added to the atmosphere of gravity. He presented a slip of paper to Helen and waited, butler style, while she read it. Mystified, she passed it to Peter, who read it aloud.

"The cemetery. Tonight. Just like the old days. XXXX Mike."

Peter returned the slip to Helen, who returned it to Pez. They regarded Pez as he made a solemn show of putting his finger to his lips to say "keep it a secret" before handing each a cricket clicker. He bowed and tramped away, while Helen and Mike watched in silence.

"Helen," said Peter. "Whatever this is, you just got one more day."

CHAPTER 35

MOON OVER VOLNEY

THE VOLNEY cemetery crowned the hill overlooking the town. The hill had an almost perfectly proportioned gumdrop shape, and it was the only rise in the prairie for miles. You could think of it as a mound, and many people did.

Over the years, teams of archaeologists, usually from the University of Missouri, would show up and poke around and then depart unrewarded, but still absolutely sure that something significant was under there. To this, the people of Volney merely shrugged. It was their hill. That was it.

The crest was bare when the hill was set aside by the Bellamann family at the founding of Volney. It had now matured into a particularly pleasant, landscaped setting – nicely wooded below the crown, and absent the precious sterility of manicure at the top.

The cemetery ground was an open space surrounded

by a grove. It was split down the middle by a white gravel path that led to a majestic oak tree. The tree was planted by Bayard Bellamann, Volney's founder, in 1859. It was at least 150 feet tall and the limbs spread just as wide – numbers often argued at the Big Three Barber Shop. It was 12 feet around at its base – that you could measure. The tree was also considered to be blessed. Rising like a tower as it did over the prairie, it had never been struck by lightning.

To the right of the path and to the front, just at the point before the hillside sloped away, was a bench that provided a view overlooking Volney. On the other side of the path was a sundial placed in memory of Bayard Bellamann. Ornamental shrubbery wove around the crown of the hill, partially concealing a small, clean, well-tended pond, known locally as The Duckless Pond, behind the tree. It was an illegal swimming hole of sorts. It was the nighttime pool of choice for teenagers who liked to hang their shirts on the "No Swimming" sign that Helen Bellamann had personally placed there.

The shrubbery was trimmed low on the Volney side of the hill to keep the view open.

The shrubbery climbed high enough on the east side of the plot to create an arbor that served as an entranceway. A winding footpath from the Jesse James Rock Park led up the hill and through the arbor. The grass was immaculate, due to yet another of Helen Bellamann's volunteer organizations. The footpath remained unstoned, yet another of Helen's frustrations.

The gravestones themselves were also well kept. There were dozens – a century's worth. Many were "modern," meaning they were substantial enough to sit upon, especially the very wide ones that served as markers for an entire family. None were tall. This was considered unseemly.

If you let yourself, you could be flooded with tranquility just by stepping through the arbor and onto the cemetery ground.

On this night, the massive tree blackened the crown of the hilltop as a rising moon silverplated the rest of the world. The tranquility was broken by the sound of a splash from the pond, and the sight of Susannah, in cutoff jeans and sleeveless blouse, running through the cemetery with an armful of clothes. She crossed the path, stopped, and looked back toward the pond. Brush's voice rose from the shrubbery.

"Hey! . . . Hey!"

He rustled through the shrubbery and came into view to the right of the wide path, opposite Susannah. He was wet and stripped bare. He was concealed from the waist down by the bushes. He gestured toward the clothes in Susannah's arms. "Hey!"

Susannah made a Lorelai-quality coquette pose. "Come and get 'em, big boy."

"I will, you know," replied Brush. His tone was grim, severe, and roguishly fake. He started to step away from the shrubs.

As he took a step, Susannah abruptly deflated and slumped onto a gravestone. She spoke to the ground.

"It's no use. I'm just pretending."

Brush, now concealed up to the waist by a gravestone, stopped his advance, one gravestone behind the bench. Even when he didn't know what Susannah was thinking, he knew what she was thinking. He knew by her tone and posture that whatever he thought this night would bring was over. The moment, the night, needed to be about her. He spoke to her in a soft voice, still trying to muster the fake severity. "Sannah, if you won't give me my pants, then look in the pocket."

Susannah rummaged through the pile of clothes until she found the pants and searched the pockets. She pulled out Brush's ring box. She opened it and dropped the pants.

"I didn't exactly picture the moment like this," said Brush.

"But tomorrow," said Susannah. The words came out, breathless, slightly choked, and alight with wonder and joy. "What about tomorrow? School? Chicago?"

"We're staying here," said Brush. "I'm not going anywhere, especially without my clothes."

Susannah slowly lifted to her feet. She held the ring to her bosom and spoke to the sky.

"I want now to stand still and make the past and future move around us. Nothing moves unless we move because here we are, even though every moment now is changing."

She looked back to Brush and spoke with an intimacy polished by their bond. "You are the only person in the world who can understand what I just said."

Brush acknowledged her with a look, his expression readable through the moonlight.

Her tone changed. "Don't you want to be a famous painter?"

"All I want is to be in control of my life again."

"You can be. You are in control, if it's you about you."

"I'd feel a lot more in control of me about me if I had my pants on."

"No, I mean you have to think about you. Not the dairy. Not your dad. Not the town. And not me. This, this . . . oh, my."

She reached into her back pocket and produced a sheet of paper. It was the note she had written alone in her bedroom the night before. Brush gave her a look that said, "what's this?"

Susannah responded to the look. "I wanted to able to say this right, so I wrote it down."

She started reading.

"I think we belong together. I think there is a reason why you and I were put here at this place and time . . ."

Brush tried to interject, but she stayed him with her hand.

". . . but there is also a reason why you are such a great artist. I think this is the time for us, but not the place. The meaning is clear to me. . ."

A rustling sound and then footsteps approaching the arbor cut her short. Brush dove behind his stone. Susannah ducked down behind hers, sprang back up, nabbed Brush's clothes, and hit the ground again as Duck stepped into the clearing in full Double Secret Agent Mode.

He cased the joint, saw the coast was clear, and assumed his usual whistling saunter. He made his way to the path in the middle of the plot and went down the path to the tree. For a moment, he went back into

Double Secret Agent Mode, warily looking both ways before reaching into a large knothole. The sound of metal on metal emerged from the knothole, followed by the thud of a closing lid. Duck rose from the knothole with a tallboy beer in his hand.

He pulled a can opener from his pocket and then peered through the shadow of the tree at the can. It had a pull top, a new invention just that year. He replaced the opener, studied the pull top and fingered it open. The hissing from the can was met with the sound of tinny clicks from outside the arbor. Duck instantly went back into Double Secret Agent Mode and hustled behind the tree. He peered around, all stealth, to see Mike passing through the arbor, holding a blue blazer in one hand, and lamely clicking a cricket toy with the other. Duck vanished behind the tree.

Mike, seeing the cemetery empty, pocketed the clicker, trudged glumly to the bench, and held up the blazer. He tugged a tri-folded sheet of paper from the lapel pocket and tossed the blazer toward the bench. It missed and draped over Brush's stone, directly behind the bench. Mike took an uneasy seat on the bench. The cemetery grew silent. Duck peeked around the tree trunk, and monitored Mike up ahead in the moonlight, his back to the cemetery. Duck took a Double Secret Agent quaff from his tallboy.

Duck slid behind the tree when he saw Lorelai, frisky and dolled up in a revealing summer dress, silently pass through the arbor and sneak up behind Mike, clicker at the ready. Brush, all eyes and breathless, watched her slink above his stone. Intent on her target, Lorelai never looked either way. She clicked in Mike's ear. He leapt up.

"Dammit, Lorelai!"

Lorelai shoved him back down and leaned in, giving Mike a closeup eyefull of high definition cleavage, and spoke in a baby version of her ukelele voice. "Did the cricky wicky scare Mikey wikey?"

Mike looked away from the cleavage, indifferent and weary.

"Yeah, you got me," he said. "So, why don't we just get this over with."

"Oh, you're no fun."

Lorelai skipped around the bench, clicking skyward in all directions. She plopped on the seat and squirmed up to Mike. She began to poke, tickle, and pester him until he retreated to the farthest end of the bench.

Susannah, who had edged up to the stone behind and to their right, used the misdirection to half rise, intending to pass Brush's clothes across the path. She strained to reach him, eyes on the bench, then dove back down when Mike turned her way.

Mike grabbed Lorelai's hands and pulled her up short.

"Lorelai, please," he said.

Lorelai freed her hands, dropped the tease and went instantly into business mode.

"Have you got it?" she said. As she spoke, Lorelai dipped her fingertips into her cleavage and pulled out a pen. She held it aloft.

Mike one-handed the contract and spoke towards it. "Yeah, I . . ."

Lorelai snatched at it, but Mike did not let go.

He was overwhelmed by the wrongness of it all. It wasn't guilt. It went deeper than guilt. It was a disquiet that invaded and occupied every fiber of his being, and refused to withdraw. It had been there, the disquiet, waiting on the outside when he typed the contract earlier that day. The invasion of his inner core began later, when he signed it.

The second Lorelai touched the contract, Mike's entire self went into revolt. Revulsion overcame him. This could not happen. He gripped the contract tighter. He added his other hand to the grip.

"Lorelai, I've been thinking."

Lorelai gently pulled the contract toward her until Mike's knuckles pressed against her bosom. She went into her seductive voice. "About what it was like, just us two, back then?"

Behind them, Susannah retreated to a safer distance behind the bench, crawled across the path toward Brush's hiding place, clothes in hand, and found a hiding place behind a gravestone. Meanwhile, Brush, unaware of Susannah's shifted position, silently inched toward the path the other way, his mid-section now covered by Mike's blazer, just in case. Mike's voice rose above the cemetery as he gently tugged the contract back toward himself.

"Dammit, Lorelai, there never was just us two."

Lorelai pulled the contract, and Mike's knuckles, back to her bosom. She remained in seductive mode. "Only because you never explored the possibilities."

"I don't want to be your fourth husband, Lorelai."

"If not the wedding march, perhaps the sheet

music?"

This made Mike's eyes roll, involuntarily. He stopped tugging, which made Lorelai ease, too. Mike looked up from the contract and into Lorelai's eyes. She searched for that fervent and fierce look that meant her wiles were working. None. His voice was all business.

"Lorelai, I don't want to do this. It's not right."

"It's my land. Don't be a poot."

"Well, yes, it's legal."

Lorelai leaned in for the kill, never releasing the contract. She whispered in Mike's ear.

"So am I."

"Lorelai, wait. Just stop."

"Oh, no, we're not stopping. You've signed it already. I know!"

The gentle contest for control of the contract abruptly became an all-out tug of war. Brush, still covered by Mike's blazer, seized the moment to hustle across the path as the contract moved back and forth under a crossfire of words.

"Lorelai, it's not right."

"Why be fair to Helen? What has she done for you? Nothing but make demands and belittle you."

"We were engaged."

"You lure me out here . . ."

"Lure? You? Me? This was your idea!"

"Just like ten years ago. When I was a child!"

"Child! We're almost the same age!"

"I was your victim!"

Mike clenched the contract and held it, unmoving.

"If the name Mike Rutherford means anything

around here, it means a square deal. Let's just tear this up
and start . . . "

"I served your lust! And now your greed!"

On the word "greed," Lorelai yanked the contract
with one hand and poked the pen into Mike's wrist with
the other. He went off balance and fell off the bench,
which gave time for Lorelai to step away, unfold the
contract, and sign it. She held the pen and contract aloft,
and spoke to the sky.

"There! Now who's the smart one!"

Mike came up from the ground, steadied himself,
and confronted Lorelai.

"Lorelai, I want that contract now. It was signed
under . . . under duress."

Lorelai gently folded the contract, moving without
haste, and then moved quickly to shove it down into her
cleavage. There wasn't a scintilla of seduction in her voice,
now. "Come and get it, big boy."

On hearing this, Susannah and Brush popped up to
realize they had exchanged sides of the path. When Mike
moved closer to Lorelai, they ducked back down.

Mike went into negotiating mode. Never taking his
eyes off Lorelai's now precious bosom, he managed to
keep his voice calm.

"Okay, never mind about Helen. We can take a walk.
You and me. Just give me the contract. The rest can . . .
can wait."

Lorelai answered in a tone that evenly mixed
petulance with menace.

"No. I'm going to show her. I'm going to show
everybody."

This was punctuated by a clicking sound outside the arbor. When Lorelai attempted to yell, Mike covered her mouth with one hand and went after the contract with the other. It was too far down her cleavage. For a moment, Lorelai checked Mike's eyes to measure his reaction. His hand was, after all, plunged between two of her finest assets. She saw only determination, which iced her own resolve. Mike, now with his hand on her mouth and an arm around her, pulled her toward the path.

Duck looked out from behind the tree to see them scuffling up the path toward the tree. He vanished behind the tree again.

Brush and Susannah both used the moment to retreat deeper into the cemetery, still on opposite sides of the path, Brush escaping into the shadow of the tree.

Mike and Lorelai circled, still grappling, behind the tree as Duck emerged in the limbs just above them. He managed to conceal himself behind the summer leaves and the massive trunk. From there, he could peek out, unseen, over the cemetery. When he saw Susannah, prone behind a gravestone, he gave a little, stealthy wave. She put her finger to her lips. He nodded in understanding, although he didn't understand. When he spotted Brush in the dark, but visibly naked, on the other side of the cemetery, his eyes widened. He frowned for a moment before putting a finger to his own lips, figuring it meant something, or maybe the right thing, in the situation. Brush just looked back at him and shrugged.

Carl Holland came through the arbor and looked around. He clicked his way to the bench and took a seat, leaned back, and surveyed the crown of the hill.

He was, he knew, alone. He wasn't on the bench long before another clicking sound came through the arbor and Lillian entered. She, too, scanned the cemetery, her eyes lighting up when she spotted Carl at the bench. He had risen upon her entrance. He clicked toward her. She clicked back.

Lillian came to the bench, a little extra sparkle in her step.

"Carl! Well, this is a surprise. Where's Brush?"

"I don't know. Been looking for him. Susannah, too. Thought they might be here. Swimming."

Brush's head popped up, wide-eyed with dread, just over his stone. Susannah's eyes followed. They exchanged "now, what" glances in the half-light, and both shrugged in exactly the same way at exactly the same time. They slid back behind their stones.

Lillian Persons had been in business long enough to know that luck happens when preparation meets opportunity. She had already decided to avoid any mention of Elizabeth and the dreadful night they'd had before. She took a half step toward Carl, and replied, "That's a first. So . . . so . . . so, what are we doing here? Alone."

"Pez's note said to be here like the old days. Whatever that means."

Mike, mortified, poked his head out from behind the tree. Below him, Lorelai's legs kicked in the air. Above him, Duck stood, breathless and unmoving in the one spot that kept him invisible from Mike directly below and the others in the cemetery before the tree.

"I don't have any plans," said Lillian. "Why don't we

just wait and see?"

By the time she finished the sentence, she had positioned herself and Carl in the middle of the bench seat with room to spare on both sides, which seemed fine to Carl. He looked up into the night and spoke to it.

"Full moon."

Lillian followed his gaze and then lowered her eyes to take in his profile. "Romantic."

Behind them, Susannah frantically signaled Brush, who was now barely visible in the deepest shade of the tree, a plan to exchange the clothes. Her arms went up in frustration when she couldn't see Brush's signals in the dark. Brush moved toward her, away from the safety of the shadow, signaling until Susannah accidentally slapped a gravestone and they both dove back down behind stones.

"Did you hear something?" said Carl, half turning.

"Well, my heart's pounding a little," said Lillian, who arrested Carl's cheek and turned his face toward hers. Now that she had Carl's full attention, she wasn't letting go of it.

Susannah used the moment to hop up and throw the lump of clothes toward the stone Brush had used for cover. She followed, just as, unseen behind her, Brush crawled across the path, the opposite way. As he crossed the path, Mike's blazer slipped off his back.

Lillian edged closer to Carl, her hand still on his cheek.

"Tough night ahead, Carl? I mean Brush . . . tomorrow and everything."

"It looks like he's not going to Chicago, which isn't

like him. Usually, when he says he's gonna do something, by God he does it."

"So . . . so, you won't be living all by yourself after all?"

Carl shrugged. Lillian slid her hand to his temple and began to stroke, which startled Carl, but he got used to it, fast. Brush, peeking over his gravestone, watched in astonishment. He'd never seen his father in a tender moment with a woman. The gentle stroking relaxed Carl. He settled into the bench and spoke as much to himself as to Lillian.

"Ya' know, he just doesn't think like a farmer. I'll tell ya', the boy has a way of getting into the damndest fixes."

Brush jolted. He surveyed himself, naked in the moonlight, then peeked over his stone. Susannah popped up only to realize they had switched sides. Brush gestured toward Mike's telltale blazer, now visible at the edge of the path ahead. Susannah pointed to herself, dropped, and crawled toward the blazer.

"You've always said Brush was good with the cows," said Lillian, still stroking.

"Well, they've all got names, thanks to him."

Brush popped up and cringed. Susannah popped up and beamed at him. Carl, adjusted his seat, erasing what little space there was between himself and Lillian, and went on.

"He's the hardest worker I know, but as a dairyman, he makes one helluva painter. The only way he could retire is if I outlive him."

Brush, staggered and abashed, rose again to protest. Susannah rose with him and halted him with a gesture that said, "Are you nuts?" They both lowered. Lorelai's legs briefly kicked out from behind the tree.

"You ought to tell him that," said Lillian. "It would make it easier for him to go."

"I'd tell him he has time. A kid thinks three years is forever. An adult thinks it's a car loan. And I'd tell him don't be afraid of change. Everything changes all the time. Trees grow. Dogs die. You can't stop time. But see, he can."

"How?"

"When he paints something, it's forever."

Brush's expression shifted, his indignance giving way to something like appreciation. Carl wasn't overly generous with praise, but he wasn't particularly critical, either. Like everyone else in Volney, he thought if a thing was good enough, it spoke for itself.

Even in Brush's dicey state, the moment caused him to exhale. He wanted to hear more. Carl, his thoughts gathered, gave him more.

"I'd tell him don't worry about me. Funny, the other night with Elizabeth. When I got home, I realized. It didn't hurt. Neither one of us needs her anymore. In a strange way, I was glad she came."

Relief flowed over Brush's face. The father had finally caught up with the son and found peace in the absence of Elizabeth Holland. Brush also sensed a slipping away. He'd come to know and understand his father more in the last few days than in all the days before. Now, he could feel their inevitable parting. Susannah's face relaxed with his, then tightened with bittersweet resignation. She could feel events turning away from her. Brush, she knew, had just grown nearer to Chicago.

The pair vanished when a new set of clicks came from the arbor, bringing Duck's apprehensive face from behind a cluster of leaves. Duck withdrew as Helen and Peter, in deep conversation, clicked their way into the cemetery, the rising moonlight defining them. Mike, struggling, peeked out over his shoulder and around the tree, becoming instantly crestfallen at the sight of them together.

Peter and Helen spotted Carl and Lillian, and approached the bench. They all clicked at each other.

"So, you are the source of the mysterious missive?" said Peter.

Carl and Lillian responded together, "No."

"Has anybody seen Mike?" said Helen.

Carl and Lillian again responded together, "No."

Carl caught Peter's eye. "Peter, about last night. Elizabeth . . ."

Peter stopped him with a shake of his head. "The show was already over, champ. She just pulled the curtain down."

Out of the corner of his eye, Peter spied Mike's blazer on the path. He went to it and lifted it up and turned to the bench.

"What have we here?"

If a cringe could make a sound, one would have been heard across the crown of the hill as Mike, Susannah, Brush, and Duck huddled deeper into hiding.

"Mike!" said Helen. "That's his blazer. He never leaves it." She swiveled her gaze back and forth across the cemetery. "He's up to something. What's this all about?"

Mike's cringe turned into a grimace as Lorelai twisted to bite his hand.

"There was only the abstruse invitation from Pez," said Peter, examining the jacket, while, behind the tree, Mike's eyes widened in horror, and then pain as Lorelai's teeth, suddenly freed, dug into his arm before he clamped a hand back over her lips.

"Same with us," said Lillian.

"What is 'just like the old days?'" said Helen.

Seeing Peter distracted by the jacket, Susannah attempted to crawl across the path behind him, but she caught his eye. He spoke loud enough for all to hear.

"And whaaaaaat, pray tell, do we have here?"

Susannah vaulted up, all smiles, and managed to conceal her panic. She came to Peter and whispered.

"Just . . . just please help me."

Peter, mystified and delighted at the same time, decided to wing it.

"So, it's hide and seek is it?" he announced to all.

"Oh, my God," said Susannah, petrified. She hurried toward Peter signaling "no" in vain.

"We have pieced together the mosaic, people," said Peter. "Susannah here says it's hide and seek."

As soon as the words left his lips, Susannah waved another frantic "no." She rushed toward the crowd, one eye on the cemetery behind, and cried out, "No!"

Before she finished the word, she observed Brush scampering to a safer hiding place under the darkness of the tree. In a flash, she switched modes and addressed them all ever so casually.

"I mean . . . okay."

"Hide and seek?" said Helen. "For adults?"

"I don't think we're supposed to look here in the graveyard," said Susannah.

"Oh, let's have a look," said Peter and he stepped among the stones.

Mike, Duck, and Brush cowered in alarm. Lorelai writhed. Susannah grew goggle-eyed as Carl, Lillian, and Helen searched, approaching the tree. Susannah grabbed Mike's blazer from Peter and held it aloft.

"Perhaps. . . perhaps Mr. Rutherford left a clue in his jacket."

The others took the red herring and came away from the tree. Duck and Mike silently breathed a sigh of relief as Lorelai, rested briefly, smoldering and exhausted, her eyes shooting malevolent lightning bolts at Mike. The struggle renewed.

Lillian took Mike's jacket. As she searched it, Peter took Susannah aside.

"I should like to paint you, miss," he said.

"Paint . . . me?"

"As a model. You. Alone on the prairie in your simple dress."

Brush peered up over his stone, stunned. Peter Basque was a never empty basket of revelations. They layered each other. Still, all surprises that came from him became unsurprising with time, which was why, in an instant, Brush was no longer stunned.

Susannah, though, was stunned.

"Will I look like a . . . a person?

"If you mean, will it be a narrative piece. Realistic.

Yes. You on the autumn prairie. Regenerative."

"Brush already painted one like that."

"I know. Shall we say a Sunday in October?"

"Why are you being . . . normal?"

"Because I have stood at the feet of a child."

From behind his stone, Brush chewed on what he'd just heard. Another revelation, this one refusing to be unsurprising. What did Peter mean? Why was he being normal? Where was the hollow and deflated man he'd left behind that morning?

Behind the tree, Mike and Lorelai paused again, chests heaving, as though in a time-out. They eyed each other – darts flashing and launched back into the struggle.

Helen had overheard Peter. She came over to him. "October? You, here in October?"

Peter didn't mind answering. He just didn't want to do it right at that moment. He shrugged. Helen was about to press him for more when Lillian's voice took her attention.

"Nothing," she said, and held Mike's blazer at arm's length.

"He's up to something," said Helen. "Mike. He's been acting so strange."

Behind the tree, Mike had the look of a man who's been tried and convicted. His eyes searched in vain for sanctuary. Everywhere he turned, Lorelai crowded him back into hiding.

"Strange?" said Carl. "How about Duck? Painting fire hydrants on Main Street with a sheet over his head. Green!"

Up in the tree, Duck went into Double Secret Agent Mode. Apprehension crept in. His clandestine operation was exposed. The panic didn't last long. He shook it off and decided to be happy that somebody had noticed his handiwork, even if it was supposed to be a secret. Peter returned to business at hand.

"Hide and seek!" he announced. "A welcome diversion."

Peter's declaration was punctuated by the sound of clicks coming up the footpath. He stage-whispered to the group.

"I say let's hide."

Duck and Brush shrank back behind their covers. Mike grew bugeyed and gripped Lorelai harder, even as she grew prematurely triumphant. Out in the cemetery, Lillian dragged Carl behind a large headstone on the right side of the path, away from the others. Peter dove behind a stone on the left side. Helen remained standing, reluctant and annoyed, until Peter reached up and pulled her behind an adjacent stone. Susannah just stood there until the clicks reached the arbor and she, too, dropped behind a stone.

Calwood, Mokane and Bloomfield clicked in, muttering.

"You say 20 pounds," said Mokane. His tone dripped with skepticism.

"Yup," said Calwood. "Five-gallon bucket. Twenty pounds."

"And how much is it going to take?" said Mokane.

"One coat?" said Calwood.

"All right," said Mokane.

Calwood weighed the question. He drew on his cigar and pulled it from his lips. He waved his cigar and answered.

"Ten thousand gallons, give or take."

Mokane swelled in triumph.

"Now, Mr. Muttonhead Genius," he said. "Now, how much does your battleship weigh?"

Calwood ignored the jab. He replaced his cigar to his lips, put his hands on his hips and turned his eyes upward and spoke to the sky. "Paint loses weight when it dries."

Mokane raised a finger, poised to offer a riposte, when Bloomfield interrupted him.

"Let's sit on Mildred," he said. The trio was now at the front of the cemetery near the center. They all sat on a wide monument on the front row and beside the path. They faced the view of the town from behind the sundial. Peter, Helen, and Susannah were directly behind them, a few rows back. Carl and Lillian remained unseen on the other side, behind a wide stone near the bench. Brush was hidden in the shadows, several rows behind Carl and Lillian. Duck, deathly still, peeked out from the branches and took in the entire cemetery. Below him, Mike and Lorelai squirmed.

Calwood chewed on his cigar. Mokane lit his own cigar. Bloomfield bit off a knot of chewing tobacco.

"I always liked Mildred," said Calwood.

"Mildred talked too much," said Mokane. "Never had much nice to say."

"She had a touch of vinegar, alright," said Calwood.

"Always gossiping," said Mokane.

"Downright unpleasant," said Calwood.

"Meaner'n a snake," said Mokane.

"Come to think of it, I couldn't stand her," said Calwood. He half turned to take in the cemetery and wondered aloud, "I wonder how this snipe hunt will make Mike any money."

Bloomfield spoke to no one in particular.

"When I was a kid. Howard Bellamann . . . lessee, Howard would have been Bayard Bellamann's grandson . . ."

"Howard was Helen's grandfather," said Mokane.

"Yup, that was it," said Bloomfield. "Grandson."

Bloomfield turned to Mokane and spoke knowingly. "Howard was Helen's grandfather. Anyway, when I was a kid, Howard Bellamann hired me to come up here with him and tend to the grass and bushes. He told me that one of these graves isn't a grave. It's a hole where Jesse James buried a pile of loot. Gold from a train robbery. Said there was a fortune in there and he thought maybe he knew which grave it was."

All except Carl and Lillian, and including Mike and Lorelai, peeked out, all eyes and highly alert, from their hiding places. A pregnant, expectant silence hung over the cemetery. Bloomfield chewed in the silence for a moment before speaking.

"Wish I had paid better attention."

Behind him, every face, now rueful, slid back into hiding.

"That's another fortune Mike Rutherford will never get his hands on," said Mokane.

"Another?" said Calwood. "What other?"

"Helen's money," said Mokane.

"Nah," said Calwood. "Mike can make his own money. It ain't greed that makes him take what Helen dishes out."

"She's cooking her seed corn," said Mokane. "Not getting any younger."

"Starting to spread," said Calwood. "Getting broad across the beam."

Helen rose slowly from behind her stone, eyes of steel, hands to her hips.

"But Mike's in his prime," said Mokane.

Behind the tree, Mike couldn't help but glow a bit.

"About nine forty-five," said Bloomfield.

"Anybody with eyes can see that Mike loves her," said Calwood. "And Helen is a fool if she thinks Mike's the first man Lorelai waltzed off the dance floor."

"You can bet lot of men in Kansas City know what she likes for breakfast," said Mokane.

Lorelai's eyes turned to slits of malice as Calwood continued. "He should never have brought Lorelai up here that night."

"Deer that bite?" said Bloomfield.

"No!" Mokane shouted into Bloomfield's ear. "Mike shtupped Lorelai right here the night of Helen's big party."

"No, he didn't," said Bloomfield.

All heads except Carl and Lillian gradually re-emerged from hiding, alive with anticipation. Established Volney lore had just been challenged by three words. Bloomfield went on.

"I saw the whole thing. We were at Helen's party that night when I remembered I forgot to water grandma. So, I left and came up here."

He thumbed backwards toward a gravestone near the rear of the cemetery. "They didn't see me. They didn't even look around. Mike had enough party punch down his throat to stagger a bull. I ought to know. I spiked it."

"So did I," said Calwood. "Every new punchbowl, too."

"So did I," said Mokane.

Bloomfield didn't hear them. He went on.

"Lorelai dragged him in here and tried to get him to lay down right there. He went down all right. Face first."

"What about Lorelai?" Calwood shouted into Bloomfield's ear.

"She was hoppin' mad," said Bloomfield. "Tried to wake him up. Pounded on him. Jumped on him. Then she tore out of here. Snagged her dress on the sundial. Nice dress, too. Yellow. I waited and she didn't come back. I couldn't wake Mike, either, and I couldn't lift him, so I just left him here."

"Why didn't you tell anyone?" shouted Mokane.

"Who would want to talk about something like that?" said Bloomfield.

Of course, everyone in Volney, with the exception of Mike and Helen, did, and had. In the silence that followed, a sermon decrying the evils of idle chatter played out on the unhidden faces behind the codgers. Helen, her expression a tortured seesaw of emotions, slowly dropped down behind her stone as all other heads slid back into hiding. Behind the tree, Mike and Lorelai exchanged white hot venomous glares. The graveyard grew absolutely quiet.

"It's so sad when people get crossways with

themselves," said Bloomfield. "They get so snagged up in what they won't do, they go blind to what they can do."

Peter, in the shadow of his stone, played with his fingers. It was his way of dealing with discomfort. It was as though the old man on the gravestone up there was speaking directly to him, and it made him uneasy. An old man who he so easily disregarded, now seemed to peer directly through him, to know him in a way that Peter had long dreaded anyone's knowing. He shifted as though people were watching him. The Act. The act that he had so recently discarded, was still alive and breathing, because, he instantly knew, he had failed to confront it properly. "Snagged up in what they won't do." Peter stopped and eyed his fingers. An apprehension had weighed on him since his confrontation with Brush that morning, an apprehension that had grown into an unwelcome concession. He was no longer an artist. He was, at best, just another showoff.

In their own ways, Helen and Brush were equally stirred. Three words – "no, he didn't" – had budged a stone weighing on Helen's heart. She almost felt it shift. Moving it was one thing, though. Removing it was another. It had been there so long. But the eviction had begun. There in the growing silver light, she was coming to know in a rush of judgments that it was she who had kept the stone there, clutched and guarded and burnished, all along. Even as she felt the stone falling away, she could feel it being replaced by another burden. She had work to do. A life to fix.

For Brush, it was a simpler revelation. It wasn't even a revelation. He did want to be a painter, and he knew he never wanted to be anything but.

Bloomfield lowered his basset hound eyes to the view of Volney below.

"When you can't see your gifts, you can't be grateful. Without gratitude, the biggest thing you've got is your own puny gimcrack self."

Peter looked up from his hands. Gratitude, now that was new. How many flowery, windblown discourses had he poured forth on the topic of inspiration, every word fabricated on the spot, none of them sincere? Peter didn't try to count. He couldn't if he tried. But, every one of them had one thing in common – they were untranslatable. Untranslatable because, to Peter Basque, inspiration was a theory, a pile of words, the jargon of the inner circle. True inspiration couldn't possibly be a gift, and was therefore beyond explaining. For him, artistic inspiration was like a cake he'd never tasted, even though he could name all the ingredients. That the cake could be made by a force outside himself – his puny, gimcrack self – had never crossed his mind. And if it's not a gift, it doesn't require thanks. "Gratitude," he whispered the word to himself.

Bloomfield bit more off his tobacco plug and tucked it in his cheek.

"The biggest you'll ever be is the day you realize just how small you are, especially in a small place. You see the passage of time different when you live in a small place. I am today the oldest person in Volney. There was a time when I was the youngest. In a small place, you watch things arise, and bloom, and wither. I've watched myself do it. When I was in bloom, I wanted to be immortal. I didn't call it that. I didn't know that was what I wanted, but it was. I wanted to be bigger than me. But life got in the way and I'm glad it did."

Calwood and Mokane nursed their cigars, watched the night sky, and remained silent, listening. Bloomfield continued.

"I didn't know about myself. I didn't know the difference between the ordinary knocks of life and mean, hard misfortune."

Bloomfield observed Calwood and Mokane, then he, too, looked up to the night sky, peering over his glasses. He spoke quietly.

"I didn't know that the stars don't go away just because there are clouds."

Bloomfield rose and addressed what he thought was an audience of two.

"I didn't know to be content with what I'd been given and thankful for what I'd been spared."

Bloomfield's eyes again traveled over Volney below.

"There are people who can be immortal. They can at least get a shot at it. Brush Holland, he's one of those people."

Brush, alerted at the sound of his name, peered over his stone, He watched Bloomfield retake his seat on the gravestone several rows ahead in the moonlight. Immortal. He wanted to hear more. Bloomfield gave him more.

"I hear people talk about artists who've been gone for hundreds of years. They talk about them like they're still here today. People may talk that way about Brush someday, because he's good enough. Now, that other artist . . ."

"Peter Basque," said Calwood.

"What?" said Bloomfield.

"Peter Basque," yelled Mokane.

Peter listened to his name bouncing about up ahead and smiled a bit. It was attention, appreciated even in this moment of unease.

"Peter Basque," said Boomfield. "Now, he's given up on immortality."

Peter's smile faded. Bloomfield went on.

"I've never seen anything he's painted, other than the buildings in Volney, but I can tell he quit trying a long time ago. He withered himself. It's written all over him. He's a man who presents you with his faults and never gives you enough time to learn his virtues. He has forgotten why he was born."

As soon as he heard the words, Peter knew them to be true. Too true. He felt the words working their way inside him. He was, at first, surprised he found a place to put them. He was also surprised at their fullness. For the first time that he could recall knowing, Peter Basque felt something like shame. It came as a pang, but there it was. Shame. Peter was enough of a student of people to know that shame requires an unveiling. Shame hibernates in the dark, but there in the moonlight, there was no place for shame to hide. In that moment, Peter understood that he was undergoing an awakening, a revelation from himself to himself. It was he who had been witless to his own secret. He had forgotten why he was born. Bloomfield wasn't finished.

"People say they wait for Judgement Day. Well, in a

Sunday way that is true, but in an everyday way, there's more. Judgement Day is every day. What are you gonna do with your God-given gifts? What did you do with the days behind you and what are you gonna do with the days you got left? Why were you born in the first place?"

Transformations come slow, until they come fast. Peter's shame was transforming at a gallop, turning itself into a need, a chest-tightening drive to overhaul himself, to fix everything all at once, to put an end to desires that pointed only inward. His was a goosebump-swelling acceptance of liberation that turned every vision of escape into an urgent possibility. Urgency. He wasn't accustomed to that. It overwhelmed him.

And then a deep breath and an exhale, and he was overcome by a recognition – he was grateful. This was a first for him, and he knew it. He was astonished by it. His first encounter with gratitude wasn't accompanied by a rising angel choir. It was just a small, happy thing there inside him. A life of directionless longing had brought him to this place and to this moment, and he was grateful for that.

As if in punctuation of Peter's thoughts, Calwood and Mokane spoke at once. "Amen."

The cemetery again grew silent. On the bench and behind the stones, the faces of all were cast skyward. Each person drawing answers from the stars and the moon, each different and yet the same.

Bloomfield leaned forward to spit tobacco.

"Don't spit on Mildred!" Calwood and Mokane said as one.

Bloomfield rose and walked to the stone where

Carl and Lillian were hiding. Before he could spit, Carl, tousled and smudged with lipstick, and Lillian, mussed and unbuttoned, popped out of hiding.

"There ya' go, Bloomfield," said Calwood. "Two snipe already."

"We, uh, we were playing hide and seek," said Lillian.

"I've gotta try that version," said Calwood.

Peter, Susannah, and Helen emerged from their hiding places.

"I believe we've got a quorum," said Calwood.

As Helen approached the bench, Peter detected a rustle behind the tree. He glanced to see Lorelai's legs kick in the air and vanish behind the tree. He turned in full astonishment to see Susannah looking directly at him. Her eyes pleaded him to say nothing. Peter gave her a wink. Whatever this was, he was in for it.

"Did everyone here get the same message from Pez?" said Helen. "Why would he say, 'just like the old days?'"

Peter, one eye on the tree, now detected Duck in the limbs above. He again questioned Susannah with his eyes. She offered a helpless shrug in answer.

"Have we done this before?" said Lillian, primping her hair and adjusting her blouse.

Helen headed toward the bench, followed by Carl and Lillian. Calwood, Mokane, and Bloomfield arose. A low muttering came from the group as they related the mystery to each other, while Peter, still near the tree, witnessed Brush in the shadows crawling between two stones. He turned, wide-eyed, to Susannah as she scurried to him.

"Just, get me . . . us . . . all of us, out . . . of this," she said. "I'll do anything."

"Brush has to go," Peter answered. "You're the only one who can make him."

"I can't. He won't."

"Don't tell me you don't know you're the strong one."

Susannah deflated. Resignation overtook her.

"Susannah, the only way to keep him is to let him go."

Peter watched her as a new resolve pushed her resignation away. She took a deep breath. "He'll go. Just get us out of this."

Peter gave her a nod and started toward the bench. Susannah grabbed his arm and whispered, "Lorelai. She's got a piece of paper. Helen can't see it."

Another nod from Peter assured Susannah. He turned up the path to see Helen heading his way.

"Something is up and I'm going to find out what it is," she said.

Peter swept passed her to the group at the front and opened his arms to the town below.

"Behold," he shouted, one eye on the view, the other on Helen. "Our town! In the moonlight! Returning the glow of the heavens!"

All except Helen turned toward the view. A moment of silence was followed by a gasp or two.

"It does rise from the prairie," said Lillian.

Carl spoke in a quiet voice. "It looks like, well there in the moonlight . . ."

Lillian moved closer to Carl and put her arm around him. "Like what, Carl?"

Behind them, Helen spoke as much to herself as to

the group.

"Expensive perfume that smells cheap. Lorelai!"

Lillian gave Carl a gentle squeeze.

"Go ahead, Carl."

"I smell a rat!" said Helen.

"With the grain towers rising up, it's, it's like . . . Oz."

"It is," said Mokane.

"Oz," said Calwood. "Well dog my cats."

Oohs and aahs murmured from the group as Peter turned toward the view and, for the first time, regarded it for what it was. The scene stopped him in his tracks. From the very beginning, he had thought of the painting of Volney as part of The Act. Even as the paint project and the people who devoted themselves to it evolved before his eyes and became meaningful, the whole thing was still part of The Act. It had to be. The Act was all he knew. Even though he had folded it, he had yet to replace it with anything workable. He had winced the night before when Elizabeth read the art critic's column in the newspaper. He winced because the critic's assertion was dead on accurate, and he had nothing to counter it.

Now, spread below him, the town in pink was cast in silver by a full moon. It slumbered in soundless harmony. What he saw wasn't shock art. It wasn't a large-scale version of a red-splotch canvas. It wasn't an expression that couldn't be expressed. It wasn't something that was tossed off and then tossed away. In his fever to get the thing done, he had failed to understand what he'd done.

It was a meditation.

"Oneness." He breathed the word.

"Peter!" Susannah's voice shook him from his reverie.

He turned to see Helen heading around the tree.

Peter rushed to the tree just as Helen rounded the right side and Mike and Lorelai emerged, scuffling, on the left. Peter scooted behind the tree, got in front of Helen and pretended to stumble in the dark, which halted her. From there he played the role of a bumbling assistant while managing to keep the massive tree trunk between them and Mike and Lorelai.

All four circled the tree while the group at the front of the cemetery, prompted by Susannah, remained focused on the view of the town. Duck and Brush, both bugeyed, watched the scene as all four circled the tree until the two couples were reset. Peter and Helen were once again on the path in front of the tree. Mike and Lorelai were again hidden behind it.

Helen turned away from Peter and the tree and marched up the path to the crest of the hill. She planted herself in front of Susannah.

"Susannah, what is going on here?" she said.

Susannah pointed toward the bench and made a lame effort at distraction.

"I think, I think there's a clue carved in the bench!" she said.

"To the bench!" shouted Peter as the others turned toward it.

Helen, her voice now gentled, addressed Susannah.

"There's nothing at the bench, is there Susannah?"

All eyes turned to Susannah. Helen went on.

"Whatever this is, I think you'd better get it off your chest."

Susannah was at the end of her rope. When Helen

didn't take the bench red herring, Peter was at the end of his, too. He gave Susannah a mild shrug and a look that said, "game over?" Susannah needed time to gather her thoughts. Time, the one thing she was out of. She made her way, unhurried, toward the crest of the hill overlooking Volney, eyes down, as all watched.

She stood at the crest, motionless, eyes sweeping the view in vain. There was no answer coming from down there. All the others except Peter came up behind her. She turned to face them.

"Well, it's just . . . It's a thing. A thing. Yes. A thing that you have to, have to, well, think about and, and, and adjust! . . . errrgh!"

Peter, still near the tree, heard a low thump followed by a low groan. Lorelai emerged from behind the tree, makeup and lipstick smeared and hair mussed. Susannah, facing the cemetery, now saw her. Words escaped her, so she started doing a little dance. She had no idea why. It looked stupid and left her little audience at a thorough loss, but the distraction worked.

Lorelai swept one hand across her hair and raised the contract in the air with the other. She shouted, "Helen!"

Susannah, eyes wide and desperate, lunged forward, grabbed Helen and prevented her from turning. The rest of the group watched Susannah in utter bafflement. At that instant, Duck emerged from the limbs above Lorelai, snatched the contract from her hand and replaced it with a tallboy and vanished back into the leaves.

Susannah released a very perturbed and indignant Helen, and all turned to see Lorelai, staring at the beer in her hand in even more bafflement.

"That's a new look for you, isn't it Lorelai," said Calwood.

"A beer?" said Helen.

Peter leapt right in. "Of course! Mike's throwing a party!"

Duck emerged from behind the tree. "That's right, Miz Helen, Mr. Mike's throwing a surprise party. Right here."

Duck reached into the knothole in the tree, rustled around a bit and emerged with beers for all. Peter again seized the moment.

"You had us all in suspense, Duck. You and Susannah must have come out here early to . . ."

"To leave the clue and hide the surprise," said Duck, beaming at himself. "Susannah, did you forget to hide the clue in Mr. Mike's jacket?

Susannah jumped at the sound of her name. "Me? The clue? No. I mean yes!"

Duck turned toward Lorelai and spoke in a stage voice, "Miz Lorelai, you shouldn't have let on. They would have found it sooner or later. Party!"

Duck tossed confetti – the torn-up contract – into the air, leaving Lorelai to glare mutely at every lowering shred.

"Party!" said Peter, who took an armful of tallboys from Duck and passed them around.

"Party!" said Susannah.

"What are we celebrating?" said Lillian as Peter handed her a can.

"The finished paint job!" said Susannah.

"And a going away party for Brush!" shouted Duck as

he pointed toward the stone where Brush was concealed. Susannah froze in panic. Peter stepped over and gently lowered Duck's arm.

"Who can't show up 'til later," said Susannah.

Duck leaned over and whispered to Peter, "Don't worry. My lips are a seal."

Mike came out from behind the tree, bent over and clutching his groin. Duck raised his tallboy and shouted, "Mr. Party!" Hurrah's and attaboys from the group followed.

Duck leaned over when Mike neared him. He whispered, "Now, who's the slow one?"

"A toast," called Susannah. All lifted their cans to the sky. Helen, who had not accepted a beer, spoke toward the ground.

"Well, I know I'm not invited to this party. The way I've been behaving."

Helen looked up and turned to address Susannah. "Especially to you."

Helen's ever-present composure disappeared. Mike deflated as he watched her start to walk toward the arbor. He deflated more and turned away when he saw Peter intercept her.

"Helen, stay," said Peter. "It's a terrible thing to imagine one life to be a dream while living another that is an illusion."

"Here we go again," said Calwood.

"You know it deep inside," Peter continued. "The life you imagine waits while the life you are living lingers, ticking the days away. You feel it deep inside. No day feels truly done. Tick and tick and tick until you forget that there was a day when the life you imagined seemed real. Was real. And so possible."

Peter held Helen by the arm and led her over to Mike, who's back was turned to them.

Peter spoke to Mike's back, "And you become unaware that bit by bit, and ever so gently, you adjust the life you've accepted into an argument. An argument against your own dream. And over time the argument creates the illusion. You become the one thing between you and who you are meant to be."

Peter raised his voice, loud enough to ensure Brush could hear. "And that is how songbirds become crows."

"Anybody want to take a shot at explaining that one?" said Calwood.

Mike moved toward the arbor exit. Peter gently grabbed his arm. "Stay. Please."

Mike stopped. Peter leaned to Helen and whispered. "You don't want to go back there. You don't want to do what you did. You don't want to be that person."

Peter spun Helen back toward the crowd and spoke to all. "You know, when I'm not invited somewhere, I know there are only two possible reasons. One, they don't know me. Two, they do know me."

"That's what I mean," said Helen. "They do . . .'

Peter stayed her with his hand.

"Everyone here knows you," he said. "And I think they want an RSVP."

Helen watched as the group before her nodded in agreement and smiled in welcome. Susannah offered her a beer. Before Helen could reach for it, Peter spun her back with one arm just as he moved Mike forward with the other, bringing them face to face. Peter spoke to Helen in hypnotic mode.

"And methinks you've always been one person's guest of honor."

He gave Mike a little prod. Mike regarded Peter with a mixture of gratitude and wonder and shuffled toward Helen as Peter faded backwards. Mike took a deep breath.

"My door has always been open," he said.

"Everything is changing. Everything," said Helen. Her voice was tender and unguarded. Mike shuffled closer.

"Oh, there's plenty that hasn't changed," he said. "The way my day can't begin until I see you. The way even though I know you, I want to know you more. The music I hear when you walk into a room - the music no one else can hear. The moonlight in your eyes right now."

Mike hesitated. He grew tongue-tied. And then he felt a light, ever so familiar and welcome touch on the wrist and looked to see Helen with eyes that said, "more." He did have more.

"Helen, the future doesn't have to come down a new highway at seventy miles an hour. Sometimes it's standing right in front of you. Waiting."

Helen never took her eyes off Mike's while he spoke. Now, her hand left his wrist and she turned away. Mike took on a look of bottomless despair.

Helen turned back to him, lunged forward into him and planted an overwhelming kiss that gobsmacked Mike. For a moment he flailed. Then his arms tightened around her. His wide eyes closed as a decade of desire overtook them both.

It would be an understatement to say this was one very persistent kiss. It went on and on and on. The witnessing group became abashed. Feet began to shuffle.

"They're a lot more entertaining when they squabble," said Calwood.

Peter whispered to himself, "And I guess now we both know why I stayed."

Mike attempted to end the kiss, but Helen would have nothing of it. His arms began to flail again. He grasped her arms and, exerting all his force, peeled her back. Her eyes remained closed, and her lips pursed as Mike gasped for breath.

"Oh, Mike," she whispered. Her eyes came open and she gazed at his. "I feel like I've been acting just . . . just nuts."

"That means we for sure have a quorum," said Calwood. Helen kept her eyes fixed on Mike's.

"And my door is open for you." she said. Her eyes traveled over Mike's shoulder and landed on Lorelai. "But that will require someone to make room in Bellamann House."

Lorelai went into a low-beam pout as Lillian stepped up and offered two beers to Helen, while Mike remained gaga from the kiss. Helen took them both. Lillian raised her can.

"And now the toast!" she called.

"To Oz!" said Carl.

All replied as one, "To Oz!"

"To the yellow brick road!" said Peter. "And to Brush Holland."

All replied as one, "To Brush!"

"Who's gonna make this town proud," said Carl.

"He will make me proud," said Peter. "If he were here right now, I'd tell him I've got a studio in Chicago he can have tomorrow. It may require a bit of tidying up."

"I think everyone here has spoken to Brush tonight," said Susannah. "I wish he was listening."

All raised a toast as Brush leaned back against his gravestone and looked skyward. If you could have looked down from above, you might have detected there in the moonlight the return of a sense of wonder to his eyes.

Calwood and Mokane polished their beers off in one shot. Helen handed Mike his beer. She pulled hers open and took a hefty belt. A chorus of clicks coming through the arbor interrupted the toast. Townspeople poured in. Calwood looked at them and then at his beer.

"If we're gonna have a party, we're gonna need a lot more of these," he said. "We've really got a quorum now."

"I move we go straight to Person's Cafe," said Lillian. "Where I've got a walk-in cooler full of leftover champagne from last night."

"I second!" called Helen.

"All in favor?" called Mike.

The people of Volney, with the exception of Lorelai, answered as one, "Aye!"

"But we can't party late," said Helen, which elicited groans all round from the crowd. She waved them off, and continued.

"Because we've got one more house to paint!"

Cheers and attaboys arose over the cemetery as Helen whispered to Mike, "With lots of rooms to fill."

Her voice rose to a shout, "And a traveler's plaza to

build!”

Another round of cheers and attaboys echoed over the hill. The crowd began to file through the arbor and down the hill. Susannah lingered, her eyes glancing toward Brush’s stone.

“I’ll stay her and clean up,” she said. “Yes. Clean up. That’s what I’ll do. Look at this mess.”

“What mess?” said Carl. He took Susannah’s arm. “This is no night to be alone.”

He and Lillian ushered Susannah, who kept glancing over her shoulder, away, as Calwood, Mokane and Bloomfield headed toward the arbor.

“I had snipe once,” said Calwood. “It tastes like chicken.”

“So does rattlesnake,” said Mokane.

“His battleship’s late?” said Bloomfield

“Was Mike in the Navy?” said Calwood.

“You can’t bring a battleship to Volney,” said Bloomfield.

“Just shut up,” said Mokane. “All of you. Just shut up.”

Peter stayed back as the crowd passed down the hill. He watched as Lorelai composed herself. She began to smooth her hair.

“Don’t do that,” said Peter, coming toward her.

“Oh?” said Lorelai.

“Please,” said Peter.

“Oh?” said Lorelai.

Peter, now near Lorelai, reached up and tousled her hair.

“The perfection of your hair has always annoyed me,” said Peter. He tousled more. “There! A tawny mane!”

"Oh?" said Lorelai.

"But your Olympian vanity has always charmed me," said Peter.

"Oh." said Lorelai. Instantly, her old come-hither mode returned. "Well of course it does."

Peter took her by the arm. "Shall we join the others?"

Lorelai went into a mix of pout and resignation.

"No," she said. "There was a . . . problem tonight."

"I know."

"You do?"

"I don't know it all."

"It's about the land for Mike's Traveler's Plaza."

"What about it?"

"I own it, and now, I'm not selling it to him. Maybe."

Peter gently grasped her other arm and turned her to face him. He started to go into hypnotist mode, then thought better of it. He addressed her in a quiet, intimate way.

"Lorelai, I've been late to the party my whole life. And, in these days here, I've come to understand why. I thought I was the party."

He released her arms and walked to the crest of the hill overlooking Volney and swept his arm across the view. "I thought all this was a party, an extension of me."

His arms dropped to his sides. "It's not. This is genuine. It's the real thing."

He turned back toward Lorelai. "It's genuine because the people here are the real thing."

Peter moved back toward her and gently grasped her arms again. "Lorelai, I think maybe you've been late to the party, too. Don't you think it's time to join?"

Lorelai Bellamann had never been spoken to in this way, mostly because she couldn't allow it. She had acted out her life behind a bubbly barricade. The barricade was skin deep. The minute anyone attempted to go deeper, her bubble machine went into overdrive. Now, Peter had taken her deeper, and much to her surprise, she hadn't released the bubbles.

A sense of relief came over her, like a weight was lifting. Who knew bubbles could be such a burden? She caught Peter's face in the moonlight. Every trace of the rock n' roll warthog was gone. There was a real man standing before her and speaking to her as a real woman. It was all new to her, but she knew she liked it.

"What say we both go to the party," said Peter, and slid one of her arms around his. "They've seen our faults. Let's let them have a long look at our virtues. You can decide about the land later."

They walked toward the arbor and the path to Volney. As they passed through the arbor, Peter's eyes grew wide when he heard her murmur, "If I'm leaving Bellamann House, I might be looking for a roommate."

The cemetery rested in silence. Ever so cautiously, Brush raised his head above his stone and scanned the hilltop. He started to rise when the sound of clicking sent him diving back down. Pez stalked in from the opposite side of the cemetery, clicking steadily. He passed behind the first three rows of headstones and stopped. He bent down and came back up with Brush's clothes. Pez sized them up and tucked them under his arm. He stalked away through the arbor, clicking.

Brush again rose cautiously. He began to make his

way to the spot where he knew Susannah had left his
clothes.

CHAPTER 36

BREAKING HOME TIES

DAYBREAK can spread an elegance over everything it touches, including a pickup truck weathered into a thousand colors. Susannah and Brush stood before hers. They were in the glow of their sanctuary tree.

Brush had just carved the year into it, Susannah assisting. Neither had slept.

Brush surveyed the new day. He sensed, as he had countless times, the way the scent of grass and soil changed in late summer before becoming dormant. He was pretty sure he'd never have that sense, or scent, in Chicago.

Chicago. The inevitable moment had arrived. Susannah went first. She steeled herself and handed Brush the box with the wedding ring. She hugged him hard, kissed him lovingly on the cheek and scurried toward the door of her truck.

Brush halted her, "Sannah."

She stopped, but she felt like she was still moving. She was electric with tension. The meadow was utterly still. Time seemed suspended. Brush continued, "Now is standing still."

Susannah turned to him, hesitant, and searched his face. She signaled "more" with her hands. Brush continued.

"The past and the future move around us."

Susannah stepped toward him. Another "more" signal. Brush continued.

"Nothing moves unless we move."

Susannah stepped closer. Another "more" signal.

"Because here we are, even though every moment now is changing."

He held out his hands. She came to him and grasped both his hands in the manner of a bride giving her hands to a groom. Brush continued.

"You're all I know."

"Brush, you know so much," said Susannah. "People don't know how much . . ."

"You're all I want to know."

"But you are going to a new place."

"Sannah, it's me."

"To become a new person."

"I'd like to hear the rest of your note."

Susannah hesitated. Brush gave her a look that told her she had no choice but to go ahead. She reached into her pocket and produced the note she had begun reading in the cemetery. She took a deep breath, found the point where she had been interrupted, and began to read.

"The meaning is clear to me. If I don't give you up

now, I'll never have you. It breaks my heart to know I won't be with you on your greatest adventure. But you must go or neither of us will ever know the truth about us."

When she finished, Brush took the note from her hands.

"See, that doesn't make sense."

"Sometimes I think I never make sense."

"It's the part about you not being with me on my greatest adventure."

"But, Chicago . . ."

"When you are my greatest adventure."

"A new place."

"Where we can become one person."

"The produce stand . . ."

Brush stayed her and lifted her left hand and spoke in mock curiosity.

"Do they wear rings in Chicago? I mean, the girls?"

Brush slipped the wedding ring on her finger. He stepped back and drank her in. She was already sublime in the sunrise. Now, a new radiance returned the light. Brush continued.

"I don't have an engagement ring, so we'll have to make that ring good for both."

"Brush, are you sure?"

"Sannah, it's mostly just a matter of confidence, but we have the chops to back it up."

"Chops."

"Trust me, we've got 'em in spades."

They embraced again, Brush stroking her temple and running his fingers through her hair. The embrace

lingered until Brush paused and momentarily grew
distant. Susannah leaned back and gave him a "what's up"
look. Brush answered.

"What's an entree?"

***

Man Street Volney was again blockaded.

The Holland Dairy truck was parked adjacent to
Lillian's Café and shaded at an angle from the morning
sun by the awning of McIntire Grocery. Carl Holland sat
on the running board facing the street, hat in hand. He
had the look of a man who wanted to be there and did
not want to be there at the same time. Brush, now in a
new suit and tie, sat at his side, eyeing the old highway
in the distance. The suitcase painted "Chicago" was at
Brush's feet.

Nobody spoke. There was too much to say.

Brush watched as, bit by bit, Main Street came to life.
His eyes widened as across the street Pez, wearing Brush's
clothes, emerged from the hardware store and began
to clear away the leftover buckets and tools from Paint
Project Headquarters. Using the sawhorses, Pez blocked
off Main Street in front of the store. Duck came out of the
store to assist. He and Pez lifted the long table that had
been the nerve center of the project and moved it out into
the blocked off area.

Duck went back into the store and returned, toting
one of Peter's large red-splotch paintings. He placed
it on the table. Pez came out of the store with another
red-splotched painting and did the same. The two went

back and forth until the table was piled high. Peter, once again wearing his hat and cape, came out of the store to supervise. He watched the pair trace a line around the table and then measure it with a tape measure. All three examined the line and nodded in agreement.

Lillian emerged from her cafe next door, spotted Carl, and made a beeline to him. Mike came out of the bank and headed their way. Susannah pulled her pickup to the curb and exited the cab. She stayed beside the truck, leaving Carl and Brush to themselves. Calwood, Mokane, and Bloomfield muttered up the sidewalk as Lorelai walked up from the opposite direction. All stopped at the Holland Dairy truck, Lorelai at a distance. Helen emerged from the Post Office Museum and walked toward the group. All, with the exception of Brush and Susannah, were quietly hungover.

They heard Peter, across the street, shout "Duck! Pez!" and point across the street toward the group at the Holland Dairy truck.

Duck and Pez came across the street and ushered all toward Paint Project Headquarters. They arranged the group around the traced-off border line as Peter, in full costume, took center stage.

"Could it be that it is September which really brings in the new year?" he said, arms spread, preacher style. "We awaken from the summer. The autumn wind quickens."

The sound of gasping air brakes turned all heads. A Greyhound bus was parked at the stop outside the Post Office. All eyes returned to Peter.

"Our intentions take life in the face of decay," he said.

"And school begins."

He handed the repaired scholarship contract to Brush. Peter continued.

"So, it is fitting that you, my friends, should witness this day on this day as we bid adieu to Brush, who is taking a new road. And tomorrow it will be a very new road, indeed. And to me."

The bus driver approached the rear of the group. Mike went into mayor mode.

"Welcome to Volney. Mike Rutherford. If there's anything we can ever do . . ."

"You could clear the street," said the driver. "I've gotta bus needs to get through. Last time I drive up this old two-lane."

The bus driver turned to go. Peter called out, "Duck!"

Duck quickly got an approval nod from Mike and collared the bus driver.

"We have one fare for you, my good man," said Peter. "But first, our ceremony."

The bus driver tried once to shrug off Duck. He knew enough not to try again and stood there on tiptoes.

"But I thought Brush was leaving with you in your bus," said Carl.

"Brush can't go where I'm going," said Peter.

"Where are you going?" said Helen.

"Nowhere," said Peter. "Why don't we call this a rebirth. Pez?"

Pez went behind the table, reached under and produced a kerosene can. He carefully doused the canvasses on the table. Pez returned to the traced-off border line.

"Please hold your positions," said Peter. He lifted his arms. "New life! It begins amid the death throes of the old."

He dropped his arm. At the signal, Pez tossed a lit match onto the pile, which burst into flames as Peter's voice arose over the group. "Now, by God, it's a work of art!"

The group jumped back at the burst of fire. A dozen loud conversations broke out as the flames erupted. Peter's voice arose again.

"New life! For the best student I never had!"

Peter removed his hat and cape and tossed them to Brush, who mulled them a moment and tossed them to Pez, who mulled them for a moment and put them on as Peter escorted Brush to center stage. He presented Brush to the group before him as the fire snapped and ebbed behind him. For a moment, the scene froze in place, as though awaiting a snapshot. Duck broke the moment.

"Brush, you take care of Brush, now."

Duck saluted as Brush's eyes traveled over the group. Mike gave a thumbs up. Pez tapped his temple with his index finger. Lorelai mimed donning a beret. Calwood and Mokane rubbed thumb and forefinger together in the universal sign for money while Bloomfield mouthed the word "Spam." Helen brought her hand to her cheek, beginning a gesture. She stopped and gently let it drop toward Susannah, who blew Brush a kiss that was both melancholy and hopeful. Lillian, standing beside Carl, patted her heart. Carl just stood there with a half-smile, equally melancholy, equally hopeful.

The bus driver put his finger to his temple and

described a circle.

On a nod from Mike, Duck released the driver, who paused in dread as Peter came to him. After Peter handed the driver a bus ticket, he retreated to his bus, fast, with Brush trailing, as Duck and Pez removed the blockades.

The group watched in silence as the two stepped up into the bus, the door closed, the sound of air brakes expelled, and the bus eased past them and out of town, Brush waving at the window.

All watched until the bus and the window disappeared in the distance.

CHAPTER 37

RESTORATION

SUSANNAH muttered as she clanked under the hood of her pickup. She labored in the shade beneath the Welcome to Volney sign, now painted pink, and with the population decreased by one. She slammed the hood shut and tossed an empty can of oil into a box containing several full cans in the rear of the bed. She slid into the truck and fired it up. She eased the truck, laden with her belongings, up near her produce stand and braked for a parting look.

Symington Produce, now operated by two high-school girls, was overrun with customers. The girls looked up long enough for a hasty goodbye wave and returned to business. Susannah waited as a stream of cars passed by, all coming from the new interstate highway access into Volney. She lurched forward through the first gap she saw and created a minor honk-fest.

She drove to the new overpass and slowed before a large green sign. "Kansas City, Denver" pointed one way. "St. Louis, Chicago" pointed the other. She wheeled the truck across the overpass and toward the ramp for St.

Louis and Chicago.

To her right, heavy machinery was grading dirt across a construction site fronted by a sign that read "Future Site of Pinktown Travelers Plaza."

Behind her, downtown Volney was crawling with tourists. There was a line outside Lillian's, and there was also a table outside the café that served up "Pinknic Lunches" in paper bags, these for the steady stream of pilgrims who hiked up the soon to be paved path to Round Hill Cemetery, where they spread blankets and took in the view, often to the sounds of a bluegrass band with a flutist playing along. Inside, Lillian could be seen head-to-head with Carl Holland at her café counter. They were laying plans for "The Perfect Person's Ice Cream Shop" at the traveler's plaza.

There was also a line backed up at Frank's 66 station, where two squads of young men in pink uniforms busily pumped gas, checked oil, and wiped windshields clean.

Across the street at the Five and Dime, Mattingly was doing a brisk trade in hand-carved pink miniatures of Bellamann House and other trinkets on a sale table outside.

At a worktable under the awning fronting Callaway Hardware, young men and women, all local, were bent and intent as they hammered out small, metal relief sculptures of the Round Hill Oak Tree.

The Historical Society also had a sales table, this one featuring reprints of Jesse James wanted posters.

The Big Three Barber Shop displayed a Robert Garrett original landscape in its window along with a hand-written note that said, "More Inside."

A team of horses pulled a pink carriage packed with tourists ready to share a smile as it clip-clopped the back streets of Volney, pausing at Bellamann House, now stunning in multiple shades of pink.

***

There were two items of new business already on the agenda for the next Volney town meeting. The first was to consider licensing for a beer garden adjacent to the duck pond. The controversy was already brewing. The second was to set the date for The Second Annual Volney Paint Fight.

***

In Chicago, Spencer Grisaille was the only person not in motion. People streamed right and left, around him, before him, and behind him in the brightly lit open spaces of The Chicago Institute of Art's contemporary wing. On every wall around were huge horizontal photographs, maybe eight feet wide each.

The pictures told the story of the painting of Volney, beginning with a shot of the truck driver hurling his clipboard at the site foreman. It was followed by a shot of bedlam at the town meeting in Person's Cafe. There was a shot of townspeople organizing Paint Project Headquarters as Duck and Pez rolled 50-gallon barrels in place along Main Street. The list went on:

Townspeople laden with painting gear stacking ladders against storefronts.

319

Lorelai painting trim on a facade, ballerina style, in a beret.

Carl at work with a spray gun.

The townspeople, working as one, chipping, masking, and painting as tractors with front end loaders maneuvered them.

The firetruck poised by the grain towers as the paint crew sprayed.

A residential street, picket fences, mailboxes, trellises, porches, homes – all in shades of pink as the volunteer painters of Volney lunched in the shade.

The paint fight on Main Street in full melee.

The bank of Volney in pink. Pez, in front, offering the photographer candy while Duck pointed to a pink fire hydrant.

Calwood, Mokane, and Bloomfield on their bench with a pink squirrel.

Mike and Helen tending a garden outside Bellamann House, glorious in pink.

The final shot, twice as big as the others, anchored the central room of the wing. It showed Volney in the moonlight as viewed from the cemetery.

Spencer moved to the central room and stood near the massive photo of Volney. He had the look of a man who knew just how lucky he was.

"Contemporary wing. All of it," he said.

***

Fall was as crisp as a new apple. New colors thrived on the prairie outside Volney. Among the colors,

320

Peter Basque labored close up to a huge canvas. Long horizontal. Maybe 10 feet wide. You'd need a pickup to move it. The painting was almost complete. It depicted the prairie surrounding him, centered by Lorelai, windblown and winsome. The image was atmospheric. She was magnificent. She demanded a second and third look.

Peter laid down his brush for a moment and took it all in and spoke almost to himself, but just enough so Lorelai could hear it.

"Perfect."

CHAPTER 38

AFTER

LATER THAT fall, an article appeared in a Sunday edition of the St. Louis Globe Democrat. It was written by the art critic under the headline:

"The Taste of Crow, Served on a Pink Platter."

"This writer has been forced to eat crow from time to time, but I'm here to say that this time it never tasted so good.

"Why am I dining on crow? Because I've just returned from two places. The first was Peter Basque's ongoing exhibit at the Chicago Institute of Art. The second was the town of Volney, 60 miles from my desk. Yes, I drove five hours north in order to compel me to drive one hour west.

"Basque's hit exhibit is the outcome of a project I lampooned in early September – the painting of an entire town in a single hue, in this case pink.

"Where to start? Let's go to the exhibit. It consists of 42 massive photographs, all horizontal, that take up the entire Contemporary Wing of the Art Institute. The photos are arranged to progress clockwise so as to tell the story of the pink paint project from beginning to end. But this is no documentary. It is a story. And a true one.

'The truth is in the photography. Basque, using a camera that fit in his shirt pocket, positioned himself in the middle of the narrative. There is only one photo in which the subjects are looking directly at the camera – an enigmatic shot of two men in front of the bank. They stand side by side while one points toward a fire hydrant and the other, dressed in Basque's notorious hat and cape, presents the viewer with a Pez candy dispenser. I interpreted it as a ritual offering.

"The rest of the shots are candid, with people behaving naturally as people do when unaware of a camera. The tone and complexion of the exhibit shifts as the photos progress. In the early photos there is an antic, breathless, almost comic urgency. This fades into a more orderly presentation as the actual project organizes and passes into a more structured phase. Donuts seemed to have played a special role.

"This sets the stage for the final series of shots, the photos that elevate the exhibit from documentary to art. That these images rise above documentary is even more remarkable because the photos are unretouched. They are straight from the camera. Basque entertained no monkey businesses in the darkroom, something we too often see on gallery walls.

'By placing himself at the center of the story, Basque places you there, too. This, combined with the astonishing size of the photos, has the effect of making you feel you are in the action. It made me feel that way.

'It is here that we, the viewers, come to understand we are not looking at pictures. We are looking at people. And it is here where the character of the people of Volney begins to come through, especially as we gradually grasp the underlying nature of the project. It isn't a stunt, another Basque headline grab. It's the people of a town joining as one to confront an unsure future.

"It's the villagers against the dragon.

"We come to understand this on our own. There is no tedious, affected artist's statement from Basque and no long-winded, thumb-sucking expositions accompanying each photo on display – a practice this reviewer wishes all exhibits would adopt.

"Other than 'Volney, Missouri, August, 1963' the exhibit has no expanded title. Basque's notes for viewers consists of two sentences. "In August, 1963, the people of Volney painted their town pink. Here they are." Each photo has a brief caption that places the image in the project timeline.

"The people of Volney were, and are, united in one desire – to keep their little town alive in the face of a faceless, unstoppable adversary, namely the inexorable progress of Interstate 70, which has already cast one crossroads village after another into the past.

"As we watch Peter Basque's project enter its final phase, in which the people of Volney assemble as one to finish off the job before the new highway opens, his

pictures imbue those people with nobility, or maybe the
people imbued themselves and Basque just clicked the
camera. That's the mystery of art. What isn't a mystery
is the growing affection for the people of Volney that
emerges in the composition and framing of the images as
the photos progress to the end. It's palpable.

"It's impossible to look at these photos and miss the
humanity in each moment.

"And with the presence of that affection comes an
absence – Peter Basque himself. His too-famous, red-
splotched signature appears nowhere in the exhibit or
anywhere else in the museum. The man who may be the
art world's most zealous self-promoter is also nowhere to
be seen in these photos. Nowhere, that is, unless you peer
into the depths of one shot. I spotted him in the reflection
of the hardware store window. There he was, taking the
photo, and, remarkably, shooting from the hip. I won't tell
you which photograph. You find it.

"The final picture in the series, which is twice as big
as the others and in the center room of the entire exhibit,
is a moonlit reverie shot from a hilltop. I won't describe
it because I can't. Go see it. If you do, you will take the
image home in your heart.

"Which is exactly what I did with Volney itself. It's
worth the trip, if for no other reason than to view the
town's most prominent feature – the Victorian-style
Bellamann House – in pink splendor.

"Volney is a town that works hard to live up to its
motto: "Where People Come to Smile." It is my hope that
the people of Volney will accept what I've written here
as an apology for calling the place 'Bumpkinville' in an

earlier column. As further penance, I purchased a small pink replica of Bellamann House which I can see here on my desk as I type.

"There is something of a mystery here. Two people I interviewed said they personally witnessed Basque setting fire to a piled-high stack of his expressionist paintings.

"Other people on Main Street were circumspect and protective about Basque – some of whom even referred to him as "Petey" – who apparently now makes his home in Volney. None would tell me where he lived or what he was up to lately. I did spot a man who bore a strong resemblance to Basque, but that person couldn't have been him because he was clean cut and seemed to have many friends. He was also wearing light blue instead of his ever present black.

"People on Main Street did say that Basque was often seen at the barber shop, which makes sense – I found the clientele there to be uncommonly conversant on the subject of art theory. And, curiously, the barber shop is also an art gallery of sorts. The shop is a small space, but one wall is hung with original landscapes by a painter named Robert Garrett. The landscapes are well-executed, if commonplace, and apparently are the fathers of thousands of prints. The barber explained that Garrett recently passed away suddenly and his accumulated paintings – a large body of work – were bequeathed to something called The Keep Volney Pink Committee.

"So, there it is. Something happened in Volney, Missouri, last August. It was certainly special. It may have been magical. Whatever it was seems to have run deeper than the painting project itself.

"But we'll probably never know exactly what happened. When I finally tracked down Peter Basque – and that, surprisingly, was no easy task – he spoke from the phone at the barber shop. When I asked him why he even started the project, his answer was "I don't know, and that's the best part."

THE END

ACKNOWLEDGEMENTS

This story was inspired by a Norman Rockwell painting – "Breaking Home Ties."

...and then Peter Basque entered the scene.

ABOUT THE AUTHOR

STEVE STINSON is an artist and writer in Southwest Virginia, where he lives with his patient wife in the world's smallest five-bedroom house. He has published thousands of drawings and stained his share of canvasses with a misguided brush. He got his first writing gig at age 16, producing headlines for the daily paper in Fulton, Missouri, a place that will always remain his hometown. When he was young and limber, he was a juggler in children's shows. Today, he is known as "Bebop" to his many grandchildren, all of whom are reasons for America to be hopeful. He thinks all things look better from the seat of a bicycle, that white bucks are required at Easter, that birdsong is heaven's whisper, and that Rachmaninoff's Symphony No. 2 is the sound of thinking. Given his druthers, he'd choose to be dancing in the kitchen with his bride.

Also by Steve Stinson:

Adult fiction:

Flip

Adult non-fiction:

Bullet Bill Dudley: The Greatest 60-Minute Man in Football

Children's fiction:

Grumpypants

Where Kent Went

Darien the Crustatarian

Squiffy & the Vine Street Boys in 'Shiver Me Timbers!'

Hay-Hay's Dog Has Her Day-Day

Whit's Matching Shoes

Ice for Rent – Bad Poetry in Motion

Owen's Choice

Go, Trippy, Go!

The First Traffic Jam in Callaway County

One Pedal More, Please!

Cecil, the Steadfast Sea Oat

The Hunt for Smitty

Today, I am a Jew

www.ingramcontent.com/pod-product-compliance
Lightning Source LLC
Chambersburg PA
CBHW071156100726
47908CB00002B/399